RAVES FOR
JAMES PATTERSON

"Patterson knows where our deepest fears are buried...There's no stopping his imagination." —*New York Times Book Review*

"James Patterson writes his thrillers as if he were building roller coasters." —Associated Press

"No one gets this big without natural storytelling talent—which is what James Patterson has, in spades." —Lee Child, #1 *New York Times* bestselling author of the Jack Reacher series

"James Patterson knows how to sell thrills and suspense in clear, unwavering prose." —*People*

"Patterson boils a scene down to a single, telling detail, the element that defines a character or moves a plot along. It's what fires off the movie projector in the reader's mind." —Michael Connelly

STEAL

For a complete list of books, visit JamesPatterson.com.

STEAL

JAMES PATTERSON
AND HOWARD ROUGHAN

GRAND CENTRAL
PUBLISHING

NEW YORK   BOSTON

Copyright © 2022 by James Patterson
Excerpt from *Run, Rose, Run* copyright © 2022 by James Patterson and Dolly Parton

Grand Central Publishing
Hachette Book Group
1290 Avenue of the Americas, New York, NY 10104
grandcentralpublishing.com
twitter.com/grandcentralpub

First Edition: February 2022

Grand Central Publishing is a division of Hachette Book Group, Inc. The Grand Central Publishing name and logo are trademarks of Hachette Book Group, Inc.

The publisher is not responsible for websites (or their content) that are not owned by the publisher.

The Hachette Speakers Bureau provides a wide range of authors for speaking events. To find out more, go to hachettespeakersbureau.com or call (866) 376-6591.

ISBN 9781538703526 (trade paperback) / 9781538709177 (large-print paperback) / 9781538703533 (ebook)

Library of Congress Control Number 2021948178

Printed in the United States of America

LSC-C

Printing 3, 2022

BETTER THAN BETTY, DEADER THAN DEAD

ONE

CARTER VON OEHSON MIXED himself a tall gin and tonic from behind the polished mahogany bar of his father's billiard room, topping it off with a squeeze of lime.

"Remember," his father once told him, "never put the used wedge of lime in your drink. Toss it and reach for a new one. Anything less is sloppy."

Carter never forgot that piece of fatherly advice, if for no other reason than he was only nine years old at the time.

A von Oehson man is never too young to learn the finer points of life.

Nor will he ever be deprived of the finest education. After boarding at Phillips Exeter, Carter was now a freshman at Yale. Never mind that he was whip smart and probably could've gotten in on his own. It didn't matter if he had the grades or test scores. What Carter had was his name—von Oehson—and, more important, the man who gave it to him.

Mathias von Oehson, Yale class of '86, ran the world's most profitable hedge fund. *Fortune* magazine listed his net worth north of twenty-four billion dollars, a hundred million of which was earmarked for his beloved alma mater upon Carter's graduation. Of course, Carter had only just submitted his application to Yale when his father made that hundred-million-dollar pledge to three of the university's senior trustees over some butter-drenched porterhouses at Peter Luger. Timing is everything. And for Mathias von Oehson, so was his only son going to Yale.

In fact, Carter's enrollment had never been discussed between the two of them. It had always just been assumed. *Like it or not, Carter, that's where you're going.*

But, oh, how Carter liked it.

The all-night parties at Durfee Hall. The infamous naked run through Bass Library. Taking in a dome show at Leitner Planetarium while completely stoned out of your gourd, and afterward eating an entire coal-fired large pepperoni from Pepe's Pizzeria. An Ivy League education at its absolute finest.

Best of all—what Carter *really* liked—was that a mere thirty minutes away, a straight shot south on I-95 in his matte-black BMW M8 coupe, was his parents' home. One of their houses, at least.

It was a sprawling Nantucket shingle in Darien, designed by Francis Fleetwood, that overlooked Long Island Sound and measured twenty-six thousand square feet with an estimated value of fifty-four million dollars. And most of the time it just sat there. Empty.

Except when Betty was coming over. *Betty was one of Carter's best-kept secrets.* She was also late.

Carter glanced again at the Patek Philippe strapped to his wrist with a preppy blue-and-white nylon band. He and Betty had had many dates, and he couldn't remember another when she had kept him waiting. Time was money, after all. Her time, his money.

The thought of calling her flashed through his mind as he took a sip of his gin and tonic, but that idea was quickly rendered moot by the melodic chime of the front doorbell.

In ripped jeans and a faded polo shirt, Carter strode barefoot across the white Italian marble of his parents' foyer. In some ways Betty's arrival was the best part. The anticipation. The initial slow climb of a giant roller coaster before the ride of his life. And always, always, always the same two words when he opened the door.

"Hello, handsome," she would say.

Not today, though.

Carter blinked a few times, confused. But also a bit mesmerized.

She was auburn hair, lush and long. She was tanned skin, even now, in the month of December, accessorized with a full-length mink that left little doubt that not much was worn underneath it.

"You're not Betty," he said.

"No," she replied, slinking up to his left ear and whispering in a Russian accent. *"I'm better than Betty."*

TWO

She breezed by him, planting a three-inch stiletto heel in the middle of the foyer and turning around. Her jade-green eyes shifted to his hand. "What are you drinking?" she asked.

Carter glanced down as if reminding himself. "A gin and tonic."

"*Boring.* You have any tequila?"

"That depends. You have a name?"

She shook her head, playfully disappointed. "Do you always ask so many questions?"

"That was only one."

"One too many," she chided him. "Besides, Betty told me you like a little mystery."

"So, you and her are—*friends*?"

"Something like that. She had to travel somewhere last minute but thought you would like me." She dropped the mink just enough to expose the curve of her naked breasts, slightly larger than Betty's. "You do like me, don't you?"

Um.

"I think you're very pretty," said Carter, sounding way more like a schoolboy than he wanted to. He cleared his throat, dropping a half octave. "In fact, I'd say you're gorgeous."

"Good," she said, pulling the mink back over her shoulders. "Now how about that tequila?"

Carter led her into the billiard room and straight to the bar. For sure, he'd impress her with his knowledge of the blue agave aging process. "Reposado or añejo?" he asked.

Or maybe not. "Shut up and pour," she said.

Carter grabbed a lowball glass, pouring a generous shot of Partida Elegante. No sooner had he handed it to her than she threw it back like a pro, so to speak. Then, without the slightest hesitation, she reached into his gin and tonic for the unused lime, sucking it dry.

Plop. Back into his glass it went.

"Would you like to help me out of my coat, Carter?"

She turned around, the nape of her long neck and everything else about her inviting in Carter a hoard of extremely impure thoughts. *Clink, clink, clink* went the roller coaster, climbing upward. Were it not for the other sound in Carter's head, his father's voice, that mink of hers would've already been on the floor, along with the both of them.

"Cigars and women. The two things in life you always take your time with, son."

That was on Carter's eleventh birthday.

Slowly, Carter reached around with both hands, feeling his way inside the front of her coat. He hated the music of John Mayer— not to mention John Mayer himself—but for the first time he sort of knew what the guy was getting at with his song "Your Body Is a Wonderland." This woman felt amazing. Her skin, soft as the mink.

Of course, a young man can only be so patient.

Carter's hands slid past her navel, his fingers tracing the edge of her lace panties. He would do a drive-by first, a little tour of the perimeter before delving in.

Suddenly, he froze. *What the…?*

There was a bulge in those panties where there absolutely, positively should not have been a bulge. Unless, of course, Better Than Betty was actually a—*Benny?*

Carter's hands snapped back. He nearly tripped over his own feet as he tried to pull away. When she spun around, the first thing he saw was her smile. Then came the second thing.

He'd felt something hard, all right, and for a split second he was relieved to know that it was something other than what he thought. The next split second, he wasn't so sure.

He could live with *The Crying Game*. But the snub-nosed, single-action .38 now aimed at his chest?

"Who are you?" asked Carter. "What do you want?"

"Again with the questions," she said.

Fine, no questions. Just a knee-jerk offer born of sheer panic and an extremely privileged upbringing. "If it's money, you can have it. As much as you want. I promise. Anything. You can have it."

She shook her head with mock disgust. "See, now you're insulting me, Carter. Do I look like I need money?"

"I didn't mean to—"

"Shut up already. You were better off asking questions."

She cocked the hammer, the metallic sound—*click!*—echoing in Carter's head and jogging loose the one and only question that really mattered now.

"Are you going to kill me?" he asked, his voice cracking.

Surprise, surprise. She shook her head no. But it was the way she did it, as if he'd just asked a tricky question with an even trickier answer.

"No, I'm not going to kill you," she explained. *"You're going to do it for us."*

BOOK ONE

THE ART OF REVENGE

CHAPTER 1

I once taught a class with a massive hangover. My head was throbbing and I wanted to throw up. It wasn't my finest hour, but it wasn't my worst, either.

During another semester, pre-Covid-19, I'd caught the flu. I had a temperature of 103 degrees and looked paler than a box of chalk. Still another time I was battling a kidney stone that had me keeling over in agony while discussing whether Freud really did have the hots for his mother.

The point being, the postal service has nothing on me. When Dylan Reinhart has an abnormal-psychology lecture to give, he delivers it no matter what.

But for the first time I simply didn't have it in me.

Still, I couldn't call in sick. Of all classes, this was one I knew I couldn't miss.

If his fellow students can show up, I sure as hell can, too.

"Good morning, everyone, although I truly wish it were a good morning," I began.

Then I just stopped. I knew everything I wanted to say, all the soothing reassurances that the grieving process is actually very healthy and that life—no matter how challenging at times or, more aptly put, how utterly effed-up beyond hope it can all too often feel like—is still always worth living. Nothing is sweeter in death. If it were, the pope wouldn't have a pope mobile.

Again, though, I just stopped. All I could do was stare helplessly at my students as they stared right back at me. I could see it in their eyes. None of us had this in us.

Suicide isn't supposed to make sense. I knew that. Hell, I'd even written about it extensively in *AJP*, the *American Journal of Psychology*. But this, what Carter had done, truly made no sense at all.

The kid wasn't born on third base. No, he had it even better. Carter von Oehson was born crossing home plate after hitting the walk-off home run to win the World Series. Game seven, no less. He was the son of a multibillionaire and *GQ*–model handsome. Literally. Carter had appeared only months ago in the magazine's September issue for a feature called "The Young Men of the Ivy League." He was Mr. Yale.

So how does this young man, my student, charismatic as all get-out and with so much going for him, decide it simply isn't enough? Why did Carter von Oehson take to Instagram a few weeks before Christmas and announce that "everything isn't as peachy keen as it seems" and that he "no longer has the will"?

Even after that post, people still didn't believe it. This was Carter being Carter. A cutup. A provocateur. He didn't shy away from drama—he courted it. Any minute now he'd show up back on campus, all smiles and laughs. That's what everyone thought.

But then those minutes became days. That's when the New Haven police were called. That's when it became news—local, tristate area, and then national. Carter's roommate explained in a TV interview, while standing in front of the century-old Harkness Tower, that last Tuesday morning Carter had left their second-floor room in the Old Campus dorm, wearing his winter coat. He had his car keys but not his knapsack.

His roommate didn't think anything of it because Carter didn't have any Tuesday classes and apparently left campus a lot on those days. Sometimes he came back Tuesday night, sometimes the next morning. But he always came back.

Then Saturday happened.

No one could blame Carter's parents for not mentioning to detectives that Carter kept a Sunfish at their waterfront Darien home. Who thinks of sailing in December? Besides, it had been months since the boat had been tied to their dock in plain sight, let alone configured. Before Carter left back in August for freshman orientation, he'd disassembled the Sunfish and stored it in the garage.

A maintenance worker at the Tokeneke Club less than a mile from the von Oehson home was the one who first spotted the boat at low tide early Saturday morning. The Sunfish was wedged along the side of a jetty that shielded the club's beach. It had been washed ashore, fully intact, save for the heavy scratches on the bow. Carter had taken the boat out, but only the boat returned.

The Coast Guard concluded its search after twenty-four hours. Divers scoured the waters around the jetty, although if Carter had accidentally drowned he presumably would've either still been floating or washed ashore. By the end of the weekend there was only one logical conclusion, especially given Carter's Instagram post. There was nothing accidental about his drowning.

"Professor Reinhart?"

I'm not sure which student had spoken up. It was a safe bet there was more than one. I had no idea how long I'd been standing there behind the lectern in a complete daze. "I'm sorry. What?" I asked.

"You stopped talking," said someone in the front row.

"Yeah, are you sure you're okay?" came a voice toward the back.

I snapped out of it. The room, my students—and most important—my purpose suddenly came into focus.

"Let's get out of here," I said. "Everybody follow me."

CHAPTER 2

THE YALE PROFESSOR HANDBOOK is decidedly unclear on the topic of spontaneous field trips. Come to think of it, it's decidedly unclear whether there's even such a thing as the Yale professor handbook. If so, I certainly haven't read it.

Besides, it's not as if I were taking the class rock climbing or bungee jumping. We were merely heading over to Woolsey Rotunda, which serves as the entrance to Woolsey Hall, the largest auditorium on campus. Even as we trudged in from the cold, though, none of my students knew why we were there. That's how I wanted it.

"Everyone, please spread out," I said.

There's a reason the Whiffenpoofs and practically every other a cappella singing group at Yale has performed in Woolsey Rotunda. In a word? Acoustics. Nowhere else on campus does sound carry, echo, reverberate, and resonate as fully and beautifully as it has in this rotunda for more than a century.

I waited in the middle as the students filled out the space around me. Then I began.

"When I was thirteen, I lost my mother to pancreatic cancer," I said. "There's no good time to lose a parent, but thirteen was especially tricky. I was obviously old enough to fully understand what had happened, the finality of it. But at the same time I was still only a kid. I hadn't lived enough to really know how to process death. All I knew was how much it hurt, and here's the tricky part: all I wanted to do was make that pain go away.

"I remember two things about the guy on the other end of the phone the night I called the suicide hotline. The first was his name—Doug. Doug talked to me for more than an hour, and at no time did he ever tell me that I shouldn't kill myself. Everyone who calls that number has reasons for doing so, and although I didn't realize it at the time, the main reason isn't that you want to kill yourself. It's that you're searching for someone, *anyone*, to give you a reason not to. And simply being told 'don't do it' isn't reason enough.

"So that was the second thing. Doug never told me that night what I should or shouldn't do. His job wasn't to give me a lecture, which is why we're here instead of back in class. What suddenly dawned on me while looking at all of you, so soon after Carter's suicide, is that words just aren't going to cut it today. How can you make sense of something that makes no sense? You can't. *You shouldn't.* So today, I say to hell with saying the right thing. To hell with saying anything at all."

With that, I gave my class a resounding explanation for why we'd marched across campus. Acoustics. At the top of my lungs, I let go with the loudest, nastiest, most primal scream I'd ever unleashed.

Half of my students were startled. As for the other half, I downright scared the crap out of them. But an amazing and wonderful thing happened as the sound of my scream engulfed the entire rotunda, the echoes seemingly weaving in and out and all around us.

One by one they started to join in. Primal screams from

younger lungs, even louder and—yes, angrier—than mine. The angrier the better. Let it all out. That was the idea. Then it can't eat you up from the inside.

When the echoes finally faded, the rotunda once again returning to silence, I looked around and smiled. Satisfied.

"Class dismissed," I said. "See you all next week."

CHAPTER 3

T. S. ELIOT HAD IT all wrong about April. Cruel, my ass. Clearly the dude had never tried riding a motorcycle round trip from Manhattan to New Haven in the month of January. Or February, for that matter.

The deepest into winter I can usually still ride my bike is December, and that's only if I catch a week early on before the mercury truly plummets. Even then I have to layer up like the kid from *A Christmas Story*.

"Is that a '62 or a '63?" came a voice over my shoulder. I was standing in the parking lot near Ingalls Rink, affectionately known as the Whale, about to strap on my helmet after climbing into my insulated clutch pants.

"Actually, it's a '61," I said, before fully turning around to see who was doing the asking.

Not that looking at him told me much. The man standing before me was wearing a black full-length cashmere coat and a Vineyard Vines baseball cap pulled down tight just above the eyes, which were covered by oversized sunglasses. Whoever he was, he was lying low.

"A 1961 Triumph TR6," he said. "I don't actually own one of those. Good for you."

There was so much to unpack with that line I didn't know where to begin. *I don't actually own one of those?* And that condescending tack-on in light of the fact that I did? *Good for you?* As if the natural order of the universe had somehow been upended by my owning something that this guy didn't?

Only that's what tipped me off as to who he was, the connotation of immense wealth combined with the strong sense that I'd heard his voice somewhere before. This was Carter von Oehson's father, in the flesh. He wasn't talking to the press in the wake of Carter's suicide, but they'd shown news clips of past interviews.

He stepped toward me. "I'm Mathias von Oehson," he said, making it official.

I removed my riding gloves so we could shake hands. "Dylan Reinhart," I said.

"Yes, I know."

I know you know. This is hardly an accidental meeting, is it? Not a chance in the world.

"I'm very sorry for your loss," I said.

"Thank you. I appreciate that. Actually, that's what brings me to campus, albeit incognito," he said. "I was hoping you and I could speak privately for a few minutes."

I glanced around. There wasn't another human being within a hundred yards. Far be it from me to point that out, though. Not to Mathias von Oehson. He was the genius, the Nostradamus, the Mad Hungarian of Wall Street, according to the litany of articles and features extolling his mastery of the financial markets. The man was the titan of all hedge funds. In other words, Mathias von Oehson didn't just manage risk. He controlled it.

"Shall we head back to my office?" I asked.

No need. Von Oehson quickly signaled with his hand. All the privacy we could ever want came rolling up to us from behind a row of parked cars. A black stretch limousine.

Except this was no ordinary prom-night limo. This was a Mercedes-Maybach Pullman, the ultimate ride for the chauffeured set. I'd never seen one in person. In fact, I could've sworn I'd read they weren't even available for sale in the United States. A brilliant US marketing strategy, if there ever was one.

The driver stepped out, but his boss waved him off. Von Oehson opened the door for me, then walked around to get in from the other side. And like that we were sitting side by side in roughly seven hundred thousand dollars' worth of comfort. *So why don't I feel the least bit comfortable?*

The reason was as clear as the stress and anguish etched on von Oehson's face, even behind the cap and sunglasses. He was about to ask me a question that I couldn't answer. He was a father on a mission. It was only natural. Carter's suicide post on Instagram was short on specifics. Very short. Von Oehson was now talking to anyone and everyone on the Yale campus who could possibly help him understand why his son would take his own life. Friends and acquaintances, professors and administrators. I was simply next on his list.

Or maybe not.

Von Oehson turned to me, removed his sunglasses, and got right down to it. "My son didn't kill himself," he said.

CHAPTER 4

"CARTER'S ALIVE?"

"I don't know for certain. I think so," said von Oehson. "But if he is dead, he sure as hell didn't drown himself out at sea."

"You're saying he could've been murdered?"

"That or, more likely, he was kidnapped. That's what I really think. Either way, they've made it look like a suicide."

I drew a deep breath, in and out. It takes a lot to make my head spin, and I was already full-on, Tilt-a-Whirl dizzy. According to von Oehson, his son might be alive. Or maybe he was murdered. Or quite possibly kidnapped. And somehow his suicide was faked?

"Have you gone to the police?" I asked.

"No," said von Oehson.

"Why not?"

"Because I can't."

There was obviously a reason behind that answer, but even more obvious was that von Oehson didn't want to share it. Not yet, at least. He seemingly had this conversation all mapped out in his head, and we weren't quite at the point where he would explain why he couldn't go to the police.

Fine, I'll play along for now.

"I could ask you a ton of questions about what you know and how you know it," I said. "Instead, why don't you simply share what you're comfortable telling me?"

Von Oehson nodded. It was the way he nodded, though. More approval than agreement. It was my first inkling as to why he'd come looking for me.

"*Peachy keen,*" he said, punching both words. "Does that ring a bell?"

"Yes, from Carter's Instagram post. He used that expression."

"Yes, and very much on purpose. *Peachy keen* happens to be the distress signal for our home alarm system in Darien."

"By *distress signal,* you mean if someone triggered the alarm while breaking into your home and then put a gun to your head."

"Exactly," said von Oehson. "That's how you would signal the alarm company when they called the house: use a code word or phrase that doesn't tip off the intruder."

"Carter knew the hidden meaning of the phrase?" I asked. "*Peachy keen?*"

"I'm the one who told him."

"Years ago, I assume. Right?"

"Yes, but it's not like he'd forget."

"So in other words, Carter wrote the Instagram post under duress," I said. "He was signaling you. Is that what you're saying?"

"You don't seem convinced."

"I'm simply weighing the possibility that it was a coincidence. Perhaps Carter just happened to have used that expression."

"It wasn't a coincidence."

"I'm sure you want to believe that, but—"

He cut me off, his hand slicing hard through the air. "This isn't about what I *want* to believe. This is what happened."

I looked away from von Oehson, my eyes darting around at all the fancy knobs, dials, buttons, screens, and hand-stitched leather surrounding me in the back of his Maybach. I said nothing. Not another word.

Sometimes you have to let your silence do the talking for you.

I'm done playing along, Mathias. Whether you're ready or not, it's time to tell me. Why can't you go to the police?

Everything he'd told me so far about Carter's disappearance kept coming back to that one question. I knew it, and so did he.

"Okay, it's like this," said von Oehson finally. "There's something else missing besides my son."

That was more than enough to get me looking back at him again.

"It's a painting," he continued. "A Monet worth more than a hundred million dollars. It was at my home in Darien. Now it isn't."

"Wouldn't that be even more of a reason for you to go to the police?"

"It would be if it weren't for one thing."

"What's that?" I asked.

"It's a stolen painting," he said.

CHAPTER 5

"I REALLY WISH YOU hadn't told me that."

"It's not quite what you think," he said.

"What do I think?"

"That I stole a hundred-million-dollar Monet."

"So you didn't?"

Von Oehson shrugged. "Technically, I did. Although I was more like a silent partner."

"Again, you should've stayed that way," I said. "Silent."

"You don't strike me as the type, Professor Reinhart."

"What type is that?"

"Someone uncomfortable knowing another man's secrets," he said. "Besides, I haven't even told you why I stole it yet. Like any great work of art, there's more than meets the eye."

"Fair enough," I said. "Go ahead. I'm listening."

Right on cue, von Oehson pressed one of the buttons on the center console between us. An image of the Monet came up on a monitor below the raised partition that sealed off the driver.

That's another thing about any great work of art. You usually know the artist just by looking at it.

Woman by the Seine," he said. "1866. Unsigned, but it hung in

Monet's studio in Giverny before he sold it. There's a photograph to prove it."

I leaned forward, taking a closer look at the stunning image of a woman in a white crinoline domed skirt. She was shielding the sun with a parasol—a Monet staple—near a bench along the Seine river in Paris. At least, one could assume it was the Seine.

"Beautiful," I said. It truly was. "I've never seen this one before."

"Most people haven't. For more than half a century it was hanging in a private room in the Hungarian Parliament Building in Budapest."

"So it was owned by the Hungarian government?"

"Funny you should ask," he said. "They certainly claim it was."

"You know differently?"

"I do. And they do, too. They'll just never admit it publicly."

"Is that why I've never heard about this? The theft of a hundred-million-dollar Monet would certainly make a newspaper or two," I said.

"Yes, to put it mildly. Part of the reason was surely embarrassment, but the main reason they kept it under wraps was to avoid the unwanted scrutiny it would've attracted. How the painting was originally obtained."

"Let me guess." Although by this point it was hardly a guess. The combination of the Hungarian government and the sketchy lineage of a painting in their possession—even the most casual student of World War II history could probably put it together. "Nazis," I said.

"Yes," said von Oehson. "The painting was looted by the Third Reich during the occupation of Hungary in 1944. After the war it quietly ended up in the hands of the Hungarian government."

"Only it was never theirs to own in the first place."

"Precisely," said von Oehson.

"How do you know, though?"

"Because it belonged to my great-grandfather. He bought it, and it was taken from him."

"So you reclaimed it," I said. "Only now it's disappeared along with your son."

"That's why I think Carter's still alive. It's not enough that they got the painting back. I'm being punished. Taxed. I suspect soon I'll be contacted about a ransom. And that's if I'm lucky."

"You really think the Hungarian government is behind this?"

"My art collection is valued at well over a billion dollars, and the only painting taken is the one that no one knows I have?"

"If you're right, someone must have known."

"Which is why we're having this conversation," he said. "I need you to find whoever that someone is, and when you do you'll also find my son."

There it was. Confirmation of what I suspected. Mathias von Oehson was looking for a hired gun. He couldn't go to the police lest he admit to grand larceny of the highest order. I was plan B.

Still. "I'm a college professor, Mr. von Oehson."

He smiled ever so slightly. "You weren't always," he said. "Let's just say you come highly recommended."

"By whom?"

"You don't expect me to reveal all my secrets, do you? What matters is that I need your help, and I'm willing to pay handsomely for it." He extended his hand. "What do you say?"

Sometimes you think long and hard about a decision. You ponder it deeply, carefully weighing the pros and cons. This wasn't one of those times. There were too many cons.

"If you truly feel you can't go to the police, there are certain private detectives, most of them ex–FBI agents, who you could turn to," I said, shaking his hand. "As for me, I'm afraid I can't help you."

"You haven't even heard my offer."

"It wouldn't make a difference."

"Are you sure? Most everyone likes my offers."

"I'm not everyone," I said.

Von Oehson laughed. A little too hard, though, and he knew it.

"I'm sorry," he said. "You reminded me of myself just there, back when I quit my first job at Goldman. I told them I was leaving that same day. I wasn't giving them two weeks. They said, 'Everyone gives two weeks,' and my response was, 'I'm not everyone.'" He bobbed his head, thinking about it. "They were right, though. I should have given them two weeks' notice. It's the right thing to do."

As I reached for the door handle and stepped out of the car, I said nothing more. Neither did von Oehson.

That should've been my first clue.

CHAPTER 6

IT WAS MIDAFTERNOON WHEN I arrived back in Manhattan. Five o'clock, cocktail hour, was still a couple of hours away, but it didn't matter. I was rounding up. After the primal-scream field trip with my students, followed by the encounter with Mathias von Oehson that flipped everything about Carter's apparent suicide upside down, it was definitely time for a drink.

Turns out, Tracy was well ahead of me.

His text was waiting on my cell when I parked my bike in the garage near our new apartment on 82nd off West End Avenue. He wanted me to meet him at Vincenzo's a few blocks away, our favorite Italian restaurant in our new neighborhood.

"You'll need to catch up," Tracy added with a couple of martini emojis. He clearly wasn't there to eat.

In fact, when I walked into Vincenzo's the first thing I saw was another round being placed in front of him at the bar. Broken Shed vodka, two olives, and only a drop of vermouth. His usual. Although not usually in the middle of a Wednesday afternoon. Something was up, all right.

First things first, though. *Where's our daughter?*

Tracy being Tracy, he answered the question even before I

asked it. "Lucinda agreed to stay an extra couple of hours," he said when he saw me approaching.

Lucinda's our go-to babysitter. She emigrated from Portugal a decade ago. We didn't hire her very often when we first adopted Annabelle because we couldn't stand being away from our new baby girl. We still can't stand it, but one of the things Tracy and I have learned about parenting skills is that they improve after having some alone time together as a couple.

Also, some alone time *apart* from each other as a couple. For me, that's my teaching and…well, yeah, some of my "extra-curriculars" over the past few years, such as chasing down a serial killer who used playing cards to announce his victims in advance and, more recently, helping to stop a major terrorist attack on Grand Central station. So much for my early retirement from the CIA.

For Tracy, he has his acting career and the amazing volunteer work he does with Harlem Legal House, putting his Yale law degree to use by helping those who aren't able to afford a private attorney. Lately, though, there have been fewer auditions and more hours spent up in Harlem. He still loves acting, but the satisfaction he gets from making sure the justice system works for everyone, and not just the wealthy, is greater than—and I quote—anything he's ever felt onstage or in front of a camera. That makes me love and respect Tracy even more.

So if that means having Lucinda watch Annabelle three after-noons a week instead of two so Tracy can volunteer more and I can still prepare for my lectures, so be it. We adore Lucinda. Annabelle adores Lucinda. Plus, how many American two-and-a-half-year-olds can already say *please* and *thank you* in Portuguese?

"Okay, then," I said, pivoting from our daughter back to Tracy. *"What's wrong?"*

CHAPTER 7

"YOU'RE KIDDING ME. WHY? How?" I asked.

But it was as if he couldn't hear me. He was rambling, trapped in his own panic. "I don't know what we're going to do. Seriously, we're screwed. The budget, our operating costs—we're already in debt up to our ears as it is. We couldn't possibly afford a lease somewhere else..."

Harlem Legal House occupied storefront office space rent-free in exchange for providing the building owner with free legal services. It was a quid pro quo, the good kind, with Harlem Legal House definitely getting the better end of the bargain. But the building was about to change hands.

"Maybe you can make the same deal with the new owner," I said.

"We already asked and were told no."

"Okay, so you'll find a new landlord who'll say yes."

Tracy just shook his head. *Fat chance.* He was right, too. The current owner was kind and considerate, two qualities rarely associated with New York City landlords.

"Besides, there's no time," said Tracy.

"What do you mean?"

"Since we don't pay rent, our lease is technically on a month-to-month basis."

He'd never mentioned that to me. "So you only have until the end of this month?"

"Not even. We have to be out before that. By Christmas."

"That doesn't seem right."

"None of this does. The owner wasn't looking to sell, but he told us he got an offer too good to pass up. The deal closes right after the new year." Tracy reached again for his martini. He was holding on to it like a life preserver. "We just feel so blindsided."

"There's got to be a solution," I said. The volunteers at Harlem Legal House were some of the best legal minds in the city.

"We were brainstorming the entire morning. It's pretty hopeless, but we're going to get together again tomorrow. Maybe there's a miracle to be had. I'm going to cancel my trip."

Tracy had plans to take Annabelle for a few days' visit with his sister, who lived in Marblehead, just outside of Boston. "You can't cancel," I said.

"She'll understand."

"Of course she will, but that's not the point."

"I know," he said. "Believe me, I know."

Tracy's sister, Rebecca, had suffered a miscarriage six months ago. She and her husband had been trying to have a child for nearly two years before that, and Rebecca was devastated. Tracy had been trying to see her since it happened, but she kept putting him off. Finally she said yes. She even made a point of asking Tracy to bring Annabelle. You don't need a degree in psychology to understand the importance of that.

The bartender came over, and I ordered a Maker's Mark, neat. He gave me a heavy pour while nodding at both of us. The guy was clearly good at reading body language.

"To better days," I said to Tracy, raising my glass. To think, I hadn't even told him about the one I'd had.

"Yes, to better days." He then mumbled something else under his breath. I immediately did a double take.

"What was that?" I asked.

"What you said, to better days."

"No, after that. To better days, but..."

"But to hell with the next two weeks. That's what we were given to vacate the building," said Tracy. "Two weeks' notice."

Son of a bitch.

I downed my bourbon in one swig, pushing back from the bar. "I'll be back soon."

"Wait. Where are you going?" asked Tracy.

"I'll explain later."

"What does that mean?"

"Just trust me," I said.

CHAPTER 8

"RIGHT THIS WAY, DR. REINHART."

The doorman didn't even ask who I was or who I wanted to see in such a damn hurry. *He already knew.* And I'm not just talking about the doorman.

"Good to see you again," said Mathias von Oehson as the private elevator opened to his penthouse apartment, sixty-five ear-popping stories above West 57th Street, a.k.a. billionaires' row. He was standing contentedly in the middle of a massive foyer, arms folded and tongue planted firmly in cheek as he added, "What a nice surprise."

Nothing takes the piss out of storming another man's castle than when the man not only knows you're coming but basically orchestrated the visit. Still, I did my best to convey exactly how I was feeling.

"Fuck you," I said, stepping off the elevator.

Von Oehson shrugged. "I suppose that's fair."

I really wanted to hit this guy. Level him. Lay him out flat on his Brazilian hardwood floor, or wherever the hell it came from. "You knew I would turn you down, that I'd say no."

"Yes, that's right," he said.

"So, before you even spoke to me this morning, you'd bought the building where—"

"Where your partner volunteers."

"He's my husband," I said.

"My mistake."

"Hardly your biggest one of the day."

"We'll see about that," he said. "As for the building, I don't technically own it yet. There's only an accepted offer."

"One that's too good for the current owner to pass up, apparently."

"I told you earlier. People tend to like my offers."

"Good. Now I want you to rescind it."

"And I want you to find my son. I believe this is what's called a standoff."

"I can think of another name for it," I said. "Front-page news."

"You're not going public with what I told you, Dylan. May I call you Dylan?"

"That depends. May I call you a prick?"

"You'd hardly be the first," he said, "and you're not going to the press because you know the difference. Not helping me get Carter back is one thing. Doing something that could harm him is another."

He was right. We both knew it. Talking to the media would put Carter at further risk, assuming he had indeed been kidnapped. What I needed, though, was for von Oehson to see the light.

"Yes, let's talk about doing harm," I said. "You're shuttering a legal aid center. Do you hear me? *A legal aid center.*"

"It doesn't have to be that way."

"You're right, it doesn't. So why do it?"

"You're here right now, aren't you?"

"Yeah, and you're lucky we're just talking."

"You'd like that, wouldn't you?" he said. "Taking a swing at me?"

"It's more than crossed my mind."

"What's stopping you?"

"You're not worth it," I said.

"An ironic turn of phrase." He glanced over his shoulder at his fifty-million-dollar apartment, give or take. As if I needed any reminder of how wealthy Mathias von Oehson truly was. "Desperate men do desperate things, Dylan. You're a father. You must be able to understand," he said.

"That much I do. But not what you've done here."

"You still haven't heard my offer, how much I'm willing to pay."

"I told you, it wouldn't make a difference," I said. "I don't need your money."

"I know you don't. That's the whole point."

"What is?"

"Why you're going to find my son and bring him home to me," he said. "What's more, you're going to do it without my paying you a dime."

That's when von Oehson finally told me his offer.

Damn, if I didn't accept it on the spot.

CHAPTER 9

THE AIR WAS DENSE with imminent snow as I walked outside von Oehson's apartment building. I texted Tracy, asking where he was. I knew I'd get a quick reply. He had to be wondering where the hell I'd run off to.

TJ's, he texted back.

Tracy had given up on the afternoon martinis and was making a quick trip to Trader Joe's before heading home to relieve Lucinda. By the time I caught up to him he was in the bread aisle. That was somewhat fitting, as he was about to learn.

"What was that all about?" he asked. "Where were you? Where'd you go?"

"I went to see Mathias von Oehson."

It took him a moment. *Mathias von Oehson?* "You mean—"

"Yeah, the hedge fund guy," I said. "His son was the one from my class. I went to his apartment down on 57th."

Tracy knew about Carter's suicide. I'd told him about it as soon as I'd found out. Even if Carter hadn't been my student, the story was all over the news. Tracy squinted. "That's where you rushed off to? You never even mentioned you knew his father."

"I don't," I said. "Or, at least, I didn't until earlier this morning. He came to see me on campus."

The more I explained, the more confused Tracy became. I couldn't blame him. "Why?" he asked. "Was it something about his son?"

"He thinks Carter is still alive, that he didn't kill himself."

"Why would he think that?"

This answer wasn't about to help. "He has his reasons," I said.

Cue the eye roll. "In other words, you're not going to tell me," said Tracy.

"It's only to protect Carter."

"Do you really think he's still alive?"

"I don't know, but von Oehson wants me to find out," I said.

"You mean, like, to help the police with an investigation?"

"Not exactly."

"What then?"

"He doesn't want to involve the police."

"Let me guess," he said. *"He has his reasons."*

"Something like that. If it's any consolation, I told him no at first."

"What changed your mind?"

"He made me an offer I couldn't refuse," I said. I at least had the good sense not to do my Marlon Brando impression. Tracy was in no mood.

"In other words, he's paying you," he said.

"It's more like leveraging me."

I watched Tracy's face as it all suddenly clicked, why I left him at the bar so quickly after he told me about Harlem Legal House and the sale of their building. "Shit. Von Oehson's the buyer, isn't he?"

"Yes, but now you all don't have to move, and you still don't have to pay rent," I said.

"That's not leverage, Dylan. That's extortion."

"Tomayto, tomahto."

"Yeah, so let's call the whole thing off."

"Absolutely," I said. "Screw him. To hell with von Oehson." I then reached into my coat pocket, handing Tracy an envelope. He looked inside.

"What's this?" he asked.

"It's a check."

"I can see that." He took it out, staring. He all but rubbed his eyes in disbelief. "Is this for real?"

"Not only is it real. It's only half of it. The first million is the down payment. The back end is another million."

"He's paying you two million dollars?"

"No. Look again. He's paying Harlem Legal House two million dollars," I said. That's how von Oehson had made out the check. "Technically, it's a donation."

"That's insane."

"Or maybe he's just a desperate father who also happens to be a multibillionaire."

"I get it," said Tracy. "I really do. This is all about his son, and he'll go to whatever lengths and spend whatever it takes. That doesn't make it right, though."

"I agree, it's messed up," I said. "Then again, so is the justice system for poor people, right? That's the whole mission of Harlem Legal House, to right that wrong. Ask some of your clients how they'd feel about an extra two million in their corner."

I watched Tracy mulling it over. It wasn't so much that I had to talk him into this. I simply had to give him enough time to make peace with it.

"What am I supposed to tell the board?" he asked.

"You tell them the good news that you've struck a deal with the new owner of the building. It's the same deal you had with the old owner. Crisis averted."

"And the two million?"

"Let's wait until we have all of it before you mention anything. In the meantime, go see your sister as planned."

"What about you?"

"What about me?"

"You've agreed to help find a man's son who everyone thinks is dead. Do you even know where to start?"

"I already have," I said.

CHAPTER 10

I WANTED TO SPEND the next morning with Annabelle, some one-on-one time, before she and Tracy headed up to Massachusetts to see his sister. Four-plus hours is a lot of time to be strapped in a car seat, so the plan was to bundle up and get her plenty of fresh air beforehand. For Annabelle, that meant going to her new favorite place. The Central Park Zoo.

After a full trip around all the exhibits, with Annabelle happily out of the stroller and tramping through the fresh snow for most of the visit, we landed on a bench by the sea lions. That's where I'd told him to meet me.

"We're just going to wait a little bit for my friend, sweetheart. He should be here any minute," I said.

Annabelle hardly minded. A fox, a giraffe, a hippopotamus, an iguana—she was on my lap and fully engrossed in the A-to-Z animal picture book I'd bought her at the gift shop, although she was having a heck of a time turning the pages with her mittens on. When I tried to help her she all but swatted my hand away. Score another one for the movement against helicopter parenting.

"I do it, Daddy," she assured me. "I do it!"

A minute later he arrived, wearing a bulky overcoat, a wool

trapper hat, and one of those ski masks with cutouts for the eyes and mouth.

"You look like you're about to rob a 7-Eleven," I said.

"Can't help it," said Julian. "We Brits don't like the cold."

It wasn't *that* cold, but I was fairly certain the ski mask was serving a dual purpose for my old friend. Warmth, yes, but also anonymity. Just in case.

Of course, the trick to being known as one of the world's most gifted and feared hackers is not to be known at all. Only a handful of people on the planet could pick Julian Byrd out of a lineup. Thankfully, Vladimir Putin wasn't one of them, nor were any members of ISIS, Al-Qaeda, Hezbollah, Hamas, Boko Haram, or the Taliban. Julian had wreaked havoc on all their hidden bank accounts over the years, in addition to either blocking or intercepting the bulk of their online communications. They'd all love to kill him. If only they knew who he was.

The fact that I did was rooted in my CIA days stationed in London, back when Julian was with MI6. After I left the agency, he soon joined it—with MI6's permission, naturally. In return the Brits got a guarantee of better shared intelligence, plus access to some advanced spyware out of a certain Silicon Valley lab disguised as an academic software developer.

"My apologies for running late," he said.

"No worries. You're the one doing me the favor," I said. "As usual."

"Yes. That is true, isn't it?"

"Plus, you actually left your Batcave and braved the weather for me."

"How could I say no? I finally get to meet this gorgeous little lady." He pulled up his mask, flashing a huge smile. "Hello, Annabelle! I'm Julian."

"Beard!" she said, pointing.

Toddlers love to cut to the chase. Julian truly did have an epic beard these days. It wasn't long, but it was big and bushy.

"Do you want to touch it?" he asked, leaning forward.

Annabelle patted away on his beard with her mittens, laughing as Julian made one funny face after another.

"Who needs the animals?" I said.

"Yeah, about that," he replied. "Who goes to the zoo in winter? I didn't even know it was open."

"Are you kidding me? This is the best time. Isn't that right, Annabelle? What was your favorite animal we saw today?"

She raised her hands in the air. "Snow leppies!"

"Little-known fact," I said. "The snow leopards actually have heated rocks in their exhibit. They're more fun to watch in the winter."

"I'm sold, professor," he said. "Let's go look at the leppies!"

Annabelle was immediately on board, she raised her arms again. "Yeah! Yeah!"

"Wait! Wait!" I said.

"Ah, yes. Business before leppies, huh?" Julian pulled his mask back down over his face and took a seat on the bench next to me. Reaching into his coat, he handed over an envelope. "Here you go," he said.

"So you were able to do it?" I asked.

"Of course I was able to."

"You said it couldn't be done."

"I always say that. Then I go ahead and do it."

I looked down at the envelope, feeling the flash drive between my fingers. "I can't thank you enough."

"Just buy me a Ferrari one day and we'll call it even," he said. "In the meantime, be extra mindful on this one."

"How do you mean?"

"The certain endeavors we engage in, the things we do, people like us. As risky and dangerous as it all is, it never really plays out in public. We never have to deal with that added component," he said.

"You mean, sunlight."

"Yes, as it were. Sunlight."

"I understand what you're saying."

"Do you?" Julian leaned forward, placing a hand on my shoulder. "Because if this von Oehson kid ends up dead on your watch, my old friend, it's a whole different kind of exposure."

CHAPTER 11

ELIZABETH REMEMBERED WHEN SHE was Pluto. The planet, not the Disney character.

It wasn't that long ago. She'd transferred into the elite Field Unit of the Joint Terrorism Task Force (JTTF) in Lower Manhattan, the only agent ever not to be handpicked by the task force chief, Evan Pritchard. He wasn't happy about it.

But Evan Pritchard knew better than to butt heads with the mayor.

Mayor Edward "Edso" Deacon held sway over the city with the kind of power not seen or felt since the days of Fiorello La Guardia. If Deacon wanted his young and pretty detective Elizabeth Needham transferred into the JTTF from his personal security detail—for reasons that he had zero intention of sharing—then, damn it, no one was going to stop him. Including Evan Pritchard.

Elizabeth got the job. Her getting the most high-profile assignments, however, was another story. She'd arrived only days before the attempted Times Square bombing. So much for easing into things. But when the follow-up attack on Grand Central station was thwarted and the terror cells eradicated, it was no longer all hands on deck at the JTTF. The natural pecking order resumed.

Elizabeth was the rookie, the newbie, the most distant planet in Pritchard's solar system. Pluto.

That was then. This was now.

While Pritchard was demanding, caustic, and sometimes a flat-out son of a bitch, he was also fair. His unit within the JTTF was first and foremost a meritocracy. The harder you worked, the more you rose in that pecking order, and no one worked harder than Elizabeth. Pritchard took notice. As sure as gravity, she began being pulled in to assist on the most high-profile assignments. He even had her move desks so she'd be closer to his office. Why bother dialing an extension when all you have to do is scream?

"Needham! Get in here!"

This morning was no different.

Elizabeth rose from her chair at the sound of Pritchard's booming voice, taking the short walk to his office. It was before 8:00 a.m., and he knew she'd already be at her desk—even though most of her fellow agents weren't at theirs.

"Needham!" he bellowed again. He sounded like James Earl Jones with a megaphone.

"One day, he might actually say *please*," muttered Pritchard's assistant, Gwen, as Elizabeth passed by. Gwen, short on height and long on chutzpah and sarcasm, had been with Pritchard for decades. His hours were her hours.

"Don't count on it," Elizabeth muttered back, adding a wink.

Elizabeth entered Pritchard's office, taking a seat in one of the two metal folding chairs in front of his massive yew desk. The chairs were purposely old and unpadded. A hard reminder, literally, that no agent should ever feel too comfortable in front of him.

"What are you working on, Needham?" he asked.

Pritchard knew what all his agents were working on, all the time. Elizabeth was half tempted to point that out. The other half, which included her brain, thought better of it.

"I'm on that offshore gambling thing," she answered.

"You mean, Rabbit's Foot?"

It wasn't a question, but a reminder. Pritchard wanted Field Unit operations to be referred to by their official name. Order and consistency was paramount to the former land component commander from Desert Storm. He never once referred to that operation as "that freeing-of-Kuwait thing."

"Yes," said Elizabeth, correcting herself. "Rabbit's Foot."

"Who are you partnered with?"

Again, Pritchard already knew the answer to the question he was asking. "Sullivan," she said.

"Anything to share?"

"Nothing yet, although that might change by the end of the day. Turkish intelligence is finally cooperating."

The purpose of Rabbit's Foot was to track large payouts by offshore gambling sites to shell companies possibly set up by terrorist groups. While the vast majority of operations that ran through the Field Unit of the JTTF were based on actionable intelligence, there were occasionally those that fell under the heading of speculative intelligence, otherwise known as a hunch. Instinct.

Elizabeth watched as Pritchard leaned back in his chair. She was certain he was about to ask her how she and Danny— Agent Sullivan—were able to pull the end run around the Turkish minister of finance, who'd been adamant about not sharing private banking information for suspected shell companies based in his country.

But that's not what Pritchard asked.

He had a different question. A real doozy. "So, Needham," he said, folding his arms. Pritchard always had his sleeves rolled up tight to his elbows. "Are you sleeping with anyone these days?"

CHAPTER 12

ELIZABETH BLINKED A FEW times, stunned. For sure, she'd misheard him. Only she was more sure she hadn't. "You know you're not actually allowed to ask me that, right?"

"Yes, and yet I still did," said Pritchard. "Imagine that."

Elizabeth had some very definite opinions about dealing with men in the workplace, and not all of what she believed was exactly feminism friendly. Context mattered a great deal. So did intent. But at the end of the day, the great Aretha Franklin said it best. R-e-s-p-e-c-t. The only way a guy ever truly crossed the line with Elizabeth was when it was clear he didn't respect her.

That wasn't the case with Pritchard. He didn't give a damn about your skin color, religion, where you were from, or even what pronoun you used. If you were extremely dedicated and an asset to the team, then he would always have your back.

But this was pushing it, to put it mildly. *He really just asked if I'm sleeping with anyone?*

Elizabeth figured her best response after his doubling down on the question was a hard stare. She crossed her arms in return, saying nothing.

"Okay, let me rephrase that a bit," Pritchard said finally. "Are you currently *dating* someone?"

"No, I'm not dating anyone at the moment." Not that that was really any of his business, either. "Why do you ask?"

"Sullivan," he said.

"What about him?"

"You know what."

"I'm not following," she said.

"Of course you are."

He was right. She was following. Elizabeth knew exactly what Pritchard meant and, as clumsy as it was, why he'd asked her such a personal question. You don't get to be the chief of the JTTF's Field Unit without having a sixth sense. Or sex sense, as it were.

"You think Danny and I are dating?"

"No, I don't," he said. "But I see the way he looks at you around the office."

"How's that?"

"The same way you look at him."

Elizabeth stared again at Pritchard. She was speechless. *Christ, have I really been that obvious?*

No, she hadn't. Pritchard was simply that good at knowing anything and everything happening in his unit. That even included things that actually weren't happening yet—but possibly could. That was obviously his concern.

"Are we really having this conversation?" she asked.

"Consider yourself lucky," he said. "We could be having it with Danny in the room."

True. That would've been worse, although it did beg the question: "Have you also spoken to Danny?" she asked.

"No, and I don't intend to," said Pritchard.

"Why not? Not that I want you to. I'm just curious."

"Because most guys are pigs, but Danny isn't. Nothing's going to happen between you and him unless you want it to happen."

"So you're telling me to make sure it doesn't?"

"Yes. That's exactly what I'm telling you."

"Does it make you feel any better to know I haven't had a serious boyfriend in more than five years?"

"No, it makes me feel sorry for you, Needham," he said. "Get a life, will you? But just don't do it with anyone here in the office." Pritchard leaned forward, resting his thick forearms on his giant desk. "There's only one thing worse than two of my agents sleeping with each other, and that's when they *stop* sleeping with each other. Do you get what I'm saying?"

"Yes," said Elizabeth, nodding. She stood up to leave.

"Where are you going?"

She sat back down, the metal chair beneath her feeling even harder now. "I thought we were done."

"I wish we were, but I got a call late last night from the mayor. In case you didn't know, I really hate late-night calls from the mayor," said Pritchard. "You're not going to like this one, either."

CHAPTER 13

THE ONLY THING ELIZABETH knew for sure was that the call had something to do with her. Anything beyond that was a blind guess. A few possibilities flashed across her mind. More than a few.

"The esteemed Mayor Deacon wants to borrow you," said Pritchard.

That definitely wasn't one of them. "*Borrow me?* What does that mean?"

"He wants you to work on something for him."

"What is it?"

"He wouldn't say, and trust me, I asked. More than once. I was actually hoping that you might have an idea," he said. "You clearly don't."

"You talked him out of it, though, right? You explained that I was neck-deep in an assignment?"

"And he explained in return that the reason he needed you wouldn't interfere for long with anything you were involved with here. It's short term."

"How short?"

"I tried to pin him down. A day? A few days? A week? He

wouldn't say for sure, but he did promise me it wouldn't be long," said Pritchard. "In fact, he used the words *I promise*."

"He's a politician."

"Yes. I'm well aware of that."

"How do I tell him no?" she asked.

"You don't. He's the mayor."

"He's not my boss. He's not even your boss."

Elizabeth recognized the look Pritchard was giving her. She used to get it a lot when she first joined the Field Unit. There was a certain watching-a-dog-chase-its-tail vibe to it.

"No matter how much you've earned your stripes here, Needham—and you sure as hell have—you still would've never set foot on this floor were it not for Deacon. I know it, you know it, and, most important, he knows it. He also knows he can make my job even harder than it already is. So if that egomaniac of a mayor wants to borrow you for some short-term assignment, I'm not going to be the one to tell him no," he said. "You're free to tell him if you want to, but that's the irony. If you were dumb enough to turn him down, you'd never be facing this situation in the first place."

There was a reason Evan Pritchard was a successful and highly decorated wartime commander. He knew how to pick and choose his battles.

"What time does he want me at his office?" asked Elizabeth.

"He said there'd be a car waiting for you out front at 9:15 sharp." He glanced at his watch. "That will give you just enough time to curse to yourself repeatedly before briefing Sullivan on your temporary leave of absence without furthering any more sexual tension between the two of you. Sound about right?"

Elizabeth faked a smile. "Perfect," she said.

Pritchard smiled back. "Good. Now get out of my office, Needham."

She did as he asked. She also did everything he predicted. Elizabeth returned to her desk while cursing under her breath, a few of the more choice words rising to the level of mumbling. When Sullivan arrived, she told him about needing to do "something" for the mayor, yet to be revealed. All the while, she was paying way too much attention to how she sounded and looked at Danny, lest she make it any more apparent—so she was told— that she had the hots for him. *Damn you, Pritchard...*

At 9:15 on the dot, she walked outside to see that the mayor wasn't merely sending a car for her. He was making the trip himself. It was as obvious as the black stretch limo hogging all the curb space right smack in front of the building. Edso Deacon wasn't subtle.

Out came his driver to open the door for her. As she slid into the seat, she reminded herself to keep her cool, that no matter what she couldn't let Deacon see that she was pissed. No way. He would enjoy that too much. The best play was to keep her mouth shut. Nothing but her best poker face.

Elizabeth took one look at the man sitting next to her, and suddenly all bets were off. It wasn't the mayor staring back at her. Deacon wasn't even in the limo.

"You've got to be kidding me," she said.

CHAPTER 14

I FLASHED MY VERY best smile. "Hey, partner!"

The art of persuasion is only about 80 percent actual persuasion, what you say and do. The other 20 percent is about making sure you have a captive audience.

I told the limo driver only one thing ahead of time. *After you open the door for her, get your tail back behind the wheel as fast as possible and drive!*

Which is not to say that it was beyond Elizabeth to do a tuck and roll from a moving vehicle. But I liked my odds. She would at least stick around and hear me out, although not without getting a little miffed at me first.

"What the hell's going on?" she asked. "I could kill you right now."

Perhaps *miffed* was being way too kind.

I've noticed over the years that Elizabeth's eyebrows tend to scrunch up when she's ticked off. The more ticked off, the more scrunched. They were pretty damn scrunched.

"Sorry," I said. "This was the only way."

"The only way for *what*?"

"That's what I'm about to explain."

"Wait. Did Deacon put you up to this? Whatever this is?"

"Actually it's more like the other way around. I did once save his life, after all. He's doing me a favor because I need you to do me a favor."

I thought it was a pretty good segue. Surely she would want to know the favor.

Nope. Not yet. "Why are we in a limo?" she asked.

"That was in case Pritchard happened to be watching."

"He's not in on this?"

"Pritchard? Hell no."

"So, in other words, you lied to my boss. That's what you're telling me?"

"Technically, it was the mayor doing the lying," I said. "But, hey, the good news is you don't have to deal with Deacon. He's not involved with this, either." I caught myself. "Well, he's not involved beyond getting clearance from Pritchard to borrow you, and then letting me borrow his personal limo."

"Great. So instead of being pissed just at the mayor I get to be pissed at both of you," she said. "And where are we going right now? It feels like I'm being kidnapped."

"Funny you should mention *kidnapped*," I said. She was about to say something more when I cut her off. I was running out of segues. *"Can I please just tell you what's going on?"*

For the next twenty blocks or so I explained everything leading up to my pulling in front of her building in a limo. There was no editing, no minor sins of omission. And certainly no protecting the privacy of a multibillionaire. Everything Mathias von Oehson had told me, from Carter and his prostitute to his use of *peachy keen* in his Instagram post to the painting stolen from the Hungarians and possibly their stealing it back, I told Elizabeth.

You either trust your partner or you don't.

"I really need your help," I said.

She didn't doubt my sincerity. Just my sanity. "You're crazy," she said. "Do you know that? What if Pritchard finds out?"

"He won't."

"The guy's like a Jedi Master. He can find out anything," she said. "He even knows all about my sex life, or lack thereof."

I shot her a look. *Who's the crazy one now?* "What on earth are you talking about?"

"Never mind."

"The mayor was very clear to Pritchard. Under no circumstances can he force you to tell him what you're needed for," I said. "Of course, knowing Pritchard, he already asked you this morning if you knew anything."

"He did."

"And you didn't have to lie."

"Is that really supposed to make me feel better?"

I slouched in my seat. "Maybe you're right. Maybe this was a mistake," I said. "The more I think about it, it's not as if I really can't do this on my own."

"*Seriously?* A psychology professor using reverse psychology?"

"Yeah. Is it working?"

"No, not even a little," she said. "But remind me again how much von Oehson is donating to Harlem Legal House."

"Two million dollars."

Elizabeth nodded slowly. That was working much better for her. "Yeah. That's a lot of money," she said.

"Does that mean you're in?"

"It means I haven't said no yet."

"So you're a maybe."

"It depends."

"On what?"

"For instance, you still haven't told me where we're going. Where does this genius plan of yours begin?" she asked.

"Where else, but at the beginning. The day Carter von Oehson disappeared, so did his girlfriend for hire," I said.

"You mean, the prostitute."

"I was trying to be politically correct."

"So says the man who just kidnapped me."

"Fine. That's where we're going," I said. "You and I are off to see a prostitute."

"Great," said Elizabeth. "My morning keeps getting better and better."

CHAPTER 15

WHEN WE ROLLED UP to the corner of East 65th Street and Third Avenue on the Upper East Side, it occurred to both of us that *prostitute* was perhaps not the right term after all. A *gentleman's escort* seemed more accurate. An expensive one, at that.

There are apartment buildings in the city, and there are luxury apartment buildings. This was definitely the latter. Even the doorman's suit was nicer than mine.

At the security desk, a guy in a guard's uniform gave us a look that all but screamed retired cop. Elizabeth did with him what I couldn't do. Flash a badge.

On the twenty-eighth floor we stepped out of the elevator and into a large foyer. A vase on the pedestal table in the center of the space held an arrangement of freshly cut flowers, mostly hyacinths. Their violet-blue color matched the vertical stripes of the wallpaper lining the hallway.

The address Julian had given me brought us to the last door on the right. A corner apartment. Again, I let Elizabeth lead the way. Not only did she have the badge, she had the better job title for the task at hand.

Within seconds of her knocking we heard footsteps approaching on the other side of the door. Elizabeth didn't wait to be asked who we were.

"I'm agent Elizabeth Needham," she said, before holding up her badge in front of the peephole. "Are you Paulina?"

"Yes," came her voice.

"Could you please open the door? We need to speak with you."

There was a pause. Pauses are fine. Just so long as they're not followed by footsteps walking away from the door. Or, worse, running. Neither was the case. A dead bolt snapped, and like that we were standing in front of a tall and slender blonde wearing a pair of sweatpants and a white T-shirt. Her hair was pulled back, she had no makeup on, and the heavy-framed glasses she was wearing looked straight out of *Revenge of the Nerds*. Still, she was absolutely, positively stunning.

"Come in," she said.

She had the Russian accent of someone who'd clearly been working over the years to get rid of it. Detectable, but only barely. She didn't inquire who I was, which meant Elizabeth didn't have to introduce me. Perfect.

I'd gone over the questioning back in the limo. I would never ask Elizabeth to follow a script, just her instincts, but there was one particular question I needed posed to Paulina Zernivik, and it had to come before any others.

"Have you heard from Carter von Oehson since his suicide?"

I watched carefully as Paulina processed the implications of what Elizabeth was asking her. I wasn't so much waiting for the answer—at least not the one she'd put into words. I all but expected her to pretend she didn't know who Carter was.

No, what mattered was the answer she'd give before even opening her mouth. The body language. The squint of recognition on hearing Carter's name. A sudden tensing of the shoulders when the brain, in a fit of panic, tells her to lie. All the unmistakable signs that she was hiding something about Carter's disappearance.

C'mon, Paulina, show me what you've got...

Only her eyes didn't narrow. Her shoulders actually relaxed. Paulina Zernivik had nothing to reveal—except relief. The kind you can't fake.

"Oh, thank God," she said.

CHAPTER 16

ONE, SHE KNEW CARTER. That was clear.

Two, she hadn't heard from him since he disappeared. Also clear.

"He's still alive, isn't he? That's what you're saying," she said. "He didn't kill himself."

"We *hope* he's still alive. We don't know for sure," I said. "But, yes, there's some evidence to suggest he didn't die by suicide."

Paulina nodded as if vindicated. "I knew it. I just knew it."

"Which is why we're here," I said. "To talk about what else you might know."

She tugged on her white T-shirt, her eyes darting back and forth at Elizabeth and me. "How did you find me?" she asked.

Well, you see, it's quite simple. It turns out the National Security Agency's global spy satellite network compiles more than one hundred petabytes of data every six months, more than the total data stored on all of Facebook's servers, and the NSA has to offload it periodically to an undisclosed data center so the network doesn't throttle itself. This network is the virtual equivalent of Fort Knox, using 256-bit encryption, but the transfer is only 64 bit because by that point the data is deemed innocuous with no national security implications and is essentially nothing more than Google Maps, albeit featuring a minute-by-minute rendering of every inch of the planet with the kind of clarity that goes well beyond what any map app could ever offer. For instance, the vehicle identification number on the black Range Rover HSE registered to your name and address, Paulina, that you've been driving to the von Oehson home in Darien, Connecticut (latitude and longitude N 41°3'4", W 73°28'45"), for a hell of a lot of Tuesday afternoons. Of course, 64-bit encryption is nothing to sneeze at in terms of data security unless you happen to be one of the world's foremost—if not the most—gifted hackers. God bless you, Julian.

That was a little lengthy for an explanation, so I tightened it up a smidge for Paulina. "We found you," I said. "That's all that matters."

"You need to be straight with us about Carter von Oehson," said Elizabeth. "You want to help us find him, don't you? Bring him home safe?"

"I do. Believe me, I want to. But there are certain things I can't tell you," she said.

I took that as my cue to be blunt. "Like his paying you for sex?"

Elizabeth shot me a look that said, *Jeez, you really do need my help, Professor Tactless.* "What he means, Paulina, is that we don't care about your profession," she explained. "That's not why we're here."

"You were possibly the last person to see Carter before he disappeared," I said. "We need to know more about the time you spent with him this past Tuesday afternoon. Did he act any different or say anything strange, something you might have picked up on?"

"No," said Paulina.

"No? Nothing at all?" I asked. "Take a minute to think it over. There had to have been something."

She didn't take a minute. She didn't need one. "I wasn't at his parents' house last Tuesday. I wasn't with him."

"Where were you?" asked Elizabeth.

"I was here in my apartment."

"Is that something you can prove?"

"I'm telling you," said Paulina. *"I wasn't there."*

"And I'm asking you," said Elizabeth. *"Can you prove it?"*

"What more do you want?" She balled her hands into fists, frustrated. Angry. "I wasn't with him. It wasn't me!"

I looked at Elizabeth. Elizabeth looked right back. Paulina looked at both of us, realizing what she'd just revealed. *It wasn't me.*

"Shit," she said.

CHAPTER 17

"IF IT WASN'T YOU at the house, then who was it?" I asked.

"I don't know," she lied. Her shoulders had tensed up so much her T-shirt looked as if it were on a hanger.

"Try again," I said.

She started walking away. "I need to sit down."

That was a good sign. People always sit for confession.

Paulina's living room looked like a page out of the Restoration Hardware catalogue. There were big pillows on top of giant sofas, set off by a huge glass coffee table with assorted knickknacks arranged just so.

She sat. We all sat. Elizabeth and I said nothing. We only stared, waiting her out. Eventually Paulina started talking.

"I was supposed to be with Carter last Tuesday," she said.

"What happened?" I asked.

"He canceled. Or at least I thought he did," she said. "I got a text about two hours beforehand." She beat us to the punch. "And, yes, I saved it."

She reached for her cell in her sweatpants, bringing up the text. We knew she wasn't about to hand over her phone, so Elizabeth and I got up to read it.

Betty it's C. Friend's
phone. Dropped smine,
shattered. Gotta get new
asap so need to cancel
today. Cool?

"Wait. Who's Betty?" I asked, reading the text again.

"That's the name I use with him," she said. "I'm Betty."

"Does he know your real name?" asked Elizabeth.

"It's funny, every repeat client wants to know my real name at some point. They think it makes them different, like we have a real connection or something. Carter never asked me. Not once," she said.

"Had he ever canceled on you before?" I asked.

She smiled slightly, as if I'd hit on something. "Never."

I sat down again, but Elizabeth remained standing. She was pacing. She was hooked. "The excuse about his phone breaking sure made it convenient for someone else to have sent that text," she said.

"Yes, but someone who also had to know who *Betty* was," I said. I pointed at Paulina. "As well as your cell number and when you saw Carter each week."

"That was another thing," said Paulina. "Something else that had me thinking he actually did send the text. Carter never used his name. It was always just *C* when he texted me. Apparently a lot of the kids on campus call him *C Money*."

"Subtle," said Elizabeth.

"So maybe Carter sent the text, maybe he didn't," I said. "The question is, what did you do about it?"

"What do you mean?" asked Paulina.

"He canceled. *Or at least I thought he did*," I said, repeating back what she'd first told us. "That means you had to have done something about it. You followed up in some way."

Again, Elizabeth and I just stared at Paulina. "I drove out to Darien," she said finally.

"I get it," said Elizabeth. "You were suspicious. You thought maybe you were losing a good client."

"Exactly," she said.

"And?" asked Elizabeth.

"And I saw his BMW in the driveway when I got there. So I parked a little down the street from the house and waited. Then I saw her," she said. "She pulled up in a red Jaguar, got out, and went inside."

"Then what?" I asked.

Paulina shrugged. "Then I went home. What was I supposed to do? I mean, I thought about waiting and confronting him afterward, but that's something a girlfriend would do. I wasn't his girlfriend."

"Did you at least get a good look at the other woman?" asked Elizabeth.

"She was tall. Long hair. Light brown, I think. Maybe not so light, I don't know. That's about it," she said. "Oh, and she was wearing a black fur coat."

"Any chance she works for the same person you work for?" I asked.

"I wouldn't know."

"What do you mean?"

"I don't know who I work for," she said.

Paulina—Betty, to Carter—was so matter-of-fact about it that I didn't immediately react the way I was supposed to react. Utter disbelief. *She doesn't know who she works for?*

"But even if I did know, I'd never tell you," she continued. "You could arrest me, try to lock me up forever. I still wouldn't tell you."

"Why not?" I asked.

"Because they'd kill me, that's why."

CHAPTER 18

ELIZABETH DIDN'T SAY A single word to me the entire way down in the elevator, nor while we walked back through the lobby of Paulina's apartment building and out the revolving doors.

But I knew what was coming. This was the calm before the storm. Hurricane Lizzie. Sure enough, the moment we hit the sidewalk...

"*What the hell was that?*" she asked, throwing her arms up in the air. "*I mean, for crying out loud, what the hell was it?*"

"Can I explain?"

"No. I don't want to hear it. I know what it's going to be. You're going to give me some fancy-pants explanation that sounds a lot smarter than it really is."

"Did you really just say *fancy pants*?"

"Shut up, I'm serious," she said. "You rope me into this thing and then you go ahead and do that. Why? Why did you let her off the hook?"

"That's not what I did."

"That's *exactly* what you did. She would've told us more, and instead you just thanked her for her time."

"That's called *keeping* her on the hook. We're going to need that girl's help, which means we need her on our side, trusting us."

"What's with all this we stuff?" she said, air quotes around the *we*. "That was you in there, acting on your own. And as for me, I already told you I haven't made up my mind yet on getting involved."

I looked at her, my best sideways glare. *Really? Don't even pretend you're not hooked, Lizzie. I saw you in there. This case is so in your wheelhouse.*

Only she wasn't looking back at me. I followed her eyeline. It was laser focused on the side view mirror of a Ford Escort parked along the curb. Something had caught her attention. "What is it?" I asked.

"My six," she said. "Right shoulder. The guy on the phone."

I glanced over her right shoulder, spotting the guy. "I see him," I said. "What about him?"

"He's talking on the phone, right?"

"Yeah?"

"So how come he's not talking? He hasn't said a word since we've been out here."

I glanced again at the guy. He was standing about twenty yards away. Long brown overcoat, phone to his ear. Maybe he was just listening to whoever was on the other end of the line. That would explain why his lips weren't moving. But it didn't account for his eyes.

For a split second they locked on to mine. He didn't flinch. He didn't panic. But how quickly he looked away was enough of a tell.

"Well, what do you know? We're being watched," I said.

"Or at least one of us is."

That made more sense. "Any reason why it's you?" I asked.

"Maybe," she said. "What about you? Your past has a funny way of never letting go."

"You've noticed that, huh?"

Elizabeth gave another look at the side view mirror on the Ford Escort. "He's still there. What do you want to do?"

"Two options," I said. "One, separate and see which of us he follows. That would be smart and sensible."

"What's the second option?"

"*This*," I said.

CHAPTER 19

I IMMEDIATELY TOOK OFF, sprinting straight at the guy. Screw smart and sensible. Sometimes you just have to go with expedient.

I thought he would run away. I was sure he would run away. Cue the action music from every cop show ever. This had street chase written all over it.

Only the guy didn't budge. It wasn't so much that he froze— more like he'd made a split-second decision. His odds were much better if he stood his ground. It stopped me dead in my tracks.

I pulled up ten feet in front of him and ignored how crazy I must have looked as I walked the rest of the way. I got up right in his grill. *"Do I know you?"* I asked.

He squinted, lowering his phone. "Excuse me?"

"Because you seem to know me," I said.

"What are you talking about?"

I pointed at his phone. The screen was black. "One of the tricks of pretending you're on a phone is to actually be on the phone."

He turned to walk away but I stepped in front of him, blocking his path.

"Get lost, asshole," he said.

"I would if it meant you'd stop following me."

"Who says I'm following you?"

"Oh, so maybe *I'm* the lucky one," said Elizabeth, with perfect timing, as she walked up to us.

"I'm not following you, either," he said.

"Man, you're really not good at this," I said, shaking my head. "When she shows up you're supposed to act as if this is the first time you're seeing her. *Who is this strange woman suddenly talking to me with this even stranger guy?* That's your play. Instead, you just admitted you've already seen both of us together. Total rookie mistake."

"Listen, I don't know who the hell either of you are, but—"

"Maybe this will help," said Elizabeth. She did more than flash her badge. She all but shoved it in his face. "Now that we have that established, it's really important from this moment on that you don't bullshit us. Do you understand me?"

There was nothing outwardly menacing about the guy. He looked average. Actually, he looked a little less than average. A bit of a shlub. The before-photo in a diet plan ad. "I'm not following you," he said, looking Elizabeth square in the eyes.

"Then we're back to me," I said. "I'm the one you're following."

"I'm sorry, I don't recall seeing your badge," he said.

"No, that's right. You didn't see it. That's because you already know who I am and that I don't have one. If you thought there was a chance, you'd never hit me with a cocky line like that," I said. "Human nature, pure and simple."

"I'm afraid he's right," said Elizabeth. "And trust me when I tell you how much it pains me to admit that Dr. Reinhart is right about anything. He's one of those Ivy League professors. Total fancy pants. Then again, you probably already know that, too. Behavioral psychology. So annoying. It's like he's living rent-free inside your head."

"Yeah, but I still don't have a badge," I said. "Agent Needham just showed you hers, though, which means you now have to show her some ID."

"Yes, and then you have to explain why you're following Dr. Reinhart," said Elizabeth.

"Tell him what happens if he doesn't," I said.

She gave him a quick head to toe. "He looks like he knows."

"You should tell him anyway. How long can you detain him for? Is it thirty-six hours?" I asked.

"No. It's forty-eight hours," she said.

"Wow. Without charging him with anything, right?"

"Yep. That's how it works."

"A whole two days," I said.

"Only it's never the days that people remember. It's always the nights."

"The nights are the worst. A slab for a bed. A rock for a pillow. Sheets like sandpaper."

"Who said anything about sheets or a pillow?"

"You get the picture," I said, smiling at the guy. "Zero stars on Tripadvisor."

This wasn't good cop, bad cop. This was crazy agent and the nutty professor. It was also damn effective. The guy didn't know what else to do—except start talking.

CHAPTER 20

"OKAY, OKAY, I GET it," he said, palms raised. "Only it's not what it looks like. I mean, it is what it looks like. I *am* following you, Dr. Reinhart. But he didn't ask me to."

He? I should've known. "He, as in, Mathias von Oehson?"

"Yes. I work for his firm."

"As a private detective?" I asked.

"No. No, it's nothing like that," he said. "Like I told you, Mathias doesn't know I'm doing this."

"So why *are* you doing it?" asked Elizabeth.

He reached into his pants pocket, removing a sterling silver business card holder. I'm pretty sure the last time I saw one of those was when I was watching Christian Bale in *American Psycho*. "Here," he said.

Elizabeth and I were both handed a card. Raised lettering. Nice texture. It even had a watermark. Richard Landau, Chief Compliance Officer, Von Oehson Capital Management.

"I've known Mathias for more than twenty-five years. We were at Yale together. I'm the closest thing he's ever had to a real friend, and I've never seen him so distraught."

Landau folded his arms as if he'd somehow made everything crystal clear for us. In a way, he had. Just not in the way he intended.

"Are you protecting him or yourself?" I asked.

"Both," answered Landau. "He's convinced his son is still alive, and the only thing he told me was that he's hired a *college professor* to find him. No offense."

"None taken," I said. "What more do you need to know?"

"For starters, that you actually know what the hell you're doing."

I nodded at his business card. "So this is about compliance, so to speak?"

"It's more than that," he said. "Our fund is worth more than one hundred forty billion dollars, and every penny of it rests on the reputation and good judgment of one man."

I got it. "In other words, Mathias von Oehson can't be seen as delusional or in denial."

"And I shouldn't have been seen at all," said Landau. "You're right, Dr. Reinhart. I'm not any good at this."

"What would happen if Mathias were to discover that you were following me?" I asked.

"To be honest, I don't know. But I wouldn't want to find out."

I glanced at Elizabeth. *Your call,* said her look.

Civilization as we know it would be nowhere without trust. We tend to remember betrayals most—Jesus and Judas, Caesar and Brutus, Benedict Arnold—but that's only because they're outliers. Suspicion isn't innate. It's a learned behavior. Just look into the eyes of a baby, if you have any doubt. What's innate is the desire to believe someone. We want to trust. We need to trust. Every day. Doctors. Pilots. A crossing guard. The elevator inspector.

As well as the chief compliance officer at Von Oehson Capital Management.

What did Richard Landau possibly have to gain by lying to us? The answer seemed to be nothing. So as I shook his hand, confident that his amateur private-detective days were over, I truly couldn't know for sure.

I'd just been played.

CHAPTER 21

HOW DO YOU TELL a man that his son was engaging the services of a prostitute once a week in his home?

If the man is Mathias von Oehson, you apparently don't use an expression like *engaging the services.*

"Do I look like a fucking choirboy, Dylan? Carter was banging a hooker here, is that what you mean?"

"Yes, that about sums it up."

"The point being, this woman was here the day he went missing?"

"Actually, no," I said, standing in the massive kitchen of von Oehson's mansion in Darien. "She apparently wasn't here. Someone else was instead."

"Who?"

"A tall brunette in a red Jaguar," I said. "That's all I know about her so far."

Von Oehson had made the trip out to Connecticut, as I'd asked, to show me where he kept his hundred-million-dollar Monet. Now I was bringing news of a mystery woman—and the hope that maybe something in the house could lead us to her quickly. The next NSA download was still weeks away, according to Julian, which meant so was that red Jaguar's VIN. That was too long to wait.

"When we first talked, you mentioned the alarm system here," I said. "But I don't see any cameras."

"No, my wife thinks security cameras are tacky. We compromised on motion detectors along the perimeter," he said. "Any room with a window or door to the outside has one."

"What about your neighbors?"

"What about them?"

"Do they have a view of your property?" I asked.

"I spent about a million dollars on trees to make sure they don't," he said. The unintended effect of that flashed across his face. He frowned. "I suppose I'm really paying for that privacy now."

"It was a long shot anyway," I said. "The off chance of a witness, someone who saw the woman here. Besides Carter, that is."

"How do you know about this woman in the first place?"

I told him about Paulina—Carter's Betty—and how she was basically duped by the tall brunette in the red Jaguar. "At this point, I have no reason to think she's lying."

"I'll give you one," he said. "She's a prostitute. I'll give you another. If she's been to the house multiple times, she probably knows the layout."

"Speaking of which," I said, "how about showing me around?"

When I'd first arrived, I followed von Oehson directly from the foyer into the kitchen. I'd basically seen only two rooms in the house. That left a mere two dozen more to cover, give or take, including the one where he kept the Monet.

"It was in here," he said, leading me into his second-floor study.

I looked at the only wall in the room that wasn't floor-to-ceiling bookshelves. Practically every square inch was covered by paintings. There was no space to be had for the Monet. Unless.

"Have you already hung something in its place?" I asked.

"As if one could actually replace a painting like that," he scoffed. But he knew what I meant. "No. It was never hanging on any wall."

He walked across the room, opening a door. I went over and took a look.

"This is where you kept it? A closet?"

A nearly empty one, at that. There were a few file boxes stacked in one corner. Nothing more.

"I didn't need to look at the painting to appreciate it," he said. "All that mattered was that the damn thing was in my possession."

I understood he couldn't exactly hang this particular painting in his living room for all the world to see. Still, for some reason I expected him to show me a secret room behind those bookshelves or some other exquisitely hidden place within the house where he and only he could marvel at his conquest. Maybe I've seen too many Bond movies.

"Did Carter know about the painting?" I asked.

"Of course not," said von Oehson.

"I don't mean the specifics of how you got your hands on it. I can't imagine you would've told him that," I said. "But it's not like it was under lock and key here. There's a chance he saw it at some point."

"I suppose."

"It wasn't boxed up or anything, was it?"

"No. It was wrapped in one of those blankets that moving companies use." He paused for a moment. "I know I just said I didn't need to look at it, but, yeah, okay, from time to time I liked to take a peek."

One of the fascinating things about the human brain is that it often processes information without telling us. We seemingly have thoughts that come out of nowhere, but the reality is that they always come out of *somewhere*. They're triggered by one thing or a collection of things that we've previously seen or heard, touched, tasted, or smelled.

I'm sure my eyes saw the telescope by the window when I first walked into the room. I suspect I maybe even saw that it wasn't aimed out the window as one would normally expect. Instead, the lens was turned around. It was facing inside the room. A little strange, if you thought about it. But I hadn't.

Not until von Oehson uttered the words "take a peek."

That's all it took. Like a robot on autopilot I walked over to the telescope and peered through the viewfinder.

"Holy shit," I muttered.

Von Oehson was convinced that Carter had intentionally said *peachy keen* in his Instagram post as a way of signaling him. He was sure of it. I was less so. But not anymore.

Carter had sent another signal.

CHAPTER 22

"THAT'S ONE SMART KID," said Elizabeth.

That was an understatement. Carter had trained the lens of the telescope on a row of books, with one of the books pulled forward slightly from all the others. Behind it on the shelf was a lowball glass that smelled like tequila, and on the glass were the fingerprints of the tall brunette in the red Jaguar.

The book Carter had chosen? *The Glass Menagerie.*

The only thing Carter couldn't know—it was safe to assume— was whether Ingrid Dombrov had a record. That was her name. The tall brunette in the red Jaguar. Then again, Ingrid was a call girl with a proclivity for kidnapping. Or even worse. As gambles go, her having a record was like Bruce Springsteen playing "Born to Run" in concert anywhere in New Jersey. It was a pretty safe bet.

"Yep. That's definitely one smart kid," I said.

I stared across the table at Elizabeth. We were in the back booth of a greasy spoon in the Financial District, only a few blocks from Wall Street. I didn't know why she wanted to meet all the way downtown, but she was helping me, not the other way around, so I didn't ask.

She'd gotten an old friend from her NYPD days to lift the fingerprint off the glass. It wasn't as if she could run it through the JTTF lab. From there, it was a simple records check. Ingrid Dombrov had been arrested a year earlier for drug possession. And like that, we had a name and address. Or at least one of us did. Elizabeth hadn't given me the address yet.

"Is there a reason you're not telling me where she lives?" I asked.

"Sort of," she said. "It's a bit complicated."

"No, it isn't." I was thinking she was still a bit conflicted about how involved she wanted to be. That was fine. I'd give her space. "You give me the address and I'm on my way. You don't have to come along. Easy as that."

We were interrupted by our waitress, coffeepot in hand. She didn't ask if we wanted refills or even look at us. She just poured.

Elizabeth waited for the waitress to walk away before leaning in. "It turns out that red Jaguar isn't owned by Ingrid Dombrov."

Okay. So what was I missing? The arrest record had all the information needed. Name, address, even a telephone number. Still, to know Elizabeth was to know there was a reason she was telling me this.

"So who owns the Jaguar?" I asked.

"According to a speeding ticket Ingrid got a few months ago, it's registered to an LLC called VOG Enterprises. The member information isn't public, but I did a little digging. *VOG* stands for Vladimir Oleg Grigoryev."

"Do I know him?"

"You're about to. Because the only way you're getting to Ingrid Dombrov is through him."

"So he's her pimp, for lack of a better word."

"He's a lot more than that. He's a *pakhan*," she said. I knew the word. A *pakhan* is a crime boss in the Russian mafia. Elizabeth began counting off on her fingers. "He's also a weapons dealer, money launderer, and, yes, he oversees a very exclusive escort service."

"How is it that you know all this about him and he's not locked up?"

"Because there's one other thing," she said.

It was the way she said it. "Shit, don't tell me."

She told me. "He's an FBI informant."

"I'm guessing a valued one," I said.

She nodded. "A *very* valued one. Which is saying a lot these days."

Newton's Third Law of Motion states that for every action there is an equal and opposite reaction. If Newton were alive today, though, he probably would've added an asterisk to the law that read, *"This does not apply to US counterintelligence, especially with the Russians."* Given their meddling with our elections, the game had changed. For every action there's now a completely unequal and overwhelming reaction on our part when it comes to informants. We try to turn every Russian on the planet who has any link to Moscow. Because that's the American way. Go big or go home.

As for me, I was apparently going to go meet Vladimir Grigoryev.

"His apartment is across the street," said Elizabeth.

That explained the diner choice. "Is he expecting us?" I asked.

"He's expecting *you*," she said. "Not me."

"So you're waiting here?"

"I'm not waiting at all. I'm on special assignment for the mayor, remember?"

I couldn't blame her. "Spa day?"

"I wish. Just a little Christmas shopping."

"I'll never tell."

"That reminds me," she said. "Our being here right now? You and me? We never were."

It wasn't hard to read between the lines. "You're not the one who set this meeting up with Grigoryev, are you?"

"Nope."

"Can you tell me who did?"

"Nope."

Fair enough. I didn't push. Someone was clearly doing her a favor, a delicate one at that. I didn't need to know who it was.

"Thank you," I said instead.

"Don't thank me yet. Grigoryev is a borderline psychopath with a god complex."

"So he's every Hollywood agent."

"I'm serious," she said. "Anyone willing to betray his own country—Mother Russia, no less—is willing to betray anyone. Whatever you do, don't drop your guard around this guy."

CHAPTER 23

I STILL DIDN'T HAVE Ingrid Dombrov's address when I walked out of the diner. But I did have Grigoryev's, and that was the only one I needed. Was he connected somehow with Carter von Oehson's disappearance?

All I knew was what Elizabeth knew. Trying to go through "one of his girls" to find out the truth would be like putting a big fat target on my chest. That's simply how the Russian mafia operated, especially with a *pakhan*. Shoot first and don't even bother asking questions. The fact that he was also a protected FBI informant meant that he might even get away with it, too.

May you live in interesting times, goes the old saying.

The pat down didn't happen in the lobby. After announcing myself to the young doorman—who looked at me dubiously, as if to ask, *Are you sure you want to do that, dude?* when I told him I was there to see Grigoryev—I was told to wait a minute for one of Grigoryev's "associates," which proved to be the kindest description ever in the history of recorded language for the steroid-addled bruiser in the sleeveless muscle shirt who grunted at me from the elevator when it opened. "Get on."

We rode up in silence to the twentieth floor, the door opening to a room that clearly hadn't been designed by the building's original architect. It was an added layer of security, a holding area. The only furniture, a small bench. Next to it, directly opposite the elevator, was a steel door. A camera was positioned over it.

The associate grunted again. "Spread."

He frisked me, then nodded at the camera. I was clean. A couple of dead bolts snapped, and the steel door opened to a thick, black curtain.

"Welcome, Dr. Reinhart," said Vladimir Grigoryev, from behind the curtain. "My apologies for the security. Occupational hazard, I'm afraid."

I'd come to see the wizard. Accordingly, when the curtain drew back, he wasn't what I expected.

The accent was a bit rough, but everything else about him was polished, right down to the wingtips. They shined like mirrors. In fact, if it weren't for the neck tattoos extending up from the button-down collar of the shirt he wore under his three-piece suit, Grigoryev could've been a fellow professor in the English department at Yale.

"Thanks for seeing me," I said, trying to hide my surprise.

He motioned for me to follow him to a large living room with two big leather couches facing each other. There was no coffee table or anything else in between.

"Please," he said, pointing at one of the couches. Like a talk-show host, he waited until I sat down before he did. He folded his legs, and didn't waste any time. "I understand you want to ask me about one of my employees."

I suppose that was one way to describe her. "Her name is Ingrid Dombrov," I said.

"Jade."

"Excuse me?"

"She goes by Jade," he said. "What about her?"

There was a certain look on his face when I'd said her name. It was as if he sensed she was the one I'd be asking about.

"Do you know who Mathias von Oehson is?" I asked.

"Of course," said Grigoryev. "A very, very rich man. But I've seen the news. About his boy. He killed himself, yes? Very sad."

"Yes. A tragedy," I said. "The reason I'm here is that Ingrid— Jade, as you say—was at von Oehson's home in Connecticut with his son the day he disappeared."

Grigoryev squinted. He definitely wasn't expecting that. In fact, he seemed genuinely confused. "Are you sure about that?"

"Very much so. A security camera outside the house showed her arrival in a red Jaguar," I said. "A red Jaguar that's registered in your company's name, as it turns out."

The car part was true. The part about the security camera wasn't. There were some things that I knew, along with how I knew them, which I simply couldn't reveal to this guy.

Of course, if it's not already another old saying, it should be. *Never lie to a Russian mob boss.*

"This is not good," said Grigoryev.

I wasn't sure which he was referring to, the message or the messenger. I also wasn't sure who he was motioning to over my right shoulder. I didn't see anyone when I walked into the living room, and when I turned around to look I still didn't see anyone. But someone could see him.

A man dressed similarly to Grigoryev—albeit wearing an off-the-rack suit as opposed to custom made—appeared from the hallway. While he had a similar physique as the Mr. Charisma who brought me up from the lobby, this guy was able to speak without grunting.

"What do you need, G?" he asked.

"Ivan, bring the car out front," said Grigoryev. "Dr. Reinhart and I need to go somewhere."

"Somewhere?" I asked. It wasn't like telling me that we were "going for a ride," but it felt a little too close to that for comfort.

"I'll explain in the car," he said.

"How about you explain now."

Sociopaths have a love-hate relationship with people standing up to them. They never want to be disrespected, but at the same time they appreciate the pushback because it reminds them of someone they truly love and admire. Themselves.

Grigoryev unfolded his legs, placing a palm on each knee. "God has ten commandments, Dr. Reinhart. I only have two. If you work for me, you never moonlight. That's my second commandment."

Okay, I'll bite. "What's the first?"

"I got word this morning that Jade didn't show for an appointment last night."

"In other words," I said, "never stand up a client."

"No. She hasn't returned any calls made to her this morning." His smile disappeared. "That's the first commandment. Never stand *me* up."

There you have it. The two commandments of Vladimir Oleg Grigoryev. With both broken by Jade, there was only one thing left to do.

"Let's go for a ride," I said.

CHAPTER 24

I TURNED TO GRIGORYEV as we sped along in the back of his black Range Rover Sentinel. "Does Jade actually know who you are?"

"Interesting question," he said. "Why would you ask such a thing?"

I glanced at Ivan, who was doing the driving. With a nod Grigoryev assured me that I had permission to speak freely.

"You said Jade hadn't returned any calls, but you didn't say you were the one making those calls."

Grigoryev smiled slightly, reading between the lines. "Are you asking me how things work?"

"I don't need to know your business model," I said.

"It's no secret how it all works. The secret is who belongs," he said. "The clients."

"What about the boss?" I asked.

"What about me?"

"You guarantee your clients' anonymity. I can only assume you'd want to guarantee your own, even among the girls who work for you," I said. "That's why I asked about you and Jade, whether she knows who you are."

We came up to a red light on Hudson Street, past the Holland Tunnel entrance. When the car stopped, so did Grigoryev. He fell silent, staring straight ahead. No response. It was so quiet I could barely hear the engine idling. Every pothole up until that point— the way the tires filled each gap with a heavy jolt—reminded me that the Range Rover Sentinel was practically a tank on wheels, with its steel-plated panels and armored privacy glass. It wasn't merely bulletproof. It was grenade proof. If the secretary-general of the United Nations could ride around the city in one, why not a bespoke suit–wearing Russian mob boss?

The light flashed green. We drove a block and took a right onto Spring Street, pulling up in front of a well-kept brownstone. For the first time, Grigoryev turned to me.

"*Berezhonogo bog berezhot,*" he said.

I took six weeks of Russian language classes when I was training with the CIA at Camp Peary in Virginia. It was geared toward KGB interaction. Key phrases and terminology in matters of intelligence. It wasn't as if I could translate Chekhov. Or, in this case, Russian proverbs.

Still, I took a stab at it. "Something about God and keeping?"

Grigoryev nodded, impressed. "God keeps those safe who keep themselves safe," he said.

With that, he'd answered my initial question. He'd also confirmed what I'd suspected. How things worked.

I had met a Paulina who went by the name of Betty, and I was on my way to meet an Ingrid who apparently was known as Jade. Both Betty and Jade worked for Grigoryev. They just didn't know it.

Except that was about to change for Jade. And I didn't have a good feeling about it.

I followed Grigoryev, along with Ivan, out of the Range Rover and up the steps to the brownstone. There was a row of apartment buzzers to the left, but I was the only one looking at them. Ivan casually took out a key, and in we went.

After a flight of stairs, Ivan reached for a second key in front of apartment 2A. He also took out a 9mm Makarov. And in *he* went. Alone. No knock, no doorbell. Just the element of surprise, immediately followed by a woman's scream.

Grigoryev took that to mean all clear.

He walked inside like he owned the place, which he clearly did. Jade must have known it, too. Her scream was still echoing, but she was otherwise silent as I fell in behind Grigoryev. As soon as I was inside the apartment, he closed the door behind us. "Hello, Jade," he said. "Do you know who I am?"

She thought for a second, terrified. "Yes. I mean, no—but, yes," she answered in a thick Russian accent. Safe bet she hadn't been in the States for too long.

After Carter had canceled on Betty, she'd seen Jade from a distance walking into the von Oehson house in Darien. She'd described her as tall with brownish hair. She was spot-on. Jade was indeed a tall brunette. Up close, not surprisingly, she was beautiful.

She was also going somewhere.

Grigoryev saw it even before I did. There was an open suitcase, half packed, on the couch behind her in the living room. He motioned to Ivan. Ivan was the last to see the suitcase but the first to do something about it.

He walked up to Jade and pressed the barrel of his Makarov hard against her left temple.

Grigoryev folded his arms. "Are we taking a trip, Jade?"

CHAPTER 25

JADE WASN'T GOING ANYWHERE. She stood rigid, a lamp-post. Frozen in a pair of black boots, black jeans, and a black turtleneck.

Then she started to shake. Her arms, legs, lips. She began to ramble, desperately trying to find a way to explain herself. There was no playing dumb. No holding back.

Nothing cuts to the chase more quickly than having a gun to your head.

"He threatened me," she said. "He . . . he told me I'd be deported if I didn't do it or talked about it to anyone. I was scared. He said nothing was going to happen to the boy. I swear, I didn't know they were going to kill him. I swear."

"Wait. *He's dead*?" I just blurted it out. I couldn't help it. How could I?

Grigoryev turned to me. If looks could kill. This was his show, not mine. More to the point, Jade was his property. Hell, everything was his property. The apartment. The building. I was his guest. My role was to observe, not interfere.

"I'm sorry," I said. "It's just that—"

He cut me off with a raised palm, turning back to Jade. "Is the kid definitely dead?" he asked.

She blinked a few times, surely trying to figure out the dynamic between the man who owned her and whoever the hell I was. In the meantime, she wasn't answering, and that didn't sit well with Grigoryev's man, Ivan. He jammed his Makarov harder against the side of her head. "He asked you a question."

"I don't know! I'm not sure," she said. "I thought he was dead because of what I saw on TV, how he had killed himself. The only thing I know is that he *didn't* kill himself. Not by choice." Tears were streaming down her cheeks. They were real. "I don't want to go to jail."

"So that explains the suitcase," said Grigoryev. He gave a quick nod to Ivan, who lowered his gun. "Now tell me this thing you did for your client."

This was the moment, what I'd come for, and I was hanging on every word as Jade explained. She was clickbait, as in the click of a lock and Carter von Oehson voluntarily opening the door to his parents' home in Darien. She had a role to play. Scare the kid to death, and have him announce on the internet that he planned to kill himself.

"Then what?" asked Grigoryev.

"Then I was done," she said. "As soon as it posted on Instagram, two men arrived in a van. They told me to leave."

Grigoryev turned to me again. *Did you get what you need?*

At least that's how I interpreted the look. I pressed my luck. "May I ask her one question?"

He shrugged. "*Kanyéchna,*" he said.

That was covered on day one of Russian class at Camp Peary. Casual KGB speak. "Yeah, sure," he'd basically told me.

I had the luxury of not having to introduce myself to Jade. She didn't need to know my name or why I was there. All I had to do was ask the question. She had to answer it. "How do you know Paulina?"

"Who?" asked Grigoryev before Jade could answer.

"You might know her as Betty," I said.

He nodded but still looked confused. Meaning, he knew who Betty was but didn't know why I was asking about her.

Jade shook her head. "I don't know her. I was just told that was her name, and that's who I was taking the place of."

Was she telling the truth? If so, she wasn't actually the one who sent the text—the supposed message from Carter that canceled his date with Betty. It actually made sense. She was a pawn in all this. Again, that was *if* she was telling the truth.

Grigoryev wasn't sold on anything yet. I'd had my one question. It was his turn again. "Were you paid to do this?" he asked her.

The second Jade hesitated, I knew he was going to kill her.

CHAPTER 26

"WERE YOU PAID?" HE asked a second time. It was one time too many to hear the razor edge in his voice.

Grigoryev already knew her answer. Jade's silence all but screamed it. Still, it was as if he needed to hear it for himself. She had to say the word out loud, which she finally did.

"Yes," said Jade softly.

The longer Grigoryev stared at her the more I could feel the room begin to spin out of control, the ground shifting beneath my feet.

"Dr. Reinhart, would you please step outside?" he asked.

"Excuse me?"

"You heard me."

"No, I'm afraid I didn't. I was distracted by your man, Ivan, reaching for his suppressor," I said.

Ivan had literally jumped the gun on their plans for Jade. I couldn't unsee what I'd seen. Not that Grigoryev really cared.

"Fine. Don't step outside," he said. "I don't give a fuck."

Jade fell to her knees, begging. "Please," she said. "Please don't! I'm sorry. I'm so sorry!"

Grigoryev cared even less about her apology. He nodded again at Ivan, who was tightening his suppressor, giving the long cylinder its last couple of turns.

Jade's eyes locked on to mine. She still didn't know who I was, but she understood enough to see that I was her only hope.

I had about ten seconds to save her life.

"Tishe yedesh', dal'she budesh'," I said.

Grigoryev turned to me. Even Ivan turned to me. His thick hand had stopped twisting the suppressor.

One good Russian proverb deserved another. Never mind that it was the only one I had in my arsenal. It applied. *Ride slower, advance farther.*

"Are you trying to tell me something?" asked Grigoryev.

"Yes," I answered. "What do you gain by killing her?"

"It's not what I gain. It's what I protect."

"What if you could also gain something?"

"What are you offering?"

"I need her help," I said.

"You need her client, you mean. The one who hired her."

"Yes, and she's the best chance I have to get him."

"Again, I ask," he said. "What do I get in return? *What are you offering?*"

"You tell me," I answered.

"Are you handing me a blank check?"

"You don't need money."

"You're right. I don't," he said.

"But no matter how much a man has, there's always something he still wants."

"Is that another proverb?" he asked.

"No," I said. "It's a promise."

"And you think you're the man to give this to me, whatever it might be? Even if you could, why the hell would I trust you?"

"Because you're alive because of me."

Grigoryev laughed hard. "How do you figure that?"

"Here," I said. "I'll show you."

CHAPTER 27

I RAISED MY HANDS slowly. No sudden moves. Ivan flinched anyway, thrusting his Makarov at me. Grigoryev waved him off. "He's clean," he said.

Damn right. Spic and span. I'd already been frisked. "Just reaching for my wallet," I said, tucking a hand in my breast pocket.

I pulled out my wallet, removing what I wanted to show him. A card. Of course, Grigoryev couldn't read it from where I was standing. He motioned impatiently for me to bring it to him.

"Whatever you do, don't drop your guard around this guy," Elizabeth had warned me.

Right advice, Lizzie. But you warned the wrong guy.

I walked over, giving Grigoryev the card. That's all it took. His eyes and trigger finger were now occupied, and in two seconds he was going to realize that he was looking at an expired coupon for a gym membership at Crunch Fitness.

But I didn't need the whole two seconds.

All at once I threw one arm around his throat, yanking his body against mine as a shield while I reached for the semiautomatic pistol he had holstered underneath his suit jacket. I'd spied it when we first sat down to talk. Before Ivan even knew what was happening, he had the business end of a short-frame Glock 29 aimed at his chest while his boss blocked him from any chance of getting off a clean shot at me.

"Drop it," I told Ivan.

I knew he wouldn't, not right away. Not until he danced with the death-wish devil in his head. He glanced at Jade, trying to figure out how fast he could train his Makarov back on her. Not fast enough was the answer.

"Go ahead, be a hero," I said. "You never know. I could always miss."

It wasn't quite reverse psychology. More like a reminder that I was a mere ten feet away from him. I wasn't going to miss.

Ivan knelt and placed the Makarov on the floor. I told him to kick it forward, then toss the keys to the Range Rover.

"Are you sure you've thought this through?" asked Grigoryev, resigned to my choke hold. He was standing perfectly still.

"Hell no," I said. "Where's the fun in that?"

Off my nod, Jade scooped up the keys and the Makarov, and got behind me. But not before a parting swipe at Grigoryev.

"Mudak!" she yelled at him. Asshole.

"It's a black Range Rover parked in front of the building," I told her. "Start it up for us and get into the backseat. I'll be trailing you by a minute."

"Okay," she said. Only she wasn't moving.

"What is it?" I asked.

"You expect them just to stay here like idiots once you leave?"

"I'll have a head start," I assured her. "Wait. Where are you going?"

She wasn't heading out the door. She instead disappeared down a hallway. Within seconds, she returned holding two pairs of handcuffs. I would've been more surprised were it not for her profession. Fittingly, the cuffs were lined with black velvet and had pink fur over the chains. Tools of the trade.

"Catch," she said, tossing one pair to Ivan. She was smart enough not to try and put them on him, which was not to say he was going to do it himself. The cuffs hit smack against his chest and fell to the ground. His arms never moved.

"Seriously?" I said.

Ivan looked at his boss. Grigoryev's neck had just enough space at the crook of my elbow for him to talk.

"*Prosto sdelay eto,*" he said, invoking the Nike slogan in Russian. *Just do it.*

Ivan put on the cuffs. As soon as he did, I turned the gun on Grigoryev, placing the barrel on the back of his head. "Your turn," I said.

"That won't be necessary. Leave. I won't be coming after you," he said. "Not today."

"What about tomorrow?"

"Tomorrow's another day."

I removed my arm from his neck and gave him a push toward Ivan. "Wrong answer," I said. "Put 'em on. Loop them around Ivan's."

I was fairly certain that making Grigoryev put handcuffs on himself was even worse than meddling in his business affairs. There's not enough rubles in the world to repair a Russian man's pride.

Sure enough. "You're going to have to kill me before I do that," he said.

I believed him. So did Jade. Without my saying a word she walked over to her suitcase, zipped it up, and made a beeline for the door. I fell in line right behind her, although never once turning my back. Out the apartment. Down the hallway. Down the stairs.

I didn't kill Grigoryev. He didn't come after me.

But tomorrow was another day.

BOOK TWO

THE MEEK SHALL INHERIT NOTHING

CHAPTER 28

A SUDDEN JOLT OF attraction mixed with a slight twinge of guilt. That's what Elizabeth felt when she originally met agent Danny Sullivan.

It was the day after the attempted Times Square bombing, the entire JTTF building was in full panic mode, and yet the first thought to cross her mind while shaking his hand was that he was a really good-looking guy. *If Ryan Gosling had a brother,* she thought to herself. She couldn't help it. She was only human, and the thought was like a doctor's tap to the knee. Pure reflex.

They'd become friendly as fellow agents but never outwardly flirted, which in a way was a form of flirtation because—as their boss, Evan Pritchard, had picked up on—they certainly were attracted to each other. There were the occasional stealth glances during group briefings and staff meetings, and if Elizabeth leaned a little to her left while sitting behind her desk, she could see Danny at his desk. His profile, at least. She liked his high cheekbones.

She didn't know much more about him beyond what would normally be on his résumé. That and a few other tidbits picked up from conversations with other agents. Danny was in his midthirties and graduated from Middlebury, where he played hockey; he joined the FBI after deciding that the analyst training program at First Boston wasn't for him. Nor was any other career in finance. He certainly had the head for it. Just not the heart.

That was maybe the most attractive thing about him, as far as Elizabeth was concerned. His desire to make a difference. Every agent possessed that to some degree, but Danny seemed to embody it. Except not loudly. He had this undercurrent of determination, an aura about him. Those who worked with him always seemed to pick up their game. It was infectious.

All the more reason why Elizabeth was dreading his call. She was sure it was coming. She'd let him down.

Well, technically, Dylan had let both of them down. Dylan's call was why she knew Danny's was only a matter of time.

"Where are you?" she'd asked Dylan, standing outside of the Moncler boutique in SoHo. She needed a new winter coat, a would-be Christmas gift to herself. She pressed the phone harder against her ear. She could hear a whooshing sound. Movement. "Are you in a car?"

"Yeah."

If he was doing the driving, he was driving fast. "Where are you going?"

"I'm not telling you," said Dylan.

"What? Why not?"

"Because whoever did you the favor and arranged that meeting with Grigoryev is going to be asking you where I am. This way you won't have to lie. You don't know."

"Shit," said Elizabeth.

"Yeah, it didn't go so well."

Dylan quickly told her what happened. "So the girl's with you?" she asked.

"Best if I don't tell you that, either." But that was as good as a yes. "I'm going to need another favor," he said.

"You've got to be kidding me."

"If only I were. Who's your friend who arranged the meeting?"

"That's not fair, Dylan. You know it's not."

"What I know—what I *need* to know—is how many people want the girl dead right now. Is it just Grigoryev?"

"Are you really asking me that? Who do you think my friends are?"

"Grigoryev is more valuable to the Bureau than the girl. That's all I'm saying."

"What about you?"

"What about me?"

"Think about it. The only person Grigoryev wants to kill more than the girl right now is you."

"Don't worry about me," said Dylan. "I'll be fine."

"No you won't."

"Yeah, you're probably right. But it sounded pretty good, didn't it?"

CHAPTER 29

ELIZABETH GOT THE CALL from Danny less than twenty minutes after she hung up with Dylan. News travels fast. Bad news even faster.

So much for her Christmas shopping. She'd been sitting and staring at her phone in a Starbucks, waiting for Danny's number to pop up. She hated Starbucks. She hated the tone of his voice even more when she answered.

"We need to talk," he said.

"I know."

"In person."

"Yeah, I know."

She offered to go to him, but he was in the office, the one place they couldn't talk. He left his desk, grabbed a cab, and came to her.

There were two things she noticed when he walked in and spotted her at a corner table. First, he looked as angry as he sounded over the phone. Second, he was still really good looking when he was angry.

"So you already spoke to Dylan," he said, sitting down across from her.

"And you've obviously spoken to Grigoryev," she said. "I'm really sorry. This is all my fault."

"You're right, it is." But he could only keep his stone face for a couple of seconds. He shook his head, even cracking a slight smile. "Damn," he said. "You're really hard to be mad at. It's not fair. You suck, you know that?"

It was the nicest thing anyone had said to Elizabeth in years. At least, it felt that way to her. "Thanks for coming to meet me," she said. "And I am really sorry."

"It's no more your fault than mine."

"No good deed, right?"

"Yeah. Now we just have to see about the punishment," he said.

"What did Grigoryev tell you?"

"He said what happened. His version, of course. Although I suspect it's very similar to what Dylan told you."

"Is that it?" she asked.

"Oh, and he added that only two other people have ever pointed a gun at him in his entire life, and they both ended up very, very dead."

"What did you say in return?"

"Nothing."

"Nothing?"

"We didn't actually talk," said Danny. "This was all in a very, very pissed-off message. When he called I just had a feeling I shouldn't pick up."

"So where does that leave us?"

"*Us*? Well, Grigoryev doesn't want to kill you or me."

"You know what I mean."

"I'm sure he wants to kill Dylan, and I'm not sure I can stop him."

"But we have to," she said. "We absolutely have to."

"It won't be for a lack of trying, I promise. There's only so many cards to play with a guy like Grigoryev, but I did buy us a little time with him."

"How?"

"A text," he said. "I told him to give me until tomorrow morning because there's something extremely important he needs to know before he does anything rash."

"What's that?"

"I don't know yet, but it's going to start with what you're about to tell me."

Elizabeth knew what he meant. Danny had done her the favor, setting up the meeting with Grigoryev, based solely on trust. He never asked her why Dylan needed to meet with a Russian gangster. If Elizabeth vouched for Dylan, that was good enough for him.

Now, as the saying goes, the situation on the ground had changed.

"How much do you want to hear?" she asked.

Danny folded his arms on the table. "Let's start with everything."

Elizabeth drew a deep breath and sighed. "You know those things that you think you want to know, only to later realize once you know them that you were better off not knowing them in the first place? This might be one of those things."

"I understand," he said. "Now tell me anyway."

CHAPTER 30

I DROVE OUT OF Manhattan as fast as I could, and kept right on driving.

It was me and a high-priced call girl on the lam in a stolen bulletproof Range Rover that belonged to a Russian mob boss who surely wanted to kill us both with extreme prejudice. Forget finishing my next book. This had TV series written all over it.

Of course, in the TV series the call girl would surely have a heart of gold. In real life, she was a bit surly and apparently had a bladder the size of a garbanzo bean.

"I need to pee again," said Jade.

Seriously? "We just stopped a half hour ago."

"I have to goddamn pee. What do you want me to do?"

"You could start by showing a little more gratitude," I said.

She huffed. "I said thank you at the gas station. *Thank you for stopping.*"

"I was talking about back at your apartment."

Jade fell silent for a few seconds, the only sound in the car belonging to Steely Dan and "Rikki Don't Lose That Number" on the radio. *You don't wanna call nobody else...*

"He's going to find me," said Jade.

"No, he won't."

"He finds everybody."

"You didn't even know who Vladimir Grigoryev was before today."

"I knew enough. I heard stories," she said. "Wherever you're taking me, he's going to find me."

I hadn't told Jade where we were headed. I hadn't told anyone. Not even Elizabeth. I wasn't merely covering my tracks. I was eliminating them.

I'd removed the SIM card from Jade's phone and disabled the GPS on the Range Rover. I had also yanked out the fuse for the emergency call button. As for any after-market tracking device, I was 99.9 percent confident there wasn't one hidden anywhere on the car. The reason was simple. You don't get to be a Russian mob boss in the United States without knowing that the FBI and NSA have easy access to them.

As for my biggest concern, I'd caught a break with Tracy taking Annabelle to his sister's house in Marblehead. I didn't know Grigoryev's next move, but I didn't want him looking for leverage with loved ones if he couldn't find me.

I glanced over at Jade. I'd tried calling her by her actual name, Ingrid, when we first started driving, but she told me not to. "Why?" I asked.

"Because I don't want *any* of this to be real," she said.

A few miles later I took the next exit off I-91 and pulled into a McDonald's so Jade could use the bathroom.

"I'm going to grab a soda," I said as we pulled into a spot. "Do you want anything?"

"Yeah, a large Diet Coke."

"Why don't we make it a small," I said.

It took her a moment. Small-bladder humor. "Yeah, that's probably a good idea," she said. There was even a hint of a smile.

"It's going to work out," I said. "You're going to be okay."

"I hope you're right," she said. "And thank you—for back at my apartment. Saving my life."

"You're welcome."

"Do you want a free one?"

"What?"

"A quickie in the backseat."

"Uh—"

"I'm kidding!" She laughed. "I totally had you!"

She sort of did. "Good one," I said.

"Besides, I can tell women aren't your thing."

I blinked. She wasn't kidding about that. "Really? You can tell that?"

"In my line of work we tend to have pretty good gaydar," she said, putting on the winter coat she'd packed in her suitcase. "You clearly prefer men."

I flashed my wedding band. "Only one in particular."

Jade went off to the bathroom, and I grabbed two Diet Cokes, plus a couple orders of fries because it's not humanly possible to enter a McDonald's without ordering fries.

"Can you finally tell me where we're going?" she asked, not long after we crossed the border into New Hampshire.

"Soon," I said. "We'll be there soon."

CHAPTER 31

WE WENT FROM A highway down to a two-lane road, then a one-lane road, and finally no road at all. At least not a paved one. After a few miles of what would generously be called a dirt trail, we arrived at a small clearing in the woods northwest of Concord.

"Whose cabin is this?" asked Jade.

"It belongs to Josiah Maxwell Reinhart, otherwise known as my father. He built it himself about twenty years ago."

Jade only heard one word of that. "Your *father*?"

"Don't worry, you'll be in good hands."

She peered out the window again. "It's the middle of nowhere, I'll give you that." She reached for the door handle.

"Not so fast," I said. "Hold up a second."

"Why?"

"Because he might blow your head off," I said. "That's why."

I hadn't tipped off my father that we were coming. Some jams you have to explain in person. So the odds that he had his Winchester 101 shotgun aimed at us at that very moment were somewhere between a sure thing and a damn sure thing. Cracking the window a couple of inches, I waved what was the best I could do for a white flag. Nothing says *don't shoot* quite like a McDonald's napkin.

My father opened his front door. He was wearing a red-and-black-plaid wool parka that looked like it came straight out of *Field & Stream* magazine, albeit an issue from 1964. His expression was far from happy, but at least the Winchester was pointed at the ground. A far friendlier greeting came from Diamond, his trusted vizsla, who immediately sprinted toward me and planted his front paws on my waist the second I stepped out of the car. "Hello, Diamond! Hey there, boy! I missed you, too!"

My father and I shook hands. He's not a hugger, never was. Turning, he gave my very attractive five-foot-ten traveling companion a once-over, head to toe. "At least tell me she can cook," he said.

"Dad, meet Jade. Jade, meet my dad," I said.

"*Perdoon stary,*" Jade muttered under her breath. Not quietly enough. I should've given her the heads-up that my father had far more Russian language training than I did.

"Did she really just call me an old fart?" He laughed. "I like her. Now tell me what the hell you're both doing here."

It was a long story, all right, but I didn't dare shorten it. You don't cut corners with Josiah Maxwell Reinhart, especially when you need a favor from him. We went inside, and over cups of kettle coffee at his pine kitchen table I explained my working for Mathias von Oehson, which led me to Jade and to the man we now needed to protect her from, Vladimir Grigoryev.

"Yeah, I know who he is," said my father. "He's a rat for the Bureau."

Which is not to say my father didn't value informants and double agents who gave him intel during his years as a CIA operative. But valuing people and respecting them don't always go hand in hand.

"Seems like everyone knew Grigoryev was an informant except me," I said.

"Who originally told you?" my father asked.

"Elizabeth."

"You roped her into the mess?"

"It wasn't a mess at that point," I said.

"I'm sure that distinction is doing her a lot of good right about now." He's had a soft spot for Elizabeth since the first day they met. "It makes sense she would know, though. She was your introduction to Grigoryev?"

"There was a middleman—or middlewoman. I'm assuming another agent at the JTTF. Elizabeth kept the name to herself."

"You'll need to change that."

"Believe me, I will."

"Still, there's no telling if Grigoryev will back off just because this other agent goes to bat for you. Do you have a plan B?"

"Is that a question or an offer?"

My father turned to Jade. She'd been sitting silent between us, sipping her coffee from a chipped ceramic mug, her head on a swivel as if she were center court at Wimbledon. "What could I possibly do to help? I'm just an old fart, right?"

"Play nice, Dad," I said. "She's had a long day."

"No, I deserved that," said Jade. Her listening to the back-and-forth with my father was clearly an eye-opener for her. "You're helping me. I apologize. Thanks for letting me stay here."

"*Na zdorovye,*" said my father.

You're welcome.

CHAPTER 32

I LEFT CONCORD RIGHT after sunset and drove nonstop, straight back down to Manhattan, arriving at a twenty-four-hour parking garage in Chelsea, on the west side of the city, a few minutes after midnight. The attendant asked how long I intended to be gone as I handed him the key to Grigoryev's Range Rover. "About ten hours," I lied. I was never coming back for it.

The night temperature had sunk into the teens, and as I walked the few blocks over to Hudson River Park I could practically feel icicles forming in my lungs. You know it's cold outside when your chance to thaw comes from walking into a hockey rink.

"You're late," said Elizabeth. The edge in her voice wasn't because I was late. She was now tasked with cleaning up my mess—or, I should say, her friend was. That only made it worse for her. Her headache was now his headache. "He wanted to talk to you before his game started."

The game had clearly started already. "Are you sure he really needs to talk to me?" I asked.

"Gee, maybe you're right. You're only asking him to save your life, so it's crazy to think he might actually want to speak to you first and see just how bad you screwed things up."

"Grigoryev was going to kill the girl," I said. "I told you that."

Elizabeth nodded, her voice softening. "I know you did."

We were standing near center ice by the team benches. New York City has tons of almost everything you can imagine except public hockey rinks. Ice time is at a major premium. The only thing crazier than the start times for many of the rec league games, especially at the Sky Rink at Chelsea Piers, are the players themselves. But that's hockey. You don't play it; you live it. The puck drops at midnight? No problem.

"Which one is he, by the way?" I asked.

Elizabeth pointed. "Number sixteen."

Right on cue, I watched as number sixteen perfectly threaded the needle on a pass to a teammate crossing the blue line. "He's good," I said.

"He played in college. Would've been drafted if he hadn't blown out his knee," she said.

The way she said it, though. I shot her a look. "Is there something I should know about you two?"

"Don't even try it. Danny and I work together. That's all we do together."

"*Danny*, huh?"

"On second thought, maybe you don't need to talk to him. Best of luck with that Russian mafia psychopath. I'm sure it will all work itself out on its own."

I cooled it with the romance talk and resumed watching some hockey. I figured I'd have to wait until the end of the first period to talk to Danny, but as soon as he skated off the ice for a shift change he came over.

"Danny, this is Dylan," said Elizabeth, in what was easily a candidate for the world's most redundant introduction.

"On a scale of one to ten, Danny, how bad did I screw up?" I asked, not wasting any time.

He needed even less time to answer. "You a fan of *Spinal Tap*? Because this one goes to eleven."

"I'm truly sorry for getting you involved," I said. "Do you think you can smooth things over with Grigoryev?"

"You stole his car, one of his girls, and you held him at gunpoint. *Smooth things over?*"

"Well, when you put it like that..."

"What I can tell him is this," he said. "He'll feel good about killing you for a day—maybe even a few days—right up until some operative, who he'll never see coming, puts a bullet through the back of his brain. If he understands that, he might back off."

"*Might?*"

"He's a *pakhan*, Dylan. *Mne nasrat', chto ty dumaesh'.*"

That was definitely outside my grasp of Russian. "What does that mean?" I asked.

"It's the polite version of what Grigoryev might tell me in return," he said. "That he doesn't give a rat's ass."

Danny was watching me intently as we talked. The more he stared, the more I began to realize what he was doing. Why I was there. Why he wanted to meet me in person.

Ask seasoned hostage negotiators what their biggest fear is on the job, and you won't be told it's the person or group who takes the hostages. Negotiators are trained for that. As long as they have a dialogue going, the odds are in their favor that innocent people won't get hurt. No, their biggest fear is what they can't control— that a hostage decides to take matters into their own hands. A preemptive strike. A hero play.

In my case, that I would kill Grigoryev before he could kill me.

That's what agent Danny Sullivan was trying to gauge. He didn't want me making his job any harder than it already was.

I wasn't ruling anything out. Never limit your options if you don't have to. But it wasn't my plan at the moment, and he needed to know that.

"Danny, is there anything I can do to help you?" I asked.

"Anything at all?" Only now I was staring back at him as hard as he'd been staring at me.

"No," he said, reading between the lines. "But thanks for asking."

"I'm the one who should be thanking you. You'll let me know once you've spoken to Grigoryev?"

"Elizabeth will. You and I never talked." He glanced at Elizabeth and then over at his team bench. There was a game to get back to. "That's my shift up next," he said. "But one last thing."

"What's that?" I asked.

"Grigoryev's girl. Is she safe?"

"She is."

"Good," he said. "No matter what, you did the right thing."

CHAPTER 33

BEFORE I LEFT THE rink, Elizabeth asked where I'd be spending the night. With a target on my back, it certainly wouldn't be at my apartment, so she offered up hers. She also asked when Tracy was due back with Annabelle.

"Not until the end of the week," I said. "And thanks for the offer, but I've already booked a hotel."

Not just any hotel.

I had Jade make one call before I removed the SIM card from her phone. It was to the client who'd hired her to set up Carter von Oehson. Ironically, her freelance gig for the guy was the only reason she knew his cell number. "Every date I had with him was arranged through Mother Hen," she'd explained. That's what she called the booker, the woman who oversaw all the escorts. What about the guy's name, her client? "He told me to call him Vincent," she said.

Maybe his name really was Vincent. Maybe it wasn't. Without a last name it didn't really matter.

What mattered was getting him alone, face to face.

Dialing *67 before his number ensured that Jade's identity would appear as "No Caller ID." This had to be a message, not a conversation. She couldn't give him the opportunity to ask questions. No one answers a "No Caller ID" call. "Straight to Voicemail," it might as well read.

Sure enough. After the beep Jade quickly explained what had happened. "He needs to hear the panic in your voice," I'd told her.

She'd been found out. Her boss—"the man who runs everything"—knew about her involvement with the rich kid's disappearance. That made her a liability. She feared for her life. She was skipping town while she still had the chance. Her flight was the next day at noon, but before leaving there was more she had to tell him. Important details.

The devil is always in the details.

She couldn't cover everything in a message, but the upshot was simple. The best way for Vincent to protect himself was by coming to see her. She'd left a room key for him with the concierge at their usual hotel. It wasn't safe for her to remain at her apartment.

Be here at noon, was how she ended the message. After that she was leaving straight for the airport. "Don't call me back. Just come." And then came the kicker, the two words I told her that she absolutely had to say before hanging up. The real secret of making someone believe you? It's not plausibility. It's vulnerability. "I'm scared," she added.

At a few minutes before noon the next day, I stood waiting in the bathroom of room 2106 of the Stafford Marshall hotel a few blocks south of the United Nations headquarters on the East Side. The door to the room—only about six feet away from the door to the bathroom—was propped open against the security latch. I'd left the key and room number in an envelope with the concierge, as Jade had told Vincent she would do. He would need the key to access the elevator. Not the room, though.

Okay, Vincent, or whatever your name really is. Don't let me down. All you've got to do now is show up...

The soft knock came at noon on the dot. It sounded almost as hesitant as the whispered voice that I heard through the crack in the door. "Jade, it's me. Are you in there?"

I waited as he waited. He knocked softly again. Whispered again. When he got no response a second time, I heard the hinges creak. He was coming in.

CHAPTER 34

THERE ARE EXACTLY FORTY-TWO muscles in the human face, and every one of his was shocked to see me.

As soon as he'd walked past the bathroom I came out behind him, loudly closing the door to the room. He spun around. I had him cornered.

"Jade couldn't make it," I said.

In a fight-or-flight world most people choose to run. This guy couldn't. That was my plan. I had to hand it to him, though. His instincts said fight.

Of course, after handing it to him, I then had to punch his lights out. Only temporarily, though. One quick jab to the solar plexus as he charged me, followed immediately by a right hook to his jaw. The bare-knuckle training at Langley will almost always leave you standing over your opponent.

"Just breathe," I told the guy as he lay flat on his back while sucking wind for dear life. He sounded like a busted accordion. "Just keep breathing. That's it. You'll be fine."

The only purchase I'd made in advance of this meeting was a roll of duct tape for $4.49, plus tax. I looped it around his ankles a half dozen times and then dragged him toward the bed, propping him up against it.

Taking a seat in an armchair opposite him, I gave him another half minute of recovery time while going through his wallet, which I lifted from the inside breast pocket of his slick Brioni suit. The bright-red stitching on the label was hard to miss.

Vincent Franchella, read his New Jersey driver's license. Turned out, he used his real first name with Jade. Who says romance is dead?

He was finally catching his breath. "Sorry about the takedown, Vincent, but you sort of left me no choice."

"Who . . . who are you?" he asked.

"You can call me Dylan," I said, since we were being honest about our first names. "I'm a friend of Mathias von Oehson."

Vincent had a lousy poker face. Those same forty-two muscles screamed *Oh, shit* all at once. "Are you a cop?" he asked.

"You should be so lucky. That would mean I wasn't allowed to kill you," I answered. I was bluffing, of course, but my poker face was a little better than his.

I watched as Vincent's Adam's apple bobbed up and down. The proverbial gulp. "Where's Jade?" he asked.

"Like I said, she couldn't make it. She's fine, for now, but you really got her mixed up in something bad. That's what you and I are going to talk about. Actually, you're going to do most of the talking."

"I don't know anything," he said.

"You know plenty. Is Carter von Oehson alive?"

Vincent stared at me, unblinking. "I don't know."

Damn. He and his face were telling the truth. I was almost sure of it. "How do you not know? You're the one who hired Jade to set him up."

"I arranged for her to do what she did, but it wasn't my money paying her," he said.

Now we were getting somewhere. Vincent Franchella of

Westfield, New Jersey—five foot nine, brown eyes, and an organ donor—was beginning to talk. All I had to do was keep asking him the right questions and listen. *C'mon, Vincent. You've got this. Walk me through every—*

Shit!

By the time I heard the double beep of the key swipe they were already bursting through the door. There were two of them, both in ski masks. The lead man was wielding a SIG pistol with a suppressor while his tail was pushing a laundry cart like an Olympic bobsledder. They knew exactly what they were doing, and who they were doing it to. Everything was happening so fast. Too fast. My only move was to raise my palms slowly in the air.

I sat staring at the barrel of the SIG while the second man pulled a long steel rod from inside the laundry cart. Before I could even figure out what it was, he jammed the electric cattle prod against Vincent, jolting him unconscious.

Out came an armful of bunched-up linens from the cart, and in went Vincent after being slung over the guy's shoulder as if he were a sack of potatoes. Then, in went the linens again to cover Vincent. It was all choreographed. Nothing was improvised.

Including my death.

Maybe they wanted Vincent alive, or maybe they wanted to kill him in a place where there'd be no blood sample from a hotel rug to identify him. Either way, they for sure wouldn't give a damn about my blood being splattered everywhere.

After watching Vincent get wheeled out of the room, my eyes swung back to the SIG aimed at my forehead. The eyes staring at me behind it were as black as the ski mask. Soulless. He edged closer to me, the barrel of the SIG only inches away. His arm was locked, his hand perfectly still. He'd done this before. Plenty of times. Snuffed out life with the simple squeeze of a trigger.

Everyone else made widgets for a living. This guy killed people. I was merely one more.

Only not today.

"*Bang,*" he said.

Then he walked out of the room.

CHAPTER 35

I'D DODGED MY OWN funeral. Actually, it was more like I'd been spared.

A minute passed. I hadn't moved from the chair in that hotel room—my heart still thumping wildly against my ribs—when the text arrived from Elizabeth. Talk about ironic timing.

> Heard from D. Something going
> down. Not sure but u should be
> good. Wasn't easy

Something had gone down, all right, but Danny had indeed come through. I owed him. I was alive. The only regret was that I was no closer to knowing whether Carter von Oehson was, too. I needed to update his father, or so I was told repeatedly via a flurry of texts that lit up my phone later that afternoon from the man himself.

There was no dodging Mathias von Oehson, nor the surreal location of where he wanted to meet.

"I'm so sorry for your loss," I said to Bethany von Oehson, Carter's mother, in the crowded vestibule of St. Sebastian's church in Darien the following morning. She was the front end of a two-person receiving line, with Mathias hearing another couple's condolences a few feet away.

I'd seen pictures of Bethany, smiling and posing at various charity benefits, but she was even prettier in person. High cheekbones, flawless skin. A trophy first wife, as dubbed by *New York* magazine. Or was it the *Post*? I couldn't remember.

I'd already introduced myself, and was about to explain my connection to Carter, when she leaned forward, her voice dropping to a near whisper. "I know who you are," she said.

"You do?"

For a brief second I thought maybe Mathias had told her about hiring me, along with all the reasons why. But that was impossible. If she truly knew everything her husband was hiding, we wouldn't be gathered at Carter's funeral. You don't bury your son when there's hope he's still alive.

Of course, Mathias was doing just that. I understood. Sort of. This was about keeping up appearances, especially in a town— and among a distinct social set—all but programmed to do "the right thing." Still, it was crazy, and I knew it. By playing along I couldn't escape feeling like an accomplice. An accomplice to crazy is never a good look.

"Yes, you're Carter's professor," said Bethany von Oehson. "I've read your book, the one about serial killers. I'm the one who actually suggested that Carter take your class."

"He was a wonderful student," I said.

"He was a wonderful boy."

The way she said boy, the sweet way only a mother could say it, echoed in my head as if I were back in Woolsey Rotunda on the Yale campus with my class. Some primal screams aren't a scream at all.

"Again, I'm so sorry," I said.

Those were the only other words I could think of to say. I glanced behind me at the slew of people waiting to greet Bethany. No one likes a Chatty Cathy on a receiving line. There was just one problem, and it suddenly dawned on me as the couple talking to Mathias moved on from him and headed into the chapel.

Do I know you, Mathias von Oehson? Or are we meeting each other for the first time?

CHAPTER 36

I WAS ABOUT TO play it safe and introduce myself when Bethany thankfully did it for me.

"Honey," she said, reaching over to tap her husband on the arm. "This is Dylan Reinhart, one of Carter's professors at Yale."

Mathias didn't flinch. He looked at me with a fixed smile, the kind you give someone you've never met before. The financial markets guru who could famously see around corners had already anticipated this moment. Of course.

"It's nice to meet you, professor. Reinhart, is it? Thank you so much for coming," he said, shaking my hand. In doing so he pulled me closer to him—and more important—away from his wife, who immediately turned back to greet the next people in line.

Mathias had me all to himself for a few moments. To anyone looking on I was extending my condolences, and we were engaging in pleasantries.

He leaned in, pushing his words through a clenched jaw that was doubling as his smile. *"What the fuck am I paying you for?"*

So much for pleasantries. "I'm getting close," I said. "Very close."

"Horseshoes and hand grenades."

"A few more days."

"Days my son may not have, if he has any at all," he said.

"Believe me. I'm doing everything I can."

"Are you?"

"Yes. Now do something for me," I said. "I want you to look over my shoulder, just casually gaze around for a few seconds. Is there anyone here you don't recognize?"

"I'm a billionaire, Dylan. I've got family here I don't even recognize."

Decent point. Money is the world's most powerful magnet.

As it stood, the odds that someone involved with Carter's disappearance would actually risk showing up at his funeral were pretty slim. Still, slim was better than none.

"Just scan the damn room, will you?"

"Fine. I'm scanning," he said.

A man's eyes will tell you everything, whether he's aiming a SIG semiautomatic at you in a hotel room or standing in the vestibule of St. Sebastian's church in Darien, Connecticut. All you have to do is look and listen. The eyes are always the first to speak.

"What is it?" I asked Mathias. His eyes were suddenly screaming. But he wasn't answering me. I stepped toward him. *What the hell is it?*

I could barely hear him, the words all but trickling out of his open and shocked mouth. "Jesus Christ," he said. "It's really him."

CHAPTER 37

A VON OEHSON MAN always knows how to make an entrance.

I turned to look. There were so many people milling about, old and young. The young were presumably classmates of Carter's, and a few I even recognized from my own class. But none of them saw what Mathias was seeing—what I was now seeing. *Jesus Christ, it's really him.*

"Carter!" yelled Mathias. "Carter!"

It set off a chain reaction. Every head whipped around, first to the grieving father calling out the name of his dead son at his funeral. Then everyone followed Mathias's eyeline to the front doors of the church. The gasps and screams were so loud that the stained glass windows in the vestibule shook, immediately followed by the near thud of Bethany von Oehson fainting to the floor. I'd caught her just in time.

Carter had a black eye and a cut lip. He looked dazed. Or was it shock? *Shock* was the right word for everyone else. No one knew what to do or say. Except Mathias. He dashed through the crowd, throwing his arms around his son. "Thank God!" he said. "Oh, thank God."

The priest took that as his cue. He'd come from inside the

chapel, having heard the commotion. He looked no less stunned but still managed to get the words out. Whatever had happened to Carter was obviously traumatic, and, as much as we all wanted to know what happened, we needed to give him and his parents some time alone together. Something like that. The priest's only goof was then announcing that the funeral was postponed. *Postponed*?

"More like canceled!" someone gleefully yelled.

Everyone laughed, save for Bethany von Oehson, who was still passed out in my arms. She was beginning to stir, though, right about the time that Mathias realized he'd left her in the dust. Who could blame him?

"Honey!" said Mathias, dashing back across the vestibule.

Carter was right behind him. He was the first person Bethany saw after Mathias gently took her from my arms. She'd come to, woozy and still a bit weak in the knees, but overwhelmed now only by tears of joy. She hugged Carter, and hugged him some more. It would've gone on for an hour were it not for the fact that others wanted to get in on the act.

Before they could, Carter spotted me. He squinted, a bit confused. "Professor Reinhart?" Subtext being, *What are you doing here?*

I didn't really have a good answer. Sure, he was one of my students, but it wasn't as if I knew him—or he knew me—outside of the classroom. Certainly, none of his other professors had showed up. As for the university president and half the board of trustees being in attendance, that was simply a matter of what's called MDM in fundraising circles. Major donor management. They were there more for Mathias than for his son.

"It's great to have you back, Carter," I said.

It was the best I could come up with in the moment, and also the end of our conversation, as those waiting to plant hugs and kisses on him moved in. The priest had given great advice, saying everyone should allow the von Oehson family some much-needed space. Everyone, in return, was now totally ignoring that advice. Once again, who could blame them?

They all wanted to know what the hell had happened to Carter. "It's a long story," he kept saying, over and over. "I'm just happy to be alive."

The more he was surrounded, the more I began to step back, fading from the crowd. I was just as curious as anyone, if not more so, to learn what had happened to Carter, but I also knew that this was hardly the right time or venue.

As for who was most curious, that was surely Mathias. For now, he would be content simply to enjoy the moment. The miracle at St. Sebastian's. But as I turned to head out the door, it was Mathias's voice I heard calling my name. He'd slipped away from the crowd, as well.

He shook his head, smiling. Smiling and crying. "I'm speechless. It feels like a dream."

"You were right," I said. "He was still alive."

Mathias nodded. The smile was still there on his face, but I could tell that his brain, as usual, was already looking ahead. I was right there with him. Call it the elephant in the vestibule. Carter was back, but the Monet wasn't.

"All I care about is that he's home and he's safe," he said. "I could give a shit about that painting now."

"Good," I said. "Hopefully, you won't have to."

We both knew, however, just how much was riding on that one word.

Hopefully.

CHAPTER 38

A VOICE MESSAGE FROM Elizabeth was waiting for me after I left the church. I listened to it from behind the wheel of my rented Toyota Camry, which stood out just a tad from almost every other car in the parking lot.

I mean, I get it, Darien. You're one of the wealthiest towns in the country, but who drives a Lamborghini to a funeral?

In the wake of the two guys bursting into my room at the Stafford Marshall hotel and making off with Vincent Franchella, I'd asked Elizabeth if she could flash her badge again. She probably would've protested more had I not hit her with my favorite Winston Churchill quote. *"A pessimist sees the difficulty in every opportunity; an optimist sees the opportunity in every difficulty."*

"Ugh," she responded. "If I do this will you promise to stop quoting famous dead people?"

"Deal. No more quips from the dearly departed," I said.

"In that case, I'll call you as soon as I have something." Hours later, she had it. "Okay, here we go," she said, kicking off her message.

She'd gotten hold of the security footage from the hotel,

tracking the two guys from the moment they arrived, which was right on the heels of Franchella. I'd given Elizabeth a description of him. He was surely being followed.

One of the guys stayed on his tail once inside the hotel, stepping onto the elevator with him just as the doors were closing. He saw where Franchella got off—my floor—then got off on the next floor and hurriedly took the stairs down a flight.

Meanwhile, the other guy headed to the laundry room in the basement where he cattle-prodded a cleaning lady, took her master key card, grabbed a linen cart, and met up with his partner outside my room. It was all very quick and clever. Even more proof that these two were far from amateurs.

"I ran both guys through facial rec but got nothing," continued Elizabeth in her message. "Their sunglasses were too big. As for Franchella, though, he has some interesting business ties."

That was putting it mildly. Vincent Franchella was head of commercial lending for the New York office of Banca Nazionale del Lavoro, based in Rome. What wasn't printed on his business card, according to Elizabeth, was his connection to organized crime. He was on an FBI watch list for suspected money laundering, and the only reason he hadn't been further investigated was that laundering cases involving possible links to terrorism always took precedence—and there were more of those cases than there were Bureau agents to go around.

"Oh, one last thing," said Elizabeth. "I checked the morgue and all hospitals. No Vincent Franchella. Of course, that hardly means he's alive and well."

That was for sure.

I drove back into the city in silence, thinking about my next move. While Elizabeth had been scouring the hotel security footage, I'd been checking the doorbell camera Tracy and I had installed outside our apartment. Maybe I truly was safe from

Grigoryev. Maybe I wasn't. Either way, no one yet had come to the door looking for payback.

I kept driving. By the time I reached the West Side Highway, I was no longer thinking about my next move. I already knew it.

To my right I could see the sunlight bouncing off the cresting caps of the Hudson River. The water looked frigid, almost angry, and yet there in the middle of it all, by itself, was a cutter sailboat about forty feet long.

It wasn't riding with the wind, it was fighting it, heading straight into the gusts. Whoever was steering the boat was blocked by the mast and mainsail, but I could imagine an old man with an unruly gray beard at the helm, shaking his fist in the air as the bow slammed up and down against the swells, the spray needling his face but never once wiping away his defiant smile.

Sometimes you take only what the wind will give you. Other times you tell the wind to go to hell.

CHAPTER 39

IT WAS A DIFFERENT doorman, but he shot me the same dubious look when I told him who I was there to see. *Are you sure you want to do that, dude?*

Sure was perhaps too strong a word, but there was no turning back now.

Two minutes later, the elevator door opened in the lobby, and out stepped Ivan. He somehow looked even bigger than when I last left him—wearing furry handcuffs—in Jade's apartment.

"Hello, Ivan," I said. "Nice to see you again."

I knew he'd be the one who'd come fetch me. I could practically hear him volunteering to Grigoryev. Insisting was more like it.

Ivan shook his head at me. "You're a stupid man," he said.

I followed him back onto the elevator. He hit the button for the penthouse and stared ahead in silence. About halfway up the building he finally spoke. "I was told I'm not allowed to kill you," he said. "Not a scratch on your face."

"I guess today's my lucky day, huh?"

Of all things, he laughed. Really loudly, too. Then he wound up and sucker punched me in the gut so hard I thought my stomach had exploded. I doubled over, dropping to one knee. The only reason I didn't throw up was that I couldn't breathe.

Ivan leaned down, looking into my eyes with sublime satisfaction as I desperately gasped for air. "Good," he said. "Not a scratch on your face."

Ding. The elevator opened.

I couldn't get to my feet so Ivan grabbed me under both my arms and threw me out like a rag doll. I hit the floor of Grigoryev's security room with a thump before rolling onto my back. Staring down at me was the man himself.

"You certainly have balls," said Grigoryev. "Brains I'm not so sure about."

My being an idiot had quickly become a recurring theme.

Grigoryev took a seat on the bench along the wall. Ivan frisked me, then stood guard in the corner, taking out his 9mm Makarov and twisting on the suppressor. It was déjà vu all over again. The only difference being that I had no move to make this time. Hell, I could barely move at all. It hurt just to talk.

"What'd you do with him?" I asked.

Grigoryev knew I was talking about Vincent Franchella but had no intention of answering my question.

"Just be happy you're still alive," he said. "How do you know Danny?"

"We have a mutual friend," I answered.

If someone had given me a hundred guesses as to what Vladimir Grigoryev was going to do next, I still wouldn't have come close. Not by a mile.

Out of the blue he stood up and began shuffling his shiny wingtips across the marble tile, back and forth, as if performing some soft shoe routine. *Is he really dancing right now?* Whatever it was, it was only the warm-up act. The main attraction followed. I was suddenly treated to a full-throated rendition of George and

Ira Gershwin's "Someone to Watch Over Me." I mean, he was really belting it out with his Russian accent. *"Looking everywhere, haven't found him yet…"*

Then, as quick as he'd started, Grigoryev stopped. "Did you know that Danny is a very good hockey player? For an American, that is."

"I did know that," I said.

"Russians always like Americans more if they can play hockey." Grigoryev bobbed his head as if sizing me up. I was still laid out flat on my back in front of him. "You don't play hockey, I'm guessing, do you, Professor Reinhart? Or is it Agent Reinhart?"

"You can just call me Dylan," I said. "And then you can tell me if Vincent Franchella is still alive. He has a wife and kids."

"Is that supposed to make me feel something?" he asked.

"Actually, yeah. It is."

"How do you think Vincent's wife would feel about his girlfriend, Jade? What would that something be? Not so good, right?"

"She'd still want to know if her husband's okay," I said.

Grigoryev thought for a moment. "Yes. He's okay," he said. "For now."

"Why? What could change later?"

"You don't get to know that," he said. I figured as much. He turned to walk away.

"Wait." I reached into my shirt pocket. "Here, this is for you," I said.

I had another card for Grigoryev. It was the parking stub for his Range Rover, including the name and address of the lot.

He nodded, taking the card. "Ivan will show you out. And if you ever come back here again, I'll shoot you myself."

"You were going to kill her," I said. "I had to do it."

He nodded again. "Yes, I've heard that about you. It's your Achilles' heel," he said. "A conscience."

CHAPTER 40

I WAS STILL ACHING from Ivan's gut punch, but at least it was officially safe to go back to my apartment. I just didn't get to stay there very long.

Von Oehson didn't text me. He called. Actually, his driver called. The guy wasn't asking me to come out to the front of my building. No, he was telling me. That's what I had to do. Eleven o'clock at night, and I was supposed to drop everything on a dime and go for a ride.

"I'll be right down," I said. Of course that's what I said. I was finally about to learn what had happened to Carter.

"Temp okay?" I was asked after I settled into the back of a Rolls-Royce Cullinan. Maybe the Maybach was in the shop. Von Oehson's driver, different from the one who'd been behind the wheel of the Maybach, had a Brooklyn accent. "Too cold? Too hot? Whattaya thinking?"

"Just right," I answered.

And that was that, the extent of our conversation. I could've asked where he was taking me—where I was meeting up with von Oehson—but I figured I'd know soon enough. Even sooner, as it turned out.

We hadn't left Manhattan. We hadn't even left the West Side. Our destination was the West 30th Street Heliport.

Von Oehson's helicopter was just approaching, its floodlights so bright I had to shield my eyes. Seconds after it touched down, von Oehson stepped out and made a beeline for the Rolls, joining me in the backseat. You always see people crouch when walking away from a helicopter. Not him. If there's such a thing as walking like a billionaire, Mathias von Oehson had the strut down pat.

"Thanks for coming to meet me," he said. "I obviously couldn't have you out to the house in Connecticut."

"That was going to be my first question, whether you said anything to Carter."

"About you? No, and he can never know."

"That's the right answer," I said. "In that case, thanks for making the trip into the city."

"It's not all for you." Von Oehson wrapped his knuckles on the burled walnut of the center console between us, apparently an unspoken cue for his driver that we were good to go. Off we went.

"Where are we heading?" I asked.

"I'm heading to my attorney's apartment. You're coming along for the ride so I can fill you in," he said. He pressed a button and up went a divider, sealing us off from his driver.

"What about the police? Have you spoken to them yet?" I asked.

"They wanted a statement from Carter this afternoon, but I was able to put them off until tomorrow," he said.

"Did you mention anything to them about speaking to your attorney first?"

"I truly hope you don't think I'm that stupid," he said. "As it is, news vans are camped out in front of my house. Not the right optics. My son miraculously returns from the dead, and suddenly I need a lawyer?"

"Okay. *So why do you need a lawyer?*"

Von Oehson unfolded a piece of paper from his pocket, handing it to me while flipping on a reading light over my shoulder. I was now staring down at a front and back copy of a deposited check from an account in his wife's name, made out to cash. The amount was seventy-eight thousand dollars.

"Impressive," he said, "don't you think?"

I was fairly certain he wasn't referring to the seventy-eight grand. Other than that I wasn't sure what to think yet. "What am I looking at?"

"A forgery."

I stared at the signature. Bethany von Oehson. Beautiful handwriting. Big swooping letters. Elegant. "This wasn't her?"

"Nope."

It was the way he shook his head. I knew right away. Carter had forged his mother's signature. "Why would he need to do that?"

"Two reasons apparently, the Rams and the Seahawks. Neither team covered the spread that week," he said.

"Carter was betting on football games?"

"Among other sports."

"So you're saying your son has a gambling problem."

"Yes. The problem is, he loses." Von Oehson caught himself. "Actually, the real problem is that he couldn't pay up. That's how this entire mess started."

CHAPTER 41

VON OEHSON WALKED ME through it. The whole thing.

He and Bethany took Carter home from St. Sebastian's church that afternoon. The three of them talked for hours. Suffice it to say, Carter did most of the talking.

He knew his mother never looked at bank statements, and when his father occasionally did he never went check by check. Even if he had spotted the one for seventy-eight thousand dollars made out to cash, Mathias von Oehson would never have questioned his wife about it. Trust played a certain role in that, he explained, but what was left unsaid—the primary reason—was the amount. A man with a net worth of more than twenty-four billion dollars doesn't blink an eye at anything less than six figures.

But over that amount? Something over a hundred grand?

That's why Carter also knew he couldn't simply forge his mother's signature again after he continued to pile up losses. When the first check cleared, his bookie had been all too willing to accept larger wagers.

"How much larger?" I asked.

"Carter owed about three hundred thousand," said von Oehson. "He tried to work out a payment plan, but this wasn't exactly Walmart."

Clearly not. "So who was it?"

"Were it only that easy. There was a go-between."

"One guess," I said. His regular Tuesday date. "A girl named Betty."

"Carter says he originally asked her if she knew someone who could take his action. Big surprise—a hooker who knew a bookie."

"So Carter never met him?"

"Not once. This Betty girl handled the money, presumably taking a cut. Until, of course, Carter said he couldn't pay up— at least not the three hundred thousand all at once. That's when they came up with their own payment plan."

"By *they* you don't mean Betty, right? Maybe she was the go-between with Carter's bets, but she was pretty convincing with me about not being involved in his disappearance. I don't think she was in on it."

"You're right. She wasn't," he said. "As for the other girl who showed up in her place, Carter thinks she was just a pawn. Her role was to gain access to the house, deliver her lines, and let the two guys in."

That tracked with everything Jade had confessed to on the drive to my father's cabin. She did her job setting up Carter and was allowed to leave. She'd been told they were going to have the kid fake his suicide, but nothing bad was actually going to happen to him. Even the gun they gave her wasn't real. It was a stage prop. That made it even easier, she explained, for her to go along with everything. She didn't ask questions. She was being paid not to.

"So what happened next?" I asked.

"Nothing short of irony," said von Oehson. "Carter was kidnapped, as I thought, but it had nothing to do with the Hungarians and the painting. It all stemmed from his gambling debt."

"I get that Carter owed a lot. But whoever was behind this, was it worth the risk? All that planning?"

"That was my first thought, as well," he said. "But I should've known. They were after far more cash than the three hundred grand." He pointed at the copy of the check in my hands, specifically the name in the upper-left corner.

Now it made sense. "So they learned exactly who Carter was," I said. Who his mother was. Even better, who his *father* was.

"The girl, Betty, had vouched for Carter with the bookie," said von Oehson. "She never revealed who he was up front, just that he was a rich kid."

"Then they found out how rich."

"They were smart about it, too. By having Carter die by suicide, as it were, there was no one for the police to look for except Carter."

"It bought them cover," I said. "But eventually they—"

"Yes, they had to show their hand. So long as they didn't ask for a ridiculous ransom, though, they knew I wouldn't be going to the police."

"How would they know that?"

"Because the only call I was ever going to receive was from Carter. That was their plan. Wait for the dust to settle and have my son get on the phone to explain everything. And once he did, the last thing I'd want to do is go public with it. Hookers and a gambling problem? The press would have a field day. People would say the kid deserved to get kidnapped. This would dog Carter forever."

"Okay. So you wouldn't go to the police," I said. "But your son just came back from the dead. In a very public fashion, no less. The police are going to want to know how. Hell, you still haven't even told *me* how."

"That's the problem," he said, slowly pinching his brow. "I don't know."

CHAPTER 42

IT WAS ONLY FITTING that we stopped at a red light as soon as von Oehson uttered those words. *I don't know.* "What does that mean?" I asked.

"Two guys in masks kidnapped my son for a ransom they never got around to asking for," he said. "They roughed him up, blindfolded him, and kept him stashed away somewhere. Then, without any explanation, they let him go. Just like that. Dropped him off in front of the church and sped off." He folded his arms. *"Why would they do that?"*

In the intelligence community, this moment is called parallel convergence. It's why intelligence agencies from different countries, even non-allies, are willing to share so much information. You simply never know when two seemingly disparate operations will intersect.

"I'll tell you why they let Carter go," I said. "They got spooked."

"How?"

"One of their own went missing."

I told von Oehson about Vincent Franchella. One minute I was talking to him in a hotel room, the next minute he was gone. Kidnapped, as well. I also told him about Vladimir Grigoryev, although I actually never said his name. All that mattered was what he was, not who. A *pakhan.*

"A what?" asked von Oehson.

"Think Russian crime boss," I said, explaining how both Betty and Jade worked for him.

"So this mobster's pissed that someone took advantage of a couple of his girls, and he lets it be known. A crazy Russian and his crew staring down some Italian wise guys."

"The wise guys blinked," I said.

"Is this where you tell me they fear the Russians because the Russians don't have rules? I've seen that movie."

"The Russians have rules." Vladimir Grigoryev sure does. Two commandments, in particular. "No, if I had to guess, what your kidnappers feared was retribution from within."

"I'm not following," said von Oehson.

"Their boss. Whoever he might be," I said. "Everything about Carter's disappearance smacks of a job that was never blessed by, let alone shared with, upper management. As soon as Vincent Franchella went missing, they panicked. They were afraid it was all going to lead back to them."

Von Oehson shook his head slowly. It wasn't disagreement. It was disbelief.

"What's wrong?" I asked.

"It's all going to lead back to them anyway," he said.

"What do you mean? The painting? You said it yourself, this had nothing to do with the Hungarians."

"You're right, it didn't."

"Now I'm the one not following," I said.

"A nineteen-year-old rich kid owes three hundred grand that he doesn't have. The two guys in masks show up to take him for ransom, and he tries to talk his way out of it. When that doesn't work, he tries to barter. He thinks to himself, what can I offer these guys in kind that my parents won't know is missing? That's when he remembers an old painting he once saw tucked away in a closet. He has no idea what it's worth, especially since it's unsigned, but if his parents own the damn thing, it has to be worth something. What did he have to lose?"

"This is what Carter told you?"

"Not at first. He never mentioned it when my wife and I got home from the church and sat him down. He'd already admitted to so much, he figured why make it even worse if he didn't have to? It's not as if we'd asked him about the painting. He assumed we hadn't noticed it was gone," he said. "Only I had."

"Did you tell him why? How you knew it was gone? The whole history behind it?"

"Absolutely not. Later, when I was alone with Carter, I explained that after he had posted his apparent suicide note, I had turned the house upside down looking for him or, at least, some clue as to what had really happened. I simply couldn't believe that he'd killed himself. That's when I noticed the painting was missing." Von Oehson sighed. "When Carter heard that, that's when he confessed."

I had to let that all sink in for a few seconds. "In other words, Carter tried to settle a three-hundred-thousand gambling debt with a hundred-million-dollar painting. Did you tell him it was a Monet?"

"And make him feel even worse? No. He'd be suicidal for real."

"What about what happened to it? Once his kidnappers got their hands on the painting, did Carter see it again?"

"He didn't see anything. He was blindfolded," said von Oehson. "He never even heard one of their names. But unless they're as dumb as rocks they're right now in the process of trying to get the painting appraised. When that happens the Hungarians are going to find out that their missing Monet has suddenly turned up in New York City. The art world is simply too small for that not to happen."

"But it probably hasn't happened yet," I said. "Which means we still have some more time—and hopefully a few more moves to make."

"Do you have any in mind yet?"

"I will."

Von Oehson smiled. "I would expect nothing less," he said, reaching into his pocket.

"What's this?" I asked. Only I could plainly see what it was. An actual check as opposed to a copy of one. He was giving me the back-end payment of our deal—another million dollars made out to Harlem Legal House.

"My son is home safely. That's what I hired you for. Nothing more," he said. "Your work is done, and I thank you."

"It wasn't entirely my work that got him back."

"All the same, he's home safely."

"What about the Hungarians? The painting?"

"That's my problem now, not yours."

"You're only half right," I said.

"How is it your problem?"

"I was referring more to Carter. He may be home, but with that painting still out there I'm not sure about the safety part."

"You think he's still in danger?"

"I'm not sure what to think, to be honest. This is more about a feeling."

"Clearly not a good one."

"Here," I said, handing him back the check. "When that feeling is gone, you can give this to me again."

CHAPTER 43

VON OEHSON LOWERED THE divider to the front seat as soon as we pulled up to his lawyer's brownstone off Central Park West. I listened to the mechanical hum of the retracting glass as the back of the driver's head slowly appeared.

"Jimmy, please take Dr. Reinhart home from here," von Oehson said. Jimmy nodded and then waited until his boss was safely inside. We both waited.

There's a time and a place for linear thinking. Sitting by myself in the back of a billionaire's Rolls-Royce at midnight struck me as neither. I'd given back von Oehson's check but held on to the copy of the one that Carter had forged to his bookie, although *bookie* seemed too quaint for the guy. Whoever he was, his signature on the back of the check wasn't going to get me any closer to identifying him. In crayon, Annabelle could write her name more legibly. Of course, that was probably intentional on his part.

Now what? The next logical move was using the bank ID code to identify the branch.

Then gain access to the bank's security footage based on the time and date.

Then rely on facial recognition software.

Then hope the guy's last known address was also his current address.

Then go have a nice chat with him. A to B to C and so on.

But by D or E it could be too late.

"Slight change of plans," I told von Oehson's driver. "Do you know O'Leary's bar in Midtown?"

Jimmy angled his rearview mirror slightly to make eye contact with me. "Does an Irishman piss Guinness?"

I took that as a yes.

Five minutes later, I was probably the only person on the planet who ever stepped out of a four-hundred-thousand-dollar Rolls-Royce to walk into O'Leary's. Not that it was a dive. It's just that the place wore its "nothing fancy" appeal like a badge of honor. This is where you went to drink pints and whiskey and nothing else. Lest you be tempted otherwise, only two wines were listed on the menu: red and white.

"Holy crap, look what the wind blew in," said Allen Grimes, spotting me from the corner of his eye while holding court at the end of the bar. He shifted an unlit cigarette to his left hand, pointing at me with his right. "Gentleman, may I present Dr. Dylan Reinhart, one of the greatest living minds in the field of human psychology. And if you don't believe me, just ask him. He'll tell you so himself."

That got a hearty laugh from the circle of red-nosed men listening in. I laughed, too. It was funny. Allen Grimes may have had his detractors in some corners of the city, but no one ever questioned his sense of humor.

"Can I talk to you for a minute?" I asked. That I wanted to do so privately was easily assumed.

"That depends," he said.

"On what?"

"How much am I going to regret it?"

CHAPTER 44

ALLEN GRIMES WAS THE man behind "Grimes on Crimes," the long-standing and exceedingly popular column in the *New York Gazette* that chronicled everything in the city that helped keep Mace purchases, gun-permit applications, and criminal defense attorney fees at all-time highs.

We'd first met through Elizabeth. Fittingly, her initial description of Grimes remains the best I've heard. "His driver's license says he's fifty, his libido thinks he's twenty, and his liver is convinced he's Keith Richards."

Way to nail it, Lizzie.

I followed Grimes to the back of the bar and an empty table out of earshot that wobbled despite a collection of sugar packets and a matchbook wedged under one leg.

"So how have you been?" I asked.

"You can skip the foreplay," he said. "What do you need?"

Fair enough. "An introduction."

"To who?"

"Frank Brunetti," I said.

Grimes laughed from his gut. "You're joking, right? You give me way too much credit."

"Do I?"

"I've interviewed the guy a couple of times," he said. "We're hardly friends."

"He trusts you, though."

"Brunetti doesn't trust anyone."

"You know what I mean," I said. "You're the only press he's ever spoken to. The word for that is *respect*."

Grimes finished what was left of his whiskey. He pushed the glass aside, folding his arms on the table. "Now you want me to risk that respect on your behalf?"

"I wouldn't ask if it weren't important."

"I'm sure it is," he said. "I'm sure it's very, very important."

He stared at me. I stared back. This was the part where I was supposed to explain why I needed a sit-down, as it were, with the head of the five families, the pope of New York. Only I wasn't saying anything.

"I can't tell you why. Not yet," I said finally. "Except this. You'd also be doing Brunetti a favor."

"How's that?"

"Again, I can't tell you."

"You're not exactly winning me over, Reinhart."

"I know. But you'll understand why soon. And one way or another you're going to have the jump on one hell of a story."

That perked him up a bit. "Why did you bury the lede?"

"I didn't want you to think I was playing you."

"You're still playing me," he said.

"What can I say? I'm not good at subtle."

Grimes looked down at his empty glass, smiling. "You know, three more whiskeys from now you would've had much better odds."

He wasn't saying yes, but he hadn't told me no. "In that case, the next rounds are on me," I said.

CHAPTER 45

"ARE YOU CRAZY?" ASKED Elizabeth.

Normally that's just a figure of speech—what people usually say in response to being told something that strikes them as a bad idea, if not downright terrible.

This sounded different. Even over the phone. Elizabeth seemed pretty convinced the following morning that I'd officially lost my mind. Bonkers. Nutsville. Cuckoo for Cocoa Puffs.

"Okay, so it might not be the *safest* idea," I said.

"Gee, you think?"

"It's the boat part, isn't it?"

"It's every part," she said. "Is Grimes at least going with you?"

"No. That would require telling him way too much."

"So you're really going alone?"

"You make it sound like a suicide mission," I said. "Frank Brunetti is not about to kill me."

"Of course not," she said. "Where would I ever get that idea? You're heading out on his yacht in international waters to basically meddle in his affairs. There's no way you could possibly fall overboard by accident."

"See? It *is* the boat part. I knew it. Do mobsters still do concrete shoes?"

"I'm serious."

"I know. I'll be fine. I went to meet Grigoryev alone, didn't I?"

"Yeah, and how'd *that* turn out?" she asked, hitting a whole new level of sarcasm. "I'm still kicking myself for helping to arrange that meeting."

"I asked you for that favor. That's on me, not you."

"Sure. At your funeral that's exactly what I would've been telling myself."

"I told you, I'll be fine."

"Yes, you will be," she said, "because I'm coming with you."

"*What?* No, you're not. You can't."

"Why not?"

"You're a federal agent, for starters," I said.

"Does that prevent me from going on a boat?"

"I don't know, let's ask your boss. I'm sure Pritchard might have an opinion about this. It wouldn't matter what special unknown assignment you might be doing for the mayor."

"Pritchard would probably love it," she said. "He hates Brunetti."

She had a point. True power is when no one can touch you, and Frank Brunetti didn't have a single fingerprint on him. For decades, the FBI—not to mention the IRS, and even the SEC— had all tried to take him down, to no avail. With the best legal and public relations teams that dirty money can buy, Brunetti had never so much as paid a parking fine. His was the kind of power that would seriously piss off a Bureau division head like Evan Pritchard.

Still. "It's not a good idea," I said.

"It's better than the idea of your going alone. Also, you have zero chance of talking me out of it."

"Zero, huh?"

"Nada," she said. "Zip."

Okay, Lizzie. If you insist . . .

CHAPTER 46

THE ONLY SURE BETS in life: death, taxes, and mobsters worshipping Martin Scorsese films.

Frank Brunetti's yacht was called *Aces High*. That made sense, given that it was a licensed offshore gambling boat, but the true inspiration actually came from Brunetti's obsession with the movie *Casino*. As he explained to Allen Grimes, the boat was named after the talk show hosted by the character that Robert De Niro played. "I've watched that flick a hundred times, easy," Brunetti went on to say in the interview.

I could only imagine how many times he'd seen *Goodfellas*.

"Welcome aboard," said the chief steward, or so read his shiny nameplate, as Elizabeth and I stepped out of the cold and onto *Aces High* a few minutes before it left from the North Cove Marina in Battery Park at exactly 8 p.m. That was another thing I'd read about Brunetti. Like Jimmy Hoffa, he was big on punctuality.

There were roughly eighty to a hundred people on board, all of us gathered in a posh stateroom with blue velvet curtains that had been converted into a bar and lounge and, of course, a cozy, high-stakes casino. There were four blackjack tables, two roulette tables, and one craps table, all of which had to remain empty until we reached international waters three miles offshore.

Everyone around us looked as if they had a lot of disposable income, although not necessarily any of it earned legally. Meanwhile, Elizabeth simply looked stunning.

"Check out the stares. I'm the envy of every man here," I said, as she and I hung out in the corner, nursing our glasses of the champagne that had been passed around.

She glanced down at her very form-fitting red dress. "Too much?"

"Just right," I assured her. "Very Christmas-y."

"So what's the plan now?"

"We're doing it."

"You mean, waiting? That's the plan?"

"Grimes got us the meeting. We just don't know when it will be."

"Are we even sure Brunetti is on the boat?"

"I'm not sure of anything right now," I said. "But he's supposed to be."

"In other words, we're betting on the come."

"Wow. Someone did her homework."

"It's a common expression." She cracked a smile. "Okay, maybe I did a little light research on casino games this afternoon. Betting on the come. It's a bet you can make on a craps table."

"I'm impressed," I said. "Did you also read that the game of craps has the smallest house advantage of all table games, with 1.41 percent on pass-line bets, or 0.606 percent if you combine it with a standard free-odds bet?"

With one look Elizabeth made it very clear that she 100 percent didn't care. "I don't get this whole attraction-to-gambling thing that people have," she said. "There's too much risk."

"So says the woman who basically risks her life for a living."

"That's different."

"Is it?" I nodded at the craps table. "No matter how big you lose over there you're still only losing money."

"Great," she said, letting that sink in. "Now I've got to go find a new line of work tomorrow."

"Assuming we make it through the night," I said. "Did you see those two bags of concrete mix on the deck when we walked on?"

"Very funny."

In a perfect world, Brunetti would have made some grand entrance at that moment and said a few welcoming words to his guests before heading over to Elizabeth and me with an invitation to some discreet parlor room for our meeting. But this was Brunetti's world. His boat, his timetable. Our waiting. And waiting, and waiting…

Two hours later, with the casino in full swing but still no sign of Brunetti, it was time for a different plan.

"Let's go play some blackjack," I said.

"You're joking, right? The minimum is a hundred dollars a hand."

"Even better."

"Better for what?" she asked.

"For how we're going to win."

"And how's that?"

"It's simple," I said. "We're going to cheat."

CHAPTER 47

THE HIGHER THE STAKES at a blackjack table, the faster the dealers. Casinos are a volume business, after all. The more bets that are placed, the better their house advantage can pay off for them—no matter how slight that advantage might be.

Not surprisingly, Frank Brunetti had hired some of the quickest hands in the business to work his tables. Watching the dealer at my table was like watching the blur of a speeding train. Only I wasn't watching the train. Just the tracks. The cards he was laying down.

"How would you like it?" the dealer asked after counting out the ten thousand in cash I'd placed on the felt in front of him. A dealer in any casino never takes money directly from another person's hand.

"Six yellows, the rest in black," I said. "Please."

Twin stacks of black hundred-dollar chips, along with six yellow thousand-dollar chips, were slid over to me, for a total of ten grand. That was followed by the two words all gamblers hear when the exchange is complete. "Good luck," said the dealer.

Subtext being, *You're going to need it.*

Not tonight, though. All I needed were some quick hands of my own along with my partner in crime.

I glanced over at Elizabeth, who was standing exactly where I'd asked her to—left of the dealer, behind the shoe of cards. I'd intentionally sat in the anchor seat of the table on the opposite side. She could see me perfectly. More important, she could see my cards.

This was all about timing. Of course, a *little* luck wouldn't hurt, either.

I looked down at two face cards on my very first hand, a combined twenty to the dealer's eight and a seven. Everybody stayed pat and the dealer hit his fifteen. Boom. He busted with another seven.

Take it away, Lizzie.

Elizabeth screamed at the top of her lungs. Every head turned, even the ones that were being paid not to. Our dealer couldn't help it. It was pure reflex. For a split second his brain forgot that he had to keep his eyes on the chips at all times.

"Oh, my God," said Elizabeth, looking up from her phone to see everyone staring at her. She slapped a palm over her forehead, the picture of embarrassment. "Sorry! I just got a text from my youngest brother. He was accepted early decision to Dartmouth."

And like that, her scream made sense to everyone. A few people even offered up congratulations.

At the same time, our dealer began quickly paying off everyone at our table. Grabbing a stack of black chips in one hand and yellow chips in the other, he moved left to right in a well-practiced, fluid motion. When he got to me, though, he stopped and cocked his head. I knew what he was thinking. He didn't remember seeing three yellow chips as part of my bet before dealing the hand. Yet there they were, staring back at him—three yellow chips at a thousand dollars apiece tucked underneath three hundred-dollar black chips.

"Is something wrong?" I asked.

"Are you sure that was your original bet, sir?"

"Of course I'm sure."

"I could've sworn that—"

"What exactly are you suggesting?" I raised my voice. *"Are you calling me a cheater?"*

All heads turned once again. Between Elizabeth and me, we were giving everyone on the boat whiplash.

"How we all doing?" asked the pit boss, stepping in. "Is there a problem?"

Nothing triggers the casino brass hierarchy faster than an unhappy customer. Not because they necessarily want to make the customer happy. They just want to get the customer to shut the hell up as fast as possible so all the other customers can resume losing their money.

"Yes. There's a problem," I said. "A really big one."

That's when I felt the hand on my shoulder. "Actually, no. There's no problem here at all, Dr. Reinhart."

I turned around to see Frank Brunetti standing behind me.

"What took you so long?" I asked.

Brunetti grinned through his clenched jaw. "Come, let's talk," he said. He nodded at Elizabeth. "And bring along your pretty accomplice."

CHAPTER 48

IT WAS A BIT like walking into the lair of a Bond villain as we followed Brunetti into another room. The look of it was midcentury mobster meets the air-traffic control tower at O'Hare International.

The surveillance cameras lining the ceiling of Brunetti's casino—the "eyes in the sky"—were doing far more than simply filming. In addition to the feeds being filtered by a real-time facial recognition platform, they were using three-dimensional thermal imaging to detect concealed weapons of any kind. It was a level of security bordering on paranoia. On the other hand, this was a guy whose life and livelihood depended on knowing who his enemies were.

Perhaps the only real surprise was that Brunetti was making no attempt to hide any of this from us. Pictures of Elizabeth culled from news stories appeared on multiple screens above a console manned by two guys who looked like they came straight out of central casting for computer nerds. The only things missing were the pocket protectors on their shirts.

Brunetti very much wanted us to see all that. He was well aware that Elizabeth was a federal agent. Despite that, he was still inviting her backstage. Why? Because he could. That's how untouchable he was. And that's what he really wanted us to know.

"Have a seat," he said.

Elizabeth and I made our way to a black leather couch that was kitty-corner to his desk, a monstrosity of glass and black lacquer. The thing practically glistened.

Opposite us were two other men, one standing and the other sitting in a matching black leather armchair. Thermal imaging would've surely revealed that they were both packing. They weren't introduced to us.

"Thanks for agreeing to see me," I said as Brunetti settled into the chair behind his desk. He gave a quick tug on both sleeves of his crisp, charcoal-gray suit. He was sporting a pink tie and a matching pocket square. At sixty-four, he looked to be in pretty good shape. Maybe a little puffy around the edges but not overweight.

"So you're a friend of Allen's, huh? He speaks highly of you," said Brunetti. "Of course, Grimes is full of shit, so who knows, right?" He laughed. He was joking. Sort of. "Okay, so we're all here now. What did you want to talk to me about?"

"A painting," I said.

"What kind of painting?"

"A stolen one."

Brunetti leaned back in his chair, amused. "That's what this is? You think I stole a painting?"

"No. I think you might know of a stolen painting."

"Are you always this cryptic, Dr. Reinhart?"

"In this case I need to be," I said. "I'm representing the owner, and he wants it back."

Brunetti looked over at Elizabeth. "And who are you representing, Agent Needham? Nice dress, by the way."

"I'm not representing anyone," Elizabeth answered. "Tonight I'm just a private citizen enjoying a gambling cruise."

"Yes, of course you are," he said. "It must be killing you, though."

"What's that?" she asked.

"To get so close to me and yet be so far. What is it with you agents wanting to take me down so badly? And I do mean badly. You all suck at it."

That got a chuckle out of his two henchmen, Thug 1 and Thug 2 (with apologies to Dr. Seuss). Meanwhile, Elizabeth was surely riffling through a hundred different comebacks in her mind, all of which were better left unsaid. But just in case she couldn't stop herself...

"Fifty million," I blurted out.

That quickly got Brunetti's attention back on me. His eyes felt like two lasers. "What was that?" he asked.

"That's how much the owner of the painting is willing to pay you to get it back," I said. "Fifty million dollars."

CHAPTER 49

"THAT'S A HELL OF a chunk of money," he said. "This must be some painting."

"It has a lot of sentimental value to its owner."

Brunetti nodded. He was waiting for me to continue. I didn't. "I'm pretty sure this is the point in our little chat here where you tell me who the hell this guy is," he said.

"Does it matter?" I asked.

"I'll let you know once you give me his name."

Good one, Frank. Don't worry, I have every intention of telling you. "It's Mathias von Oehson," I said.

"That explains the fifty million. The hedge fund guy, right? You're working for him?"

"Representing him. On this one particular matter."

"Now repeat the part you said before."

"Which part?" I asked.

"You know the one. I want to make sure I heard you right."

Oh, that part. "What I said was that I don't think you had anything to do with the painting's disappearance. You had no involvement whatsoever."

"Yet you somehow think I know where this missing painting is?"

"If you don't already know, I trust you have the ability to find out."

"I'm not sure whether that's a compliment or an insult," he said.

"I think the better word is *candid*. I'm being candid with you."

"Good. So let me be candid with you." Brunetti leaned forward in his chair, resting his elbows on the desk. He didn't raise his voice but the veins in his neck were bulging. *"I don't know what the fuck you're talking about with this painting."*

"Okay," I said.

"No. It's not okay. I don't appreciate what you're suggesting. Not one bit. Do you understand?"

"Yes. I understand," I said. "My mistake. My apologies."

My job is done here.

I stood and extended my hand to Brunetti, thanking him for his time. He clearly didn't expect to be done with me so fast. *Even better.*

"What did you buy in for?" he asked.

"Excuse me?" I'd heard him just fine.

"At my blackjack table. What did you buy in for?"

"Ten thousand," I said.

"How much did you win on your first hand?"

"I wouldn't call that winning."

"What would you call it?"

"The same thing you did. Cheating in order to get your attention."

"Yes. You switched out the black chips for yellows, I know. But what was your original bet?"

"Six hundred."

"Then that's your winnings." Brunetti turned to Thug 2. "Give him that plus his ten grand back."

"Just the buy-in would be fine," I said. "I don't deserve more than that."

"You're right, you don't," he said. "But that's the real funny thing about money, Dr. Reinhart. Those who have the most are rarely the ones who deserve it."

CHAPTER 50

JAMES BOND WOULD'VE SOMEHOW arranged for a sleek helicopter to take him off Brunetti's boat the moment the meeting was over. Reinhart, Dylan Reinhart, had no such pull.

It was another hour and a half before the cruise ended, well after midnight. Elizabeth and I couldn't even kill time discussing whether we thought my plan had worked for fear that Brunetti had the entire boat bugged or was using the latest in lip-reading software. I could manipulate the guy, hopefully, but what I couldn't do was underestimate him.

"Now what?" asked Elizabeth, once we were off the boat.

I glanced down at my phone. "Now we wait another two minutes for your Uber driver to show up to take you home. His name is Jackson and he has 4.94 stars."

"You know what I mean."

"Yes. I do. And I also know what you're thinking."

"Men always think they know what a woman is thinking. They never do."

"You're thinking you want to be the one agent who finally brings Frank Brunetti down," I said.

"Okay, maybe you know this *one* time."

"I get it. He's a smug son of a bitch who more than has it coming to him."

"So let me help you bring it," she said.

"That's not what I'm trying to do. This is just about a painting."

"Why can't it be about both?"

"For starters, it could get you fired. Or worse."

"What did you tell me back on the boat about what I do for a living? The risk?"

"All the more reason why you shouldn't be getting involved with this," I said.

"I already am."

I glanced again at my phone. "Two minutes," I said. "Jackson and his 4.94 rating can't get here soon enough."

Forget how cold it was outside. Elizabeth was fired up. "*Why are you being so damn stubborn about this?* You originally wanted my help, and I gave it to you. Now I'm asking if I can help even more, and you're giving me a hard time. Why?"

"Because things are about to get a little dicey," I said.

"*Dicey?*"

"Yes, dicey."

"So what else is new?"

"I'm talking unorthodox."

"Right," she said. "Because Dylan Reinhart normally plays it so straight."

"Was that a gay joke?"

"Shut up."

"I'm just trying to give you fair warning."

"Consider me warned."

I chuckled. I couldn't help myself. Elizabeth was about to figure out what was happening.

I was counting on her all along.

"Our ride's here," I said. "Are you ready, partner?"

She took one look at the white van with tinted windows that rolled up in front of us and immediately knew that this was no Uber. The giant logo on the side read MR. FIX-IT, framed by a wrench and hammer. Nice touch.

Julian lowered his driver's-side window, flashing a toothy grin beneath his Manchester United cap. He always sounded a little more British when he was excited. "Who's up for a bit of mischief?" he asked.

CHAPTER 51

WHO WOULD'VE THUNK IT? The best way to break into the Hungarian consulate is not to break into the Hungarian consulate. You break into a Hungarian bakery instead.

"Are you guys sure this is going to work?" asked Elizabeth.

"Absolutely not," said Julian.

I wish he'd been kidding. He really wasn't sure.

We were parked across the street from Eszter's Pastries on the Upper East Side, "Home of All Things Sweet and Hungarian," according to the shop's Facebook page.

As for Julian's intel, that came from what was commonly referred to in the CIA as the hab file. If you were on the agency's radar and did anything on a habitual basis, it was noted in the hab file. For instance, the Hungarian consulate in Manhattan ordered a breakfast pastry assortment each morning from Eszter's.

Of course, that didn't explain why we were about to break in to the place. The specifics behind it were a bit complicated. Julian took a crack at it for Elizabeth's sake, but, suffice it to say, he didn't exactly simplify things.

"You see, the entire Hungarian consulate has an STC rating over 50, while the ambassador's office meets every ICD 705 requirement, and the main conference room is a permanent skiff, complete with an RF-shielded door," he'd said. All of it with a straight face, no less.

For anyone not possessing a PhD in advanced intelligence gathering, an RF-shielded door is one that prevents radio frequencies from getting in or out. These doors are commonly used with "skiffs" (colloquial for SCIFs, or Sensitive Compartmented Information Facilities), which are relied on by governments, and anyone else with good reason to be paranoid, to negate listening devices and eavesdropping. There are both permanent and temporary skiffs, the latter usually erected when presidents and other high-ranking officials visit foreign countries and need to be assured of their privacy. Either way, all skiffs must meet certain standards, including those mandated by Intelligence Community Directive (ICD) 705. Requirements include having a sound transmission class (STC) rating above 50, a level of soundproofing sophisticated enough to mute your neighbor's Mötley Crüe CD at top volume.

In short, the Hungarian consulate was like a big can of Raid. It was really good at repelling bugs. We couldn't just walk in the front door and hope to plant a listening device somewhere.

But there was another possibility. A back door. Literally.

The consulate had a loading dock that was serviced by a guarded alleyway. While the loading dock itself was rarely used, it had a separate door that was opened frequently by staffers taking cigarette breaks. That's how the pastries from Eszter's came in at approximately 8 a.m., Monday through Friday. A delivery van would drop them off at the small gatehouse in front of the alley, and a guard would walk them back. That guard was supposed to use the front entrance of the consulate and have the pastries run through their X-ray machine like every other delivery, but that meant a much longer walk to the kitchen, which was right off the loading dock.

That's what happens when routines become ingrained. People cut corners. And if those people happen to include a security guard at the Hungarian consulate, the CIA was going to know about it.

Not that the US government is habitually bugging foreign embassies on its soil. That would be crazy, right? Unheard of. Rootin' tootin' Vladimir Putin nuts.

But if we had to, it's good to know we could. Wink-wink.

"Okay. Wait a minute, though," said Elizabeth, after taking all this in. "You guys left out the most important part."

She was right. We had.

CHAPTER 52

IT WAS TWO IN the morning, and we were sitting in the back of Julian's mobile office, *Mr. Fix-It*—an old FBI surveillance van that he reconfigured after it had been put out to pasture. Naturally, the Bureau knew nothing about this repurposing. Almost no one did.

"Which part don't you get?" asked Julian.

"I go in just before the night shift wraps up. I get that," she said. "I knock on the front door, flash my badge, get someone to open up for me, and then give a reason why I need to see the kitchen." She glanced down at the piece of molded plastic in her hand that Julian had given her. It looked like a tiny wishbone. "I jam the lock with this little doohickey when closing the door behind me, which leaves the front of the bakery all clear for you two."

"So far, so good. Technically it's not even breaking and entering. It's just entering," said Julian. "Easy-peasy, right? A piece of *torta*."

"A what?" asked Elizabeth.

"That's Hungarian for 'cake,'" he said. "It's also the answer to your question. The part we haven't told you yet."

"Yes. Once the night shift leaves. *What exactly are you two doing?*" asked Elizabeth.

Julian reached into a small black duffel bag by his feet, pulling out a pastry box. "Behold," he said, lifting the lid. "A yeast cake with almonds. Otherwise known as Hungarian coffee cake."

It looked delicious. All sliced up and ready to eat. I was hungry, too, but I knew this was hardly a snack for us. I also knew one of those slices was not like the others. So did Elizabeth now.

"Which one did you put it in?" I asked.

Julian pointed at the slice closest to him. "That's our baby right there," he said. "No, wait." He cocked his head, thinking for a moment. He turned the box around in his lap, then turned it around again. "Ah, hell. Maybe it's the other end here. I can't bloody remember," he said.

Elizabeth looked horrified. I started to laugh. "He's joking," I assured her. "It's right in the middle."

"Three slices in from the left and three in from the right. The exact middle, no matter how you look at it," said Julian. "Just make sure the meeting's early enough so no one eats it before you get there."

She wasn't amused. Or convinced. Of any of it. "Are we really doing this?" she asked.

"Of course," said Julian. "What's the worst that can happen?"

"Someone discovers it and we all go to jail for espionage," she said.

Julian shrugged. "Yeah, that sounds about right."

Elizabeth stared at me. I smiled back. "Dicey enough for you?" I asked.

BOOK THREE

YOU AIN'T SEEN NOTHING YET

CHAPTER 53

CHARLIE REXSON HAD COMMITTED economic suicide.

At least that's how most of the townspeople of Hensonville in upstate New York had pegged it. Some of them had even said as much to his face. And among those, a few managed to insert another adjective between "you've committed" and "suicide." It rhymed with *trucking*.

But Charlie didn't care. He'd owned his gun shop in Hensonville for more than thirty years and had already squirreled away enough money to retire comfortably. Not that his healthy 401(k) was the main reason he did what he did. No. What prompted Charlie to write the opinion piece that, in turn, started the boycott of his business was a crisis of conscience. That stupid devil of a kid, all of nineteen—the one who the FBI apprehended before he could shoot up a shopping mall in Albany—had tried to buy an AR-15 from Charlie only weeks before. The kid had passed the background check. Everything about the purchase was legal. But there was something about the way the kid looked at Charlie. Something off. And for no other reason than gut instinct, he refused to sell him the AR-15.

Charlie didn't blame the owner of another gun shop who

ended up selling the rifle to the kid. He blamed himself. For years, decades even, he'd bought into the slippery-slope theory. To pass any gun control law was to pass every gun control law. The left wouldn't know how or when to stop. Unless you never let them get started.

Now, thanks to one crazy-eyed kid, Charlie had experienced a change of heart, saying as much in the local newspaper. Universal background checks. Elimination of the gun-show loophole. A purchase age of twenty-one rather than eighteen for all guns. These safeguards were a matter of common sense, Charlie wrote, not the beginning of the end of the right to bear arms. If he could come to terms with that—someone who made his living selling guns—couldn't everyone else?

Apparently not.

It wasn't as if the townspeople lit torches, gathered in a field at midnight, and decided to never set foot in Charlie's shop ever again. It was just understood. If you were pro-gun in Hensonville, you were now anti-Charlie.

So when the brass bell jingled above the door to Charlie's shop a week after the piece ran, Charlie didn't even have to look at the man to know he wasn't a local. And when he did look at him, he knew *for sure* the man wasn't a local.

The median household income in Hensonville was $39,167. This man's watch alone, a giant gold Rolex, was easily worth more than that. Charlie eyed it when the man reached up to adjust his black fedora.

Of course, Charlie was just happy that someone—anyone— was willing to come into his shop. It was his first customer since the boycott began.

"I wasn't sure you were open," said the man, closing the door behind him.

Charlie could feel the blast of cold air all the way across the shop to where he was standing, where he always stood, behind the counter. The forecast had predicted snow that night. Only a few inches, though.

"Oh, sure. Definitely," said Charlie. "We're open, all right."

"It's just that the parking lot—there were no cars. A little slow today, huh?"

"Lucky for you, you just missed the morning rush."

The man smiled. "Yes," he said. "Lucky for me."

He walked toward the counter. The closer he got to Charlie, the more expensive his long black overcoat looked. *Is that cashmere?*

"So what can I help you with? What brings you in?" asked Charlie.

The man gazed left and right over Charlie's shoulders, eyeing the crowded display of shotguns and semiautomatic rifles that hung on the wall. "Hunting. That's my purpose," he said. "I'm here to hunt."

"You've certainly come to the right place, then," said Charlie. "I've got every option for deer you could possibly want."

The man smiled again.

Funny when people hear the word hunt. *They always just assume it's an animal.*

CHAPTER 54

"WHAT'S YOUR NAME, BY the way?" asked Charlie.

"Hans," said the man, extending his hand. "Dr. Hans Kestler."

"Pleasure to meet you, Hans." He had a firm grip, thought Charlie. A surgeon, perhaps? "Now tell me, did you have a specific gun or two in mind?"

"Not exactly, but that one over there is catching my eye," said Hans.

He began walking to his left, all the way to the end of the long counter. Charlie followed.

There are certain rules that any good gun shop owner lives by. First, you never fully turn your back on a customer. Second, you stay with that customer wherever they go. The first rule is about safety, the second about sales. Gun buyers need engagement to pull the trigger, as it were, on a purchase. You never just tell them about a gun. You preach it. You make them believe in the depths of their soul that owning this gun is the secret to true self-empowerment.

"So which one was it?" asked Charlie, with a quick glance at the wall behind him.

But it was as if Hans hadn't heard him, not a word. He was

staring back at where they'd first been standing. "How many feet do you think we just walked?" Hans asked.

Charlie squinted. "Excuse me?"

"The distance between here and where you were when I initially walked in," said Hans. "What is that, about ten feet?"

"Um. Yeah, I suppose," said Charlie, scratching the white stubble on his chin. "Call it ten feet."

"How fast do you think you can cover that? I mean, if you had to move as fast as you possibly could. I'm assuming that's where you keep it. Under the counter by the register?"

Charlie didn't know what the hell this guy was talking about. At the same time, he knew *exactly* what he was talking about. If gun shop owners have rules to live by, they also have a gun tucked away somewhere near the register—also to live by.

"I'm sorry, what exactly is going on here?" asked Charlie.

All he could think was that this had something to do with his opinion piece. The pushback had gone beyond a mere boycott and straight to scare tactics. If that was the case, it was working.

Charlie, as subtly as he could, took one side step toward the register and, indeed, the hidden sawed-off shotgun that was positioned under the lip of the counter.

"Ah-ah-ah, not so fast," said Hans. He even wagged his finger.

But it was his other hand that froze Charlie. Hans had pulled back one side of his cashmere overcoat, exposing a Glock 20 tucked behind his belt.

"Okay, okay," said Charlie, raising his palms in the air. "Easy now. There's not a lot of cash in the register, but whatever's there is yours."

Hans glanced down at himself. His coat. His suit. His shoes, a pair of polished wingtips that shined. "Do I look like I need your money, Charlie?"

"Then what do you want?"

"I want to give you one chance before I kill you. It's a chance to kill me first."

"This is crazy," said Charlie. "I don't want to do that."

"Trust me. You do." Hans took a few steps back. "I'm going to close my eyes and count to three. Three's fair, don't you think? Ten feet in three seconds? You might just be able to make that. It's well within the realm of possibility."

"Please—"

"I'm going to start counting, Charlie," said Hans. "What you do after that is up to you."

CHAPTER 55

ELIZABETH ELBOWED ME IN the ribs. "Stop yawning," she whispered.

I couldn't help it. We hadn't slept. "How are you not as tired as I am?" I whispered back.

"Don't you know? I always pull all-nighters to break into Hungarian bakeries."

"We technically didn't break in, remember?"

"I'll be sure to point that out in the meeting, if need be."

"Relax, this is going to work," I said. "We're halfway home. We just need to stick the landing."

"I'm pretty sure the captain of the *Hindenburg* said the same thing."

"Good one," I said. "Max Pruss, by the way."

"What?"

"He was the captain of *Hindenburg*. That was his name. Max Pruss."

Elizabeth's eyes nearly rolled out of her head. "It *so* figures that you would know that."

"That's not a compliment, is it?"

"*Shhhh.* Here she comes."

The two of us had been waiting, side by side on a small couch, in a reception area on the top floor of the Hungarian consulate on East 52nd. A young female receptionist with a pixie haircut sat at a desk across the room, fielding calls one after the other via headset. The red, white, and green from all the Hungarian flags flanking her blended perfectly with the Christmas tree and other holiday decorations that all had the tired look of having been trotted out of a storage closet once every year since the Nixon administration.

Unlike the pastries from Eszter's, Elizabeth and I had come in through the front entrance and passed through security. I even got the bonus full-body-wand treatment from a guard after my platinum wedding band triggered the walk-through metal detector. That's how sensitive the machine was, and how thorough embassies and their consulates tend to be in major cities when it comes to screening. For good reason, of course.

All the more reason we couldn't just waltz in with Julian's transmitter.

What we could bring with us, however, was the audio jamming software that Julian had installed on our phones. If the walls of the consulate had ears—and surely they did—the software was able to mimic the effect of a Druid white-noise generator, which creates a barely detectable level of audible distortion and reverberation that renders listening devices all but moot.

Still, Elizabeth and I weren't taking any chances when we were alone anywhere in the consulate, including a reception area. In other words, even with jamming software triggered, we whispered softly as we waited.

The wait was over. *Here she comes, all right...*

"Good morning, Agent Needham. I'm Dorian Laszlo," she said, thrusting out her hand with a locked elbow as we stood.

Laszlo's title was economic and trade commissioner. From her diction to her posture to her crisp, wrinkle-free pantsuit, she had the air of a perfectionist. She was also the perfect point of entry for us. Dorian Laszlo had substantial authority within the Hungarian consulate, but not so much that would allow her instincts to get in the way of covering her ass with the powers that be back in Budapest.

She also didn't have a personal assistant. That was important.

"It's very nice to meet you," said Elizabeth. "Thanks for seeing us on such short notice."

"You did say it was urgent."

"I'm afraid it is. In fact, that's why I want to introduce you to Dr. Dylan Reinhart. Dr. Reinhart is a professor at Yale and the one who first alerted my office to the situation."

"*Potential* situation, I should clarify," I said.

"Yes. Again, that's why time is of the essence," said Elizabeth.

"I understand," said Laszlo. "Let's head back to my office."

We followed her down a hallway that featured photographs, in both color and black and white, depicting various highlights of Hungarian history over the last hundred or so years. The bigger the moment, the bigger the picture. The Hungarian Revolution of 1956, the Soviet Army officially leaving the country in 1990, Hungary joining NATO in 1999. Conveniently missing from the walls were some of the lowlights, particularly anything having to do with Hungary's role in World War II.

Barbara Tuchman said it best. *History is the unfolding of miscalculations.*

After a left turn and a quick right, we arrived in Laszlo's office. It was a bit like walking into a Pottery Barn. All the furniture looked as if it had been focus-group tested. Nothing was out of place, either. The room was spotless.

"May I offer you something to drink?" asked Laszlo. "A bottle of water?"

"No, thanks," said Elizabeth.

"I'm good, too," I said.

What I didn't say was that in a few minutes I was going to change my mind and take her up on that water, or whatever it took to get Laszlo to leave her office, if only for a few moments.

But first things first.

Elizabeth and I glanced at each other. We were double checking that we'd each turned off our Druid simulators, the audio jammers. *I did, Lizzie. What about you?*

She gave me a quick nod. *Mine's off, too.*

Let the show begin.

CHAPTER 56

LASZLO MOTIONED TO THE two upholstered guest chairs in front of her desk. They looked to be positioned at exactly a forty-five-degree angle. I could practically picture her with a protractor making sure of it.

"As I said," began Elizabeth, wasting no time as we settled in, "Dr. Reinhart came to us with this information, so I think it's best for him to walk you through it. Do you mind, Dr. Reinhart?"

"No. Of course not," I said. I cleared my throat and scratched my chin, the picture of hesitation. "I do want to mention up front that I can't reveal the exact source of what I'm about to share because that could possibly put that person in legal jeopardy."

"I understand," said Laszlo. "I wouldn't want you to do that."

Not yet, you don't.

"A few days ago I was having dinner with a friend of mine who's very well connected in the art world, particularly with the top collectors. After a couple of glasses of wine, he mentioned that he'd been approached confidentially about brokering the private sale of a certain painting," I said. "So far, no big deal. Right?"

Laszlo nodded. "Right."

You always know when you have someone hanging on your every word. They answer your rhetorical questions.

I continued. "The reason my friend was telling me this story is that he was extremely conflicted. He was being offered an obscene amount of money in return for his discretion. This was no ordinary painting, it turns out. It has a history." I waited a beat. "A Hungarian history."

I didn't even finish the next sentence before Laszlo knew the exact painting, along with the exact history. All it took was one word out of my mouth. *Monet.* She didn't flinch or nod. She didn't do anything to let on—except forget to breathe.

Laszlo sat frozen, but her brain, behind her perfectly straight bangs, was surely furiously churning out various questions to ask. Two key ones, in particular. Sure enough, she asked them both. Did we know who originally stole the painting from the Hungarian Parliament Building in Budapest? And who was it who approached my friend about now selling it on the black market?

"My friend doesn't know who originally stole it," I answered. "As educated as he is about art, he didn't know the background of this particular Monet when he was first approached. Only afterward, upon doing some research, did he learn the whole story."

I watched as Laszlo blinked a few times, digesting the subtext of my saying *whole story*. She clearly knew the circumstances of how the Hungarian government originally acquired the painting during World War II. Just like anything else having to do with her government's alliance with Nazi Germany, this definitely wasn't hallway material for the walls outside her office.

"I know you don't want to reveal who your friend is," she said, ending the awkward silence. Awkward for her, at least. "But you can understand why my government would be extremely vested in knowing who's in possession of this painting."

"Naturally," I said.

"Maybe there's a way you can tell me without compromising your friend," said Laszlo.

"Maybe there is, but here's the thing. I don't know who has the painting because my friend doesn't know who has it. The person who approached him was an intermediary."

"I see," said Laszlo, unable to hide her disappointment. She looked more deflated than a party balloon the morning after. "I suppose that makes sense."

"Yes. I'm afraid it does," I said.

Laszlo fell silent, but within seconds I could see her brain churning again. She looked at me. She looked at Elizabeth. It suddenly dawned on her. There was one big question she hadn't asked.

"*Why are you both here telling me all this?*"

That was Elizabeth's cue.

CHAPTER 57

"DR. REINHART HAS ACTUALLY worked with me and the Joint Terrorism Task Force on a previous case, although *case* isn't really the right word. It was the attempted Times Square bombing," said Elizabeth. "He's too modest to say so, but he's one of the foremost authorities on the study of abnormal human behavior. His insights have been invaluable for helping us understand the mind of a terrorist."

The fact that Elizabeth was able to call me modest without breaking character was worthy of an Academy Award.

"Is that what you teach at Yale?" asked Laszlo.

"Yes. I'm a professor of psychology, but I specialize in abnormal human behavior," I said.

"Dr. Reinhart contacted me after this dinner he had because of something that was said regarding the intermediary who had approached his friend," explained Elizabeth. "We can't divulge exactly what it was, but it concerned how the possible transaction for this Monet painting would be structured. Based on Dr. Reinhart's experience with the work we do at the JTTF, it raised a red flag with him."

"I'm not sure I follow," said Laszlo.

"We're concerned that the proceeds from the sale of this painting will be used to fund terrorism," said Elizabeth.

That was now my cue.

I let go with a slight cough. It was nothing. Then it became something, one of those "went down the wrong pipe" situations that you can't control. My coughs were getting louder and louder. It was obvious what I needed.

"Let me get you some water," said Laszlo, hastily standing.

I nodded. *Perfect.*

Laszlo walked out of her office and my sudden coughing fit suddenly disappeared.

"*What are you doing?*" asked Elizabeth. She sounded angry.

"I needed her out of the room for a minute," I said.

"Why? You're doing fine."

"I don't feel fine. This makes me very uncomfortable. I still don't know why we can't tell her the truth."

"*The truth?* That a mob boss is the one who actually has their painting? We went over this."

"We don't know for sure that Brunetti has it," I said.

"We know enough to think he does. More important, we know for sure he'll sell it to the highest bidder, and the State Department doesn't want that to be the Hungarian government."

"So we really just lie to them?"

"If it means beating Brunetti to the punch, yes. It's only a matter of time before he figures out the history of that painting. So we take the Hungarians out of the bidding before the process starts," she said. "Exactly as I told you."

"You're that sure they wouldn't buy from terrorists?"

"Yes."

"Why?" I asked.

"Because this meeting is our warning to them. That's what

we're doing here. Making it very clear there'll be hell to pay," she said.

"I hope you're right."

"Even if I'm not it's still the plan. The plan you agreed to."

"I know."

Then stick to it.

I nodded to Elizabeth. She nodded back.

End of scene.

CHAPTER 58

ELIZABETH STARED AT ME anxiously at the elevator bank after the meeting. She could tell there was a problem. "What's he saying?" she asked.

I checked my phone for the tenth time in ten seconds. "He's not saying anything." That was the problem.

Where are you, Julian? Why aren't you texting me back?

I'd given him the go-ahead. We were clear from Laszlo. He was pinging the transmitter from *Mr. Fix-It* outside the consulate so he could tell us its location, where the Hungarian coffee cake had ended up within the building.

"Is it the jammers?" asked Elizabeth. "Maybe they're interfering with the GPS."

We'd already turned the Druid simulators back on, but that couldn't be the problem. "No, it's something else. There's got to be an issue on his end," I said. "Something he didn't anticipate."

Elizabeth glanced over her shoulder. "In about another ten seconds we're officially loitering."

I shouldn't have looked back at the receptionist. Damn. We locked eyes. I casually stepped to my left to block her view of the unlit elevator button.

"Are you two going down?"

I turned the other way to see a man wearing a brown, ill-fitting suit and a puzzled look. He'd must have come from the opposite hallway. Without waiting for Elizabeth or me to answer, he hit the Down button.

"Wow, that's strange," I said. "I could've sworn I'd pressed it."

"Yeah, that actually happens sometimes," he said, glancing at our visitor badges. "Either the light doesn't come on or it mysteriously goes off. It's a really old building."

Maybe. But the security measures were anything but antiquated.

I finally felt a buzz in my hand. Julian was texting. The news wasn't good. I gave Elizabeth a quick shake of my head. Julian couldn't get a reading on the transmitter. It was either blocked or not transmitting. Perhaps embedding it in a slice of Hungarian coffee cake wasn't such a clever idea after all. Not if we couldn't find the damn thing now.

Ding.

The elevator arrived, the doors parting open. The man in the brown suit took a step back, giving Elizabeth a clear path to get on first. He even stuck out a chivalrous hand as if to say, *After you.*

Elizabeth looked at me. *What do we do?*

Apparently nothing. The two of us froze. It was as if we actually had no idea how an elevator worked.

"Are either of you getting on?" he asked, jamming his foot to keep the doors from closing.

I glanced back at the receptionist again. She was now paying full attention, wondering what was going on with us.

Quick, Dylan, think of something. And it would really, really help if it was a good idea.

CHAPTER 59

THERE WERE CAMERAS EVERYWHERE. We couldn't just be riding the elevator up and down, roaming around the consulate.

Nor could we simply leave and say screw the damn transmitter. Elizabeth and I had to find it before someone else did. This wasn't a gizmo we could explain away or deny. The trail would lead back to Eszter's Pastries and, more important, Elizabeth. I could never let her take the fall for me. Not ever.

"Is everything all right over there?" the receptionist called out.

Her voice was a bit nasally but it was music to my ears. A good idea has a melody all its own.

I spun around on my heels, heading straight for the reception desk. Elizabeth had no choice but to fall in line behind me.

"What are we doing?" she whispered. *"Where are we going?"*

The answer was right in front of us.

"Hi, there. I'm Dylan," I said, giving the young woman with a blunt bob my very best Midwestern smile. Never mind that I was neither born nor raised in the Midwest. "I didn't catch your name when we first arrived."

"I'm Cynthia," she answered.

"No kidding. My favorite niece is a Cynthia." I turned to

Elizabeth. "Isn't that right? I'm always telling you how much I adore Cynthia."

"Yes, all the time," said Elizabeth, nodding with some quickly manufactured enthusiasm. "Definitely all the time."

"So, Cynthia, I was hoping you could help me out. I'm on this antibiotic that I'm not supposed to take on an empty stomach, but I haven't eaten anything yet this morning. Do you know where I can get a muffin or pastry of some kind? The closest deli or bakery near the consulate?"

Psychologists have long debated whether kindness is a learned behavior or an inherent human trait. What I've come to realize is that it's actually both. We all have the capacity for kindness, but that doesn't mean we always show it. Sometimes it requires the power of suggestion.

Elizabeth and I watched as Cynthia thought for a moment, trying to make up her mind. *C'mon, c'mon, c'mon, you can do it...*

"I'm probably not supposed to do this," she said, glancing left and right before leaning in, "but the ambassador has pastries brought in every morning to the conference room. Follow me."

CHAPTER 60

"WELL?" ASKED JULIAN, THE second we got back inside *Mr. Fix-It*.

"Piece of cake," I said.

"Very funny." He smiled, though. Julian had known me for a long time. If I could crack a joke, he already had his answer. "You got it done."

"Yeah," I said. "We got it done."

Elizabeth had distracted our new best friend, Cynthia, while I dug out the transmitter from the coffee cake in the conference room. We thanked Cynthia for her kindness and said good-bye. That was that. Until it wasn't.

A couple of minutes later, I returned from the lobby after explaining to a guard that my driver's license must have fallen out of my pocket during my meeting with Laszlo. Silly me, I hadn't put it back in my wallet after originally going through security. When we returned to Laszlo's office, Elizabeth again played the decoy by chatting her up while I pretended to look for my license.

"Desk?" asked Julian. Meaning, where I'd placed the transmitter.

"Chair in front of it," I said. "Underneath."

"Within ten feet of her?"

"Easily."

"Good. Well done."

"No thanks to you, world's greatest hacker. Give back the shiny medal they gave you, you're obviously slipping."

"You wish," said Julian. "And it's not a medal, it's actually a shiny trophy."

"Any idea what the issue was? Why you were blocked?" I asked.

"Not for sure. I can't think of a jammer on their end that would block a GPS signal. But if they can firewall that . . ."

Julian's voice trailed off. The silence that followed spoke volumes.

"In other words," Elizabeth said, "all this might have been for nothing?"

"I honestly don't know. Maybe fifty-fifty at this point," he said. "But we're about to find out."

Julian turned to his laptop, only to stop halfway. "Wait. Where did you say they had the pastries?"

"A conference room," I said.

He snapped his fingers. "There you have it."

"Have what?"

"Element 82," he said. "Pb."

He was right. He had to be. "Lead-lined sheetrock?"

"Exactly. Installed wall to wall, including the floor and ceiling."

"Across the entire building?" asked Elizabeth.

Julian shook his head. "Lead linings wouldn't make sense beyond a conference room. No one would be able to use a cell phone in their office." He squared up to his laptop. "Our odds just got better."

A lot better. Julian had only been tapping away a few moments before we heard the crackle of the transmitter coming online, followed by the sound of Laszlo's voice. It was a bit muffled by the ambient noise of her office. Not for long. He ran the sound through a souped-up audio filter, and suddenly we could hear every word, crystal clear. We were officially in. Julian had done it again.

"Okay, you can keep the damn trophy," I said.

We listened just long enough to realize that Laszlo wasn't on the phone telling the prime minister, or one of his key deputies, about her meeting with Elizabeth and me. Instead, she was making an appointment with her hair stylist. Something about a keratin treatment.

Julian hit the space bar, muting the sound. "That's enough of that," he said. "We're done here."

The days of stakeouts, with federal agents having to sit for hours and days on end in the back of vans, wearing headphones and taking notes, were long over. Well, it hasn't been that long, but they're still gone forever. Depending on your politics, we have the NSA to either blame or thank for that. Their Caltech nerds are the ones who first perfected the software that could cull through millions of phone conversations in real time. The rest of the world's intelligence agencies eventually caught up.

Everything Elizabeth and I said in Laszlo's office when Laszlo left to get me water was surely recorded, but no human being was listening to it in real time. Instead, the conversation was being filtered through a program designed to detect certain trigger words. In the Hungarian consulate those words would include the surnames of all its top officials. The reason was simple. If a visitor to the consulate was referring to any ambassador or commissioner by their last name, it was safe to assume that person wasn't in the room. What government wouldn't want to hear that conversation?

In other words, you're never truly alone in the Hungarian consulate.

Which was exactly what the three of us were banking on.

We were now using the same software to hear when Laszlo got the call from an intelligence official back in Hungary telling her about the American federal agent and the Ivy League professor who were trying to mislead her and her government regarding a hundred-million-dollar Monet, *Woman by the Seine,* that was presumed gone forever.

I was absolutely convinced that call to her would come. It wasn't a matter of if.

It was only a matter of when.

CHAPTER 61

I WAS RUNNING ON fumes, desperately craving sleep. There's only so much morally justifiable subterfuge a person can engage in before needing to recharge the batteries.

My plan was to grab a nap for a couple of hours, wake up and cook a three-egg Western omelet, and then, when I'm good and rested and calorically satisfied, clean the apartment a bit before Tracy and Annabelle got home from Marblehead. I'd really missed them both.

Yep. That was my plan. Unfortunately, Mathias von Oehson had his own plan. No sooner had I arrived home when he called my cell. If only I'd let it go to voicemail.

"Where are you?" he asked, skipping any hellos. "Are you in the city?"

"Yes."

"How fast can you get to the Yale Club?"

"Why?"

"I'll tell you when you get here," he said. "A half hour, no later. I'm on a plane this afternoon."

Then he did the most billionaire thing he could do. He hung up on me.

I could've called him back and postponed, but I'd already seen firsthand how Mathias von Oehson deals with rejection. Exhibit A, extorting me by buying the building that housed Tracy's legal aid office.

I changed my clothes and grabbed a cab.

When the Yale Club building in Midtown Manhattan opened in 1915, it was a place where a bunch of rich white guys could gather to feel extra smug about the fact that they attended Yale. Of course, times have changed. These days, the club is a place where a bunch of ethnically diverse people of all backgrounds can gather to feel extra smug about the fact that they attended Yale. That's progress for you.

"Yes, he's right over here," said the hostess. "This way."

Von Oehson hadn't mentioned whether he was in the Tap Room or the Grill Room in the club. Both served lunch, and while the more refined Grill Room would normally match his tastes, everyone knows that the Tap Room is the place to be around the holidays. Decked out with garland and poinsettias galore, with its bright-red dining chairs and massive wood beams, the room was a sight to behold. It was as if Santa had designed a ski lodge.

"There he is," said von Oehson, standing from his back corner table to greet me as I approached. He wasn't alone. "I'd introduce you to Richard here, but apparently you've already met."

"How could I forget?" I said, shaking the hand of my one and only stalker. Last time I saw Richard Landau, chief compliance officer for Von Oehson Capital Management, he was telling me that his boss—an old college chum—had no idea that he was following me.

"Nice to see you again," he said.

"You as well," I replied, although we both knew that was being overly kind. "So did you confess, junior detective Landau, or were you found out?"

"He confessed," said von Oehson, as we all sat down. "I would've fired his ass for stalking you, but he knows all my secrets." He paused, smiling. "Most of them, at least."

"I felt guilty," explained Landau. "I should've never doubted my dear friend, and I told him as much."

"Bullshit," said von Oehson. "You thought I was losing my grip, and I was."

"Well, now you're not. Carter is alive and well and home safe," said Landau.

"Yes. Yes, he is," said von Oehson with a look of overwhelming relief. He pointed at a double old-fashioned glass in front of him. Whatever he was drinking on the rocks was now just rocks. "I'd raise a toast, but I'm empty. Dylan, you want something to drink?"

"Actually, it's food that I could use."

"I was going to say, you look a little worn down."

"I had a late night," I said. "Didn't get a lot of sleep."

"Let's get you a menu, then," said von Oehson, motioning for a waiter. "In the meantime, Richard, why don't you get the conversation started. I've got to take a piss."

Landau, head of compliance, nodded dutifully as his boss got up. "Sure thing," he said.

It was a seamless handoff. Casual. Off the cuff. Very nonchalant.

It was also very unconvincing.

CHAPTER 62

VON OEHSON WALKED AWAY. As soon as he was out of ear-shot, Landau placed an elbow on the arm of his red chair and leaned toward me. "He doesn't really have to take a piss."

"No shit," I said. "What's going on?"

"He's just insulating himself."

"From what?"

"The conversation you and I are about to have," said Landau. "His stepping away gives him plausible deniability."

I deliberately placed my elbow on the arm of my chair, leaning in as he'd done. "I'm not a lawyer, but I'm pretty sure you're not supposed to admit that to me."

Landau shrugged, chuckling. "No one ever said I was good at my job."

The man who looked like the before photo in a diet plan ad when I'd first met him on the street with Elizabeth no longer seemed like such a shlub. This was confidence masked as self-deprecation.

"Okay," I said. "I'm listening."

"Mathias told me about the Monet."

"What exactly did he tell you?"

"Everything," said Landau. "The painting's entire history, the Hungarian government, how he got it back from them, and now how it's missing again—like I said, everything."

"He obviously trusts you a great deal."

"I'd like to think I'm worthy of it. I've known him a long, long time." He paused, straightening the fork and knife in front of him that didn't need straightening. "Mathias thinks he knows who has the painting."

"He couldn't tell me that himself?"

"I'm sure he could. The problem is the part that comes next, his plan to get the painting back. It's not exactly legal."

"I'm not sure if you've figured this out yet, but that guy you've known for a long, long time? Your old college chum? He's not exactly a Boy Scout," I said.

"I know. I'm well aware. Mathias has surely cut some corners along the way. This is different, though."

"Not exactly legal, as you put it."

"Let me rephrase that. It's very much not legal."

"In that case, don't tell me what it is," I said.

"From what I've been told, Dr. Reinhart, you're hardly a Boy Scout, either."

"Yeah, but that's because I'm gay. I wasn't allowed in."

Landau nodded. Touché. "You don't even want to know the name?" he asked. "Who we think has the painting?"

"Nope. Not even the initials."

"Why not?"

"That's easy," I said. "Plausible deniability."

The waiter returned with the menus. "Here you go, gentlemen."

"I won't be needing one," I said.

"Give us a minute, please, will you?" Landau asked, giving the waiter a forced smile.

The second we were alone again he started in with a revamped pitch. I cut him off with a raised palm. "Where is he? Where's he watching us from?" I asked.

Landau knew better than to play dumb with me at this point. He sighed. "The bar," he said.

"And you're supposed to give him some kind of signal, right?"

"When we're done talking, yes."

"We're done talking," I said. "Wave him over."

He sighed again. This one was actually more like a huff. Within seconds, it was the three of us again.

Mathias von Oehson had hired me to find his son. Now that Carter was home, I was seeing to the damage that had been done, making sure that the boy would remain out of harm's way. Carter had been staying out of the public spotlight, and von Oehson's lawyer had run interference with the police, stalling and muddying up their inquiry as only a fifteen-hundred-dollar-an-hour lawyer can do. Ostensibly, we were all on the same page— or painting, as it were.

"So what did I miss?" asked von Oehson, settling back in his chair.

I could've spent an hour bringing him fully up to speed. I could've explained why I didn't need his plan, or even his thoughts on who might have his Monet. I could've gotten a free lunch out of it, too. Did I mention I was starving?

Instead, I cut to the chase. The bottom line. Sometimes in life you fly by the seat of your pants. Other times you know exactly what you're doing.

"It's like this," I said. "How many millions are you willing to spend to buy your painting back?"

CHAPTER 63

"DADDY D! DADDY D!"

Annabelle called out to me in the most wonderful, happy, sing-song-y voice as I walked through the door. She ran as fast as her little legs would let her, jumping into my arms. I squeezed her tight, spinning her around.

"Anna B! Anna B! I've missed you so much! Did you miss me? Show me how much!"

She pushed her hands wide apart and giggled. "Dis much!"

"That's my girl! That's my Anna B!" I spun her around again, showering her with kisses. "Where's Daddy T?"

"He's right here," said Tracy, coming around the corner.

We formed an Annabelle sandwich as we hugged, which made our little girl giggle even louder.

"I'm so glad you're both home, safe and sound," I said.

"I think someone here was a little homesick, actually, so we got on the road earlier than planned this morning." Tracy gave Annabelle a few playful pokes to her belly. "Isn't that right, Anna B?"

"I'm afraid to ask," I said. "What did she miss more, me or her toys?"

204 • JAMES PATTERSON

"Well, to be fair, she does have some really great toys," he dead-panned. He lifted Annabelle from my arms. "Hey, sweetheart, I have a fun idea. Why don't you go to your bedroom and get the squishy fishy that Aunt Rebecca gave you so you can show it to Daddy D?"

Annabelle nodded with a big smile as he lowered her to the floor. Off she scampered, disappearing down the hall that led to her bedroom. Tracy and I would now be alone for a minute, which was clearly what he wanted.

Something suddenly didn't seem right. *Or maybe I'm the one who doesn't seem right?*

"Are you okay?" asked Tracy, taking a step back. "You look absolutely exhausted."

"I hardly slept last night," I said.

It technically wasn't a lie, but the two of us had dealt with some major trust issues in the past couple of years—all because I'd hidden my CIA past from him for a long time—so I immediately felt guilty about letting him picture me tossing and turning in our bed as opposed to what I was really doing, risking an international scandal by conspiring to bug a foreign consulate.

"What about you? How was the trip?" I asked. "How's your sis?"

"It was good," he said. "She's good."

I waited for Tracy to keep talking as he usually did, never needing much prompting to launch into a story, any story, from his daily life. He was like a walking, talking human version of the Metropolitan Diary section of the *New York Times*.

But here he was, after being away for a couple of days, staring at me and saying nothing. His shoulders tightened.

"Okay," I said. "What is it? What's wrong?"

"Who's Frank?" he asked.

"Who?"

"Seriously? That's your answer? That's what you're going with?"

"Tracy, what are you talking about?"

"I'm not home longer than ten minutes when I get a call from the lobby telling me there's a delivery for you," he said. "It's a three-hundred-dollar bottle of wine. I googled it. Three hundred and forty dollars, to be exact. A Brunello. *Great meeting you last night,* it says on the card. *Frank.*"

"Oh, that Frank," I said.

"Ah, and just like that, he remembers. What were you saying about getting no sleep last night?"

Tracy folded his arms, shifting on his feet into the universal *gotcha* pose. As he did I could see Frank Brunetti's bottle of Brunello behind him. Say that three times fast. The bottle— with a bow on it, no less—was sitting on the end table in our living room.

I wanted to promise Tracy that this wasn't what it looked like. Not even close. But that's the tricky thing about trust in any relationship. Promises only get you so far.

"Let's at least open the bottle first," I said. "Then I'll tell you everything you want to know."

CHAPTER 64

TRACY PLOPPED HIS FEET on the ottoman in our den off the kitchen. "I have to admit, this is really good," he said.

"Which?" I asked. "The Brunello or what I'm telling you?"

"Both."

I didn't quite have a second wind, and the red wine wasn't exactly helping me stay awake, but this was definitely one of those times to keep the focus no matter what. By the middle of our second glass I finished explaining everything that had happened in the days that Tracy was away with Annabelle. The one thing that absolutely didn't happen was my cheating on him. Tracy's shoulders had finally relaxed. That didn't mean I was fully off the hook.

"You should've filled me in on the painting from the beginning," he said.

"No. I shouldn't have. Von Oehson told me that in confidence. But that was then."

"And now?"

I looked from Tracy to Annabelle, who was sitting on the couch, completely engrossed in a recording of *Sesame Street* after showing me her new squishy-fishy stuffed animal. Bert and Ernie were playing the touch-your-face game (thank you, Covid-19 vaccine), and Annabelle was playing right along, smiling ear to ear. Never did the words come so easily. "My family's more important than any billionaire's secret," I said.

Tracy nodded begrudgingly. "Well played, Reinhart."

"It's always easier when it's true."

"So von Oehson really stole it, huh? The Monet?"

"Stole it back, yeah. I researched the painting after first meeting with him. It was definitely in his family," I said. "It's funny, though. As much as I had no reason to think he wasn't telling me the truth, it wasn't until Elizabeth and I sat down with this woman at the Hungarian consulate this morning that I knew for sure. The look in her eyes alone when I simply said *Monet*."

Tracy poured us a little more of Brunetti's gift. "I can't get over the history of this painting," he said. "It goes from von Oehson's family to the Nazis, then to the Hungarian government, before ending up back in the von Oehson family. I suppose it's only fitting that it's now a mafia boss that somehow has it. Or, that's what you're hoping. When will you know?"

"When Brunetti agrees to sell it," I said.

"But you already tried that on his boat. He turned you down."

"No. He turned von Oehson down. That's who I was representing."

"What, then? You go back to Brunetti with a better offer?"

"I don't. Somebody else does."

"Who?" asked Tracy.

"Someone he can trust."

"Why can't he trust you? You told him von Oehson was willing to pay to get the painting back, no questions asked."

"That's right. Only I wasn't the one he was looking at when I was telling him that."

"Elizabeth?"

"Yes, the one with a badge. The last thing Frank Brunetti would ever do was admit to her that he has this stolen painting or anything else he's not supposed to have."

"Okay. Now I'm confused," he said. "Why did you bring her with you?"

"Because I need Brunetti to think that he's smarter than me. I mean, who brings a federal agent as a sidekick to negotiate a black market art sale?"

With that, I told Tracy the full plan. The whole enchilada.

"Holy *shhhhh*—" He looked at Annabelle and caught himself. "Bleep."

"That's right," I said. "Holy bleep."

His face suddenly lit up. "I'll do it!"

"Do what?"

"You need someone to act as the broker. I'm your actor."

"No, you're not. I mean, you're an actor, and a very good one, but this definitely isn't your role."

"Are you kidding me? This is the part I was born to play," he said. "I can totally do this."

"Even if you could, I would never let you."

"Why not?"

"Because if you mess up with a guy like Brunetti, you don't get another take," I said. "You get a bullet between the eyes, or however else the mob is killing people these days."

"Talk about melodramatic."

"I'm serious."

"I know you are. So am I. I'm the reason you're involved in this whole thing in the first place," he said. "Mathias von Oehson used me to get to you."

"Maybe, but it will all be worth it in the end."

"So let me earn my share."

I had no intention of saying yes to Tracy. In fact, I'd already lined up someone else for the job. He was an ex-operative I worked with when I was stationed in London. He was still there and he owed me, which was why he immediately said yes when I called. I was flying him in at the end of the week. It was the quickest he could come.

Only suddenly it wasn't quick enough.

I stared at my phone. Julian might as well have been listening in on the conversation, given the timing of his message. He was letting me know the stars had aligned, that we were a go. One text, two words. *Tomorrow night.*

I looked at Tracy, contemplating the impossible. It's true what they say. Desperation is the mother of invention.

"What?" asked Tracy. "Why are you looking at me like that?"

"Congratulations," I said. "You got the part."

CHAPTER 65

A JUNIOR SUITE AT the Roxy Hotel, directly across the street from Frankie's restaurant in Tribeca, served as our rehearsal stage the following night. I had finally caught up on sleep, and Tracy was officially "off book," as they say in the theater world. He knew the script cold.

"He's ready," I said.

"Maybe. But let's rehearse it one more time," said Elizabeth, channeling her inner Stanley Kubrick in the pursuit of perfection. She reached for the last quarter of her turkey club. Please don't burn the toast or undercook the bacon, she'd told room service.

"Actually, that's one thing we didn't discuss," said Tracy, watching her take a bite. "Do I have a reservation to eat or am I just going to the bar?"

"You definitely don't have a reservation," I said.

As a former CIA operative I still had the ability to engineer a few minor miracles. Getting a reservation at Frankie's on short notice, however, was absolutely not in my toolbox. Ditto for Elizabeth. To think, we both even knew the owner.

Frankie's restaurant was one of Frank Brunetti's other legitimate holdings. If his gambling boat was his bread and butter, Frankie's was his pride and joy—not to mention a poke in the eye to everyone with a badge who wanted to bring him down. Reason being, the restaurant was one of the hottest reservations in town, and had been for years. The food was excellent (Brunetti had brought in a two-star Michelin chef from Rome), but what really gave the place its buzz was the mob-boss aura. Frank Brunetti himself—"Frankie," if you were a regular—was almost always in the house.

Thankfully, tonight would be no different.

Tracy went over his lines with us one more time. Once again, he nailed it. Elizabeth was sold. He was as ready as he was ever going to be, at least for the first act of the evening. We turned our attention to the second act.

"You've got the picture, right?" asked Elizabeth.

"Right here," said Tracy, patting the breast of his suit jacket. That was good enough for me. Of course, I should've known better when it came to Elizabeth.

"Show it to me," she said. "I want to make sure."

Tracy chuckled as he reached inside his breast pocket to prove he had the picture. "I know what you're doing," he said. "You just want to take another look at the guy."

The guy was agent Danny Sullivan, Elizabeth's coworker. I'd only just met him face-to-face at the Chelsea Piers ice rink after the favor he'd done for me—arranging a meeting with Vladimir Grigoryev—had spectacularly backfired. Danny intervened with Grigoryev and basically saved my life. So how do I repay him? Ask him to do another favor, of course.

But I knew he'd be on board. He was that kind of guy. Plus, it didn't hurt that he had the hots for Elizabeth. It was pretty obvious at the rink. And, yeah, given the way she was looking at the photo of Danny, the feeling was definitely mutual. Not that this was the time or place for me to point that out to her.

As for everything Tracy knew about Danny, that was next to nothing. Tracy wanted it that way, too. I'm pretty sure it was a method-acting thing. Stanislavsky and Stella Adler, all rolled into one. He wanted to think of Danny only in terms of the character he'd be playing. All he needed to know was what Danny looked like.

Tracy glanced at the picture of Danny again before putting it back in his pocket. "I swear, he looks like he could be Ryan Gosling's brother," he said. "What do you think, Lizzie?"

Elizabeth wasn't about to take the bait, glancing at her watch instead. "It's showtime," she said.

I'd convinced myself that I was okay with the idea of turning Tracy into an operative for one night, and one night only. But as Tracy stood and straightened his tie in the mirror by the door, I got this sudden jolt of regret. *What are you doing, Reinhart? Are you nuts?*

It certainly didn't help the guilt meter when Tracy casually turned to remind me that I should check in on Annabelle at some point. Lucinda had agreed to babysit her for the evening, although by now she was already snug in her toddler bed.

"Don't forget," said Tracy.

"I won't," I told him. "Same goes for you."

"What does that mean?"

"It means remember everything we talked about. Most of all, expect the unexpected."

Tracy smiled, nodded, and buttoned his suit jacket. "Don't worry," he said. "I've got this."

Maybe he did. But the second he left the hotel room to head across the street to Frankie's, I was on my phone. "He's on his way," I said.

CHAPTER 66

TRACY WALKED INTO FRANKIE'S, his ears hit first by the loud hum of a packed house. It was wall-to-wall tables, not a single one empty.

The smell came next, a mixture of garlic and basil. Also, freshly cut flowers. Yellow winter jasmine, mostly. Someone on the staff had the good sense to avoid the Christmas go-to of red poinsettias. Smart, thought Tracy.

He glanced at the stunningly attractive woman behind the reservation desk who was wearing an off-the-shoulder black dress. She flashed a well-practiced smile and was about to greet him when Tracy performed his first bit of acting: pretending to recognize someone.

"Oh, I see my friend at the bar," he said, never breaking stride.

The bar along the right side of the restaurant was crammed, as well, not a single gap between elbows. Tracy knew it wouldn't matter if he couldn't find a seat, so long as he could spot Brunetti. He scanned the dining room once, then twice. No Brunetti. And still no seat at the bar.

The tap on his back startled him. A man getting up to leave pointed at his chair, offering it to Tracy.

"Thanks so much," said Tracy. "Really appreciate it."

"Must be your lucky night," said the man, cradling a whiskey glass in his hand. His suit was slightly rumpled, and the British accent a touch garbled. That wasn't his first whiskey. Probably not his second or third, either. He took his last sip, draining the glass before landing it hard on the bar. "She's all yours."

Tracy thanked him again as he slid into the seat, scooching up to the bar. Within seconds, the space in front of him was cleared of the glass, as well as the twenty-dollar tip next to it.

"What can I get you?" asked the bartender.

He was one of a half dozen working behind the bar, and living proof of the difference between restaurants that barely make money versus those that seemingly print it. Liquor was where the real profits were. The faster you served it, the bigger your profit.

"Broken Shed martini, a drop of vermouth, two olives," said Tracy.

"Right away," answered the bartender. This was the man's job, his career. He wasn't some unemployed actor paying his rent. He was a professional. Midfifties, not midtwenties. Hadn't lost a step, though. Tracy had barely blinked before the man was filling a shaker.

Again, Tracy scanned the dining room, craning his neck. There was a sea of people eating, but the owner was nowhere in sight. His imprint on the place, though, was unmistakable. Frankie's felt like a smoke-filled room without anyone actually smoking.

"Here you go, sir."

Tracy turned back to see his vodka martini being placed in front of him. Two olives and filled to the rim, with a few ice shavings floating on the surface.

"Thank you, Salvatore."

Tracy had spotted his nameplate on the black vest over the rolled-up white sleeves as soon as he'd sat down, but waited until now to say the man's name.

"You're welcome. Enjoy," said Salvatore. He was about to seek out his next order a few seats down the bar.

"Quick question," said Tracy before he could. "Is Frank here tonight?"

Salvatore shot him a look. *Who wants to know?* Tracy didn't exactly have a "from the neighborhood" vibe to him. And by neighborhood, that meant Bensonhurst or Red Hook over in Brooklyn, not Tribeca.

"You mean, Mr. Brunetti?" asked Salvatore.

"No, I mean Frank," said Tracy pointedly.

"Are you a friend of his?"

"I didn't know he had any."

Salvatore cracked a smile. "Good one," he said. More important, it was something that an actual friend of Frank Brunetti's might say. "I think he's back in the kitchen."

"Do me a favor," said Tracy, sliding Ben Franklin's face across the bar. "Tell him there's a guy out here who wants to talk to him about a painting."

Salvatore glanced at the hundred-dollar bill for a second before scooping it up. *"A painting?"*

"Yes. That's right."

For the next minute there were only five instead of six bartenders pouring drinks at Frankie's. As for the man who came back from the kitchen with Salvatore, he was definitely from the neighborhood. The clothes alone were a dead giveaway—a black turtleneck underneath a black sport coat that looked ready to burst at the seams. This was one of Brunetti's henchmen. His muscle.

"Who are you?" the guy asked.

"I'm an art dealer," said Tracy.

"Who do you work for?"

"Myself. *Who do you work for?*"

The guy gave Tracy the once-over. Damn, his neck was thick. "Stay here," he said. He walked off, returning to the kitchen.

Tracy watched until he was gone. Then he proceeded to break the world record for finishing a martini. Stay calm, he kept telling himself, you're doing great. He'd stuck to the script. Talked the talk. Didn't let any jitters show.

Brunetti's henchman returned. "Come with me," he said.

CHAPTER 67

TRACY NODDED LIKE IT was never in doubt.

He pushed back from the bar and fell in line behind the black turtleneck and sport coat, weaving through a few tables before reaching the swinging door to the kitchen. After a quick left before a grill and prep station, they headed through another door to a wine-tasting room. The guy even turned to Tracy at one point along the way and, of all things, smiled at him. It was all very civilized.

Until it wasn't.

The door to the wine-tasting room closed behind Tracy. In front of him sat Frank Brunetti at the head of a long table with a glass of red in his hand. Over his shoulder was another henchman. This one was younger, leaner, and now coming right at Tracy with a head of steam. "You a cop?" he asked, getting right up in Tracy's grill. His breath smelled like an ashtray. "Huh? You a cop?"

"No," said Tracy.

"Then who are you?"

"You're going to mug me anyway, so go ahead. It's in the back right pocket."

Tracy turned and glanced at the guy who'd led him from the

bar into the tasting room. He was standing off to the side by some crates of wine, flashing that same smile. All along, this guy knew what was coming next.

Tracy didn't. He never saw the punch. It came so fast and hard to his gut that by the time the pain kicked in he was on his knees and falling flat on his face. He couldn't breathe. He couldn't move. It was as if his stomach were superglued to the floor.

"Yep, you were right," said ashtray breath. "Back right pocket."

He removed Tracy's wallet, handing it over to his boss. Brunetti casually glanced at the driver's license. "Nice to meet you, Mr. William D'Alexander from the Upper East Side."

At any given time, the CIA has about five thousand invented people roaming the planet as various covers for their field operatives. They possess official passports and driver's licenses from all over the world, and hold down every conceivable job as evidenced by their made-up internet profiles, including social media posts. Mr. William D'Alexander was an art dealer now living in Manhattan, after years of managing a gallery in São Paulo. There was another gallery before that in Lisbon. All the information was there in plain sight, just in case Brunetti wanted to google him at some point.

In the meantime, Tracy still couldn't catch his breath from the sucker punch. Off Brunetti's nod, he was helped to his feet. Slowly, his lungs started to work again.

Dylan had said it, and said it again. Expect the unexpected. Tracy now nodded as if nothing had happened. *What sucker punch?*

"Nice to meet you, too, Frank," he said.

Brunetti cracked a smile. Full caps, not veneers. "What do you do, William?"

"Call me Bill. I'm an art dealer."

"Do you have a gallery, Bill?"

"I used to. Not anymore."

Brunetti thumbed through Tracy's wallet again. "Do you have a business card?"

"No. Not these days."

"Why not?"

"Let's just say I don't like paper trails anymore."

Tracy stared silently at Brunetti, waiting for the subtext to land. It didn't take long.

"Do black-market art dealers actually refer to themselves as black-market art dealers?" asked Brunetti.

"I prefer the term *facilitator.*"

"And who are you facilitating for?"

"All my clients are confidential."

"Of course they are. That would only make sense. Now, would you mind removing your clothes?"

"Excuse me?" asked Tracy.

"Your clothes," said Brunetti. "Strip. Everything off."

"You're not going to at least buy me dinner first?"

Brunetti stared back at Tracy. There wasn't even a hint of a smile this time. "Do you really want that joke to be the last one you ever tell?"

Tracy started taking off his clothes.

CHAPTER 68

"SATISFIED?" ASKED TRACY, DOWN to his underwear. He swung his arms out wide, palms flat up to the ceiling. His stomach was still killing him but he wasn't about to show it. "I'm not wearing a wire."

"But you're still wearing clothes," said Brunetti.

Tracy looked down at his boxers. "You're joking, right?"

"Do I look like I'm joking?"

"Okay, but I'm drawing the line at a body cavity search."

Tracy dropped his boxers. The embarrassment of stripping completely naked for Brunetti and his crew in the tight confines of a wine-tasting room was mitigated slightly by the fact that Tracy, a graduate of the Yale School of Drama, had once performed in an off-off-Broadway adaptation of *Equus*, appearing nude onstage for five nights a week, with two shows on Wednesdays and Saturdays.

But still.

"Now are you satisfied?" asked Tracy, standing full monty.

"Shut up and put your clothes back on," said Brunetti.

Only this wasn't the time to shut up. As Tracy began to get dressed he launched right into the pitch. Everything about this deal, if it was going to happen, had to be quick. It was about impulse, not reflection. Emotion, not intellect. Tracy needed Frank Brunetti to do one thing, and one thing only, with his offer, right on the spot.

Turn him down.

"You have a painting that a new client of mine very much wants to buy from you," said Tracy. "You're going to deny that you have it, but we both know you do. My client is willing to pay you fifty million dollars for it, no questions asked. More important, there'll be no paper trail. It's the cleanest deal you'll ever make. And the most money you'll ever make in a single deal."

"What about you?" asked Brunetti.

"What about me?"

"What's your cut from this deal? Or is that confidential, as well?"

"Funny you should ask," said Tracy. "Normally I wouldn't discuss my fee, but I'm going to make an exception because God forbid you think I'm a fool for being here." He zipped up his pants. "My client offered me a choice. I could take a 5 percent commission on the back end, were the deal to happen, or a flat fee of five hundred thousand up front, regardless of whether the deal happens. Which one do you think I chose?"

"I'm pretty sure you just told me," said Brunetti.

"You're right. I did, Frank. May I call you that? Because frankly I don't give a shit what you decide."

"Of course you do," said Brunetti, "and of course I know who your client is. Von Oehson's giving you a shot at this because his first guy fucked it up for him. If it makes you feel any better, you didn't fuck this up. You did everything you could. But you're still getting the same answer I told his first guy. No."

"Are you sure I can't change your mind?"

"What do you think?" It wasn't a question.

"I think I gave it my best shot," said Tracy.

"Exactly." Brunetti took a sip of his wine. "And what's a punch to the gut and a little loss of dignity in exchange for five hundred large, right?"

Tracy reached for his jacket off the floor, sliding both arms through the sleeves and giving a tug to both lapels. He was fully dressed again, ready to leave. "For what it's worth," he said, "I totally get it."

"What's that?" asked Brunetti, handing back Tracy's wallet.

"Given what I know about the painting, especially some of the rumors surrounding it, I wouldn't blame you for not trusting my client. I mean, how would you really know until it was too late that you weren't being set up? Besides, it's a beautiful painting. You should hold on to it."

"I don't know what painting you're talking about," said Brunetti.

"Right. Of course," said Tracy, with a wink. He turned to leave, mumbling something under his breath.

"What did you say?" asked Brunetti.

"Nothing."

"It was obviously something."

"I was just talking to myself, that's all. No big deal." Tracy glanced at Brunetti's guys. He clearly wasn't leaving that wine room without explaining. "It's just that...well...it suddenly occurred to me that I was representing the wrong client."

Brunetti put down his wineglass, edging forward a bit in his seat. "What is that supposed to mean?"

"There's really only one buyer for that painting," said Tracy.

"Who?"

"The country that stole it in the first place. Who else?"

CHAPTER 69

TRACY CHECKED HIS WATCH the second he was outside of the restaurant. He was right on schedule.

He didn't have to waste time hailing a taxi, either. Patrons of Frankie's aren't exactly the Ubering type, and every cabbie in the city knew it. Five of them were lined up waiting along the curb. The taxi in the pole position edged forward before Tracy could even raise his arm.

"The Guggenheim," Tracy said, sliding into the backseat. He immediately muted the sound on the annoying promo TV underneath the Plexiglas divider, and hit his speed dial for Dylan. The way Dylan answered, sounding so relieved, told Tracy just how much he might have been second-guessing everything.

"We've got a seller," announced Tracy.

He gave Dylan a full rundown, minus his getting punched and having to strip naked. Those were details for another day. Not tonight. Not during intermission. There was still a second act to go, and a buyer to line up for Brunetti. The only true buyer there was, as Tracy had convinced him.

"Bravo," said Dylan. "I knew you could do it."

"No, you didn't."

"Yeah, you're right. I wasn't sure."

They both laughed. They both knew the truth. If Dylan didn't think it could work, he never would've let Tracy get anywhere near a guy like Brunetti.

"How's our little girl?" asked Tracy.

"Lucinda said she needed two bedtime stories instead of one but after that she fell right asleep," said Dylan. "Wait, wait—hold on a second."

"What is it?"

"Elizabeth just got a text from Danny. He's asking how close you are."

Tracy craned his neck, trying to see the next intersection. The driver was taking Amsterdam Avenue up the West Side, surely heading for the transverse at 86th Street to cut through Central Park and over to the East Side. From there the Guggenheim museum was only a few blocks north on Fifth Avenue.

"Just about to pass Damrosch," said Tracy, seeing the sign for West 61st Street. Damrosch Park, directly behind Lincoln Center, was up ahead at 62nd Street. "With traffic, I figure fifteen minutes until I'm there."

"Better make it ten," said Dylan.

"Why?"

"Danny just overheard Laszlo tell someone that she was leaving shortly."

"Shit. She can't!"

Tracy didn't mean to hang up on Dylan but he for sure would understand. There was a taxi driver that needed bribing.

Tracy leaned forward in his seat, talking through the small holes in the Plexiglas. "Excuse me, but I'm really in a rush," he said. "I'll give you an extra ten bucks for every red light you run."

Tracy had read that line in a book once. Unfortunately, the book was fiction.

The driver shot him a look in the rearview mirror, the pine tree car freshener swinging back and forth, just like his head. *Not a chance, pal.*

"Make it twenty bucks," said Tracy.

"Deal," said the driver.

Every man has his price.

An extra sixty dollars later, Tracy hopped out of the cab in front of the Guggenheim, making a beeline for the entrance. The check-in desk for the benefit on behalf of the Council of Europe Art Exhibitions had no line, the festivities having started more than an hour earlier.

"I don't see your name, sir."

"Please check again," said Tracy. Dylan had assured him he'd be on the list.

"D'Alexander."

"Oh, I thought you said *Alexander.* I didn't hear the *D*," said the man working the desk. He shifted his attention three letters down on his clipboard, his forefinger finally coming to a stop. "There you are, William D'Alexander. Which hand, left or right?"

Tracy stuck out his left hand, the man wrapping a purple band around his wrist—or at least trying to. He was fumbling with the snap. The clock was ticking. Tracy was slowly dying.

"Here, I've got it," said Tracy, taking over. He quickly fastened the band, moving past the desk.

"Don't you want a program, sir? It has a map of everything. The exhibits, the food and bar locations..."

"No, thanks," said Tracy, over his shoulder. There was no map for what—or who—he was looking for. There was also no time.

Is she even still here?

CHAPTER 70

THE ANSWER WAS YES. But just barely.

Tracy was so intent on getting inside the atrium of the museum that at first he didn't even look at the small line of people gathered at the coat check who were on their way out.

Of course, though. It made perfect sense. She'd wanted to leave.

Even from the side Tracy knew right away it was Dorian Laszlo. He'd seen plenty of photos of her, courtesy of Dylan. There were a half dozen alone on the website for New York's Consulate General of Hungary. Laszlo, the economic and trade commissioner, was always smiling and shaking hands with some American business leader. The only picture that didn't look dated, though, was the one with her and a marketing executive from Gojo Industries, the makers of Purell. They were smiling and touching elbows.

Tracy stopped on a dime. "Gordon! Is that you?"

All those photos of Laszlo were so Tracy knew who *not* to look at as he approached his old friend "Gordon," who just happened to be standing behind Laszlo in the coat-check line. At no time could Tracy even glance in her direction.

"Bill! I didn't know you were going to be here," said Danny, giving Tracy the combo handshake-and-hug.

Tracy, for sure, didn't need to glance again at the picture of Danny Sullivan in his breast pocket. This was Ryan Gosling's would-be brother, all right. Maybe even his doppelgänger. Either way, Tracy could pick him out of a lineup. He literally just had.

The original plan called for some chitchat up front before getting down to business. The conversation had to seem natural and unforced to anyone who might happen to overhear them. But that was then, this was now. Laszlo was only a few people away from handing over her claim ticket and putting on her coat. She'd be out the door. More important, out of earshot. It was time to improvise.

Tracy stepped back from Danny, tripping over his own feet. He nearly fell.

"Whoa," said Danny, reaching out to catch him. "You okay there?"

"I'm fine, absolutely fine," said Tracy, slapping the air with his hand the way people do when they've had a few drinks. "I'm pretty sure a mob boss wants to kill me but other than that everything's great." He slapped the air again. "Whoops. Forget I just told you that."

There was no wink, no nod, no anything from Danny in return. He simply said what anyone would say after hearing that from a friend. They were off script but on the same page.

"What are you talking about?" asked Danny. "What do you mean *mob boss*?"

"*Shhhh*," said Tracy. "It's nothing."

"It's obviously something. *Wait*. Is this about that meeting? It is, isn't it? You wouldn't tell me who it was with."

"I still can't tell you."

"But you said the whole thing was bullshit."

"It *is* bullshit. A mysterious painting that can't go to auction? It's probably a tax scam or something."

"You told the guy that? This mob boss?"

"Hell no." Tracy laughed. "He would've killed me, for sure. What I did was politely explain that I don't do black-market sales. He said he understood, but, hell, I wasn't listening to his words. It was his eyes. He wanted to strangle me."

"Wow."

"Tell me about it. I went straight from the meeting over to the Palm. It took me three martinis just to stop shaking." Tracy stuck out his hand. There was still a slight tremble. "Damn, I think I need a fourth. Which way to the bar?"

Danny pointed toward the atrium. "Go straight and then take a left at the giant Rothko," he said.

"Appreciate it. Hey, you available for lunch next week? We'll both get drunk and you can tell me if Sotheby's is really getting that Matisse from the Rockefeller estate."

"I'll never tell."

"We'll see about that."

The two repeated the combo handshake-and-hug before Tracy peeled off for the atrium, not once looking back. He'd done all he could do. So had Danny, who stared straight ahead, watching as Laszlo stepped forward in the line. She was next up, ticket in hand.

C'mon, you know you heard us. Take the bait. Okay, maybe get your coat first, but then take the bait. Go track him down, Dorian . . .

CHAPTER 71

TRACY REACHED THE BAR in the atrium, the spiraling levels of Frank Lloyd Wright's magnum opus rising above him. He looked up, as everyone does at first. But he still didn't look back.

He was tempted, no doubt. It was like an itch he knew he couldn't scratch. Just a peek, a glimpse, a little lookie-loo behind him—he'd make it seem oh-so-casual. Natural.

No. *Don't you dare.*

She was either heading his way or she wasn't. He'd know for sure soon enough. Until then, he would continue to—

"Excuse me."

The tap on his shoulder was even better than the words themselves. It startled Tracy. It shouldn't have, but it did. He jumped slightly out of his shoes, no acting required. He turned around, clutching his heart.

"Oh, I'm so sorry," said Laszlo. "I didn't mean to scare you."

Tracy exhaled. "No, that's quite all right." He followed that up with a squint. *Do I know you?*

"I'm Dorian," she said. "Dorian Laszlo."

She certainly was. "Bill D'Alexander," said Tracy.

Laszlo flashed a sheepish grin as they shook hands. "I have a confession to make," she said.

Tracy leaned in enthusiastically, swaying just a smidge. If she'd heard everything he'd said to Danny back in the coat check line, then he was still supposed to have three martinis sloshing around inside him.

"I absolutely love confessions, always have," he said. "My mother actually thought I was going to grow up to become a priest. It was a bit odd, considering we were Jewish."

Laszlo laughed. She was exactly as advertised, according to Dylan. Measured and precise. But Tracy could see her already growing comfortable with him, loosening up a little. Or maybe that was her angle. Her plan. "That's funny," she said. She laughed again. "Very funny."

"So, please. Tell me your sin," said Tracy. "I'm sure it's not as bad as you think."

Her voice dropped to a hushed tone. She edged closer to him. "I overheard some of your conversation back there," she said.

"Back where?"

She pointed down at the long black wool coat draped over her forearm. "I was standing in line in front of your friend you just spoke to. It's not like I was trying to listen."

"Of course. So we were talking a little too loud, huh? My apologies."

"No. If anything, I'm the one who should be thanking you."

"How so?"

She glanced left and right. They were in a crowd. "If you don't mind," she said, nodding to an area off to the side.

Tracy followed her, step for step. "Better?" he asked, leaning against the wall near the gift shop. The store closed for the event.

"Much," said Laszlo. "I assume you're an art dealer or broker of some kind?"

"I am. Yes."

"I'm also assuming you're not associated with any auction house, that you work independently."

"Right again." He took his phone out of his pocket only to put it back. "Actually, let's do it on yours," he said. "My website."

She reached into her clutch for her phone. "Ready," she said, thumbs hovering over the keyboard. Tracy gave her the address, watching her nod as his website appeared. It's all she needed to see.

"I'll get right to the point, then," she said. "That painting you mentioned to your friend—is it a Monet, by any chance?"

Tracy cocked his head, incredulous. "How would you know that?"

"That depends. How much do you know about its background?"

"Next to nothing. But something tells me the better question might be, how much do I *want* to know?"

"Here's what matters most," she said. "I've got a buyer for it."

"Who?"

"Me."

"I don't even know who you are," said Tracy.

Laszlo reached into her clutch again to remedy that. She handed him her business card.

"So the economic and trade commissioner for the Consulate General of Hungary wants to buy a Monet," he said, amused. "That must be quite a salary you make."

"My government pays well."

"Fifty million well?"

"Is that the price?" she asked.

"That's what the seller wants for it, yes. He seemed pretty fixed on the number."

"That sounds a lot like something a dealer would say."

"Not in this case," said Tracy. "Like I told the seller, I don't do black-market deals."

232 • JAMES PATTERSON

"Yes, I heard what you told your friend."

"You don't believe me?"

"No, I do. You don't do black-market deals. I understand," she said. "But I think you're going to do this one. In fact, I'm pretty sure of it."

"Okay, I'll bite. Why?"

"Because you do what you do to make money, and I'm going to guess that the last time you brokered a fifty-million-dollar painting was...never?"

Tracy looked down at Laszlo's business card again, silently mouthing every word of her job title for full effect. *Economic and trade commissioner.* In other words, this conversation was directly in her wheelhouse.

"I stand corrected, Dorian," he said. "Maybe you're not being paid enough."

"Is that a yes?" she asked.

"Are you agreeing to the fifty million?"

"I have to get the official okay from my government, but I don't see a problem." She motioned to her phone. "Your number's on the website?"

Tracy nodded. "It's there."

"Then I'll call you tomorrow," she said, putting on her coat. "In the meantime, go tell your seller that you've had a change of heart. Maybe he won't want to kill you anymore."

CHAPTER 72

THE PHONE CALL THAT officially put the exchange into motion the next morning was really a mere formality. I had no doubt that Dorian Laszlo was going to ring Tracy to announce that she and the government of Hungary were all in on Monet's *Woman by the Seine* to the tune of fifty million dollars. From an odds standpoint, her making the call fell somewhere between a lock and a sure thing. The reason was simple. We'd not only bugged her office, we'd also tapped her cell.

Tracy hadn't even returned from the Guggenheim before Laszlo had dialed the Hungarian ambassador to the United States at his home in Washington, DC. She at least had the good sense not to say anything incriminating over an open wireless network. As for her unwittingly installing malware on her cell when she visited a certain art dealer's website while in the atrium of the museum...well, good sense only gets you so far.

Julian's handiwork—a program he called Echoing—essentially hijacked the microphone feature on Laszlo's cell so we could hear every conversation she was having. *Alexa, play us some very eager Hungarians...*

Laszlo and her country desperately wanted this painting back, and I was banking on their having the same psychological makeup as the climbers who flock to Mount Everest every year. There's a one-in-sixty chance the climb will kill them somewhere along the way, but all they care about is reaching the summit.

"Winner, winner, chicken dinner," I announced as the burner phone sitting in the middle of our kitchen table rang. "With a half hour to spare, no less."

The over/under bet was that Laszlo would call by noon the next day. Tracy and I had the under, Elizabeth took the over. Too much bureaucratic red tape for it to happen before lunch, she was thinking. Normally, I'd agree with her. Only this wasn't normally.

The phone rang at 11:30 on the dot. Tracy waited patiently until the third ring before answering. "Bill D'Alexander," he said calmly.

Tracy had not only kept to the script so far, he'd improved on it. The improvising he did with Danny at the Guggenheim had saved the night, if not the deal itself. Tracy was now beyond playing the part of art dealer, Bill D'Alexander. He had become him—and Dorian Laszlo, along with her government, were about to come through with the biggest sale of his career. But this was still no time for him to sound overly enthusiastic.

"That's too fast," he told Laszlo while at the same time flashing Elizabeth and me a thumbs-up. "I need to authenticate the painting."

Tracy listened as Laszlo explained why the exchange had to happen so quickly. He kept the phone away from his ear just enough that we could hear most of what she was saying. The Hungarian ambassador was flying back to Budapest in two days, and if he didn't have the painting with him, she no longer had a job. Period. End of story.

The fifty million would be wired by her personally at the time of the exchange to whichever account Frank Brunetti wanted, so long as it was either Swiss or offshore (Caymans, preferably).

"I assumed as much," said Tracy. "I've already addressed it with the seller, and he said no problem."

As for authenticating the Monet, Laszlo explained that she'd be bringing along her own "expert" so as to expedite things. That seemed odd only because any reputable authenticator would need to spend considerable time analyzing a painting of this nature, as opposed to giving it a once-over, as it were. But then again, standing on the top of Mount Everest must be one of the greatest feelings in the world, right?

"So your guy is that good, huh? He'll know that quickly?" asked Tracy.

"Quick enough," said Laszlo.

Tracy continued to play hard to get. "I don't know," he said, his voice trailing off.

"What don't you know?" she asked.

"I don't like the idea of us all standing around waiting for your guy to do in five minutes what should normally take at least five hours."

Laszlo knew what "Bill D'Alexander" didn't. Or supposedly didn't. The painting was authentic. She wasn't about to reveal that she'd been visited by an agent with the Joint Terrorism Task Force and an Ivy League professor named Reinhart.

Of course, what she didn't know was that those same two were listening in on this conversation.

"I'd like to do the exchange at the consulate," said Laszlo.

"That won't fly with the seller," said Tracy. "His painting, his choice. But in the interest of making both sides comfortable, I pushed heavily for a neutral site."

"Fine," she said. "That's fair."

He gave her the address. The meeting was set. It would happen in two days.

Tracy was the picture of relief after ending the call. Laszlo was on board, no hitches. Then the concern kicked in—how quickly everything needed to fall into place. He looked back and forth at Elizabeth and me. "Can we actually pull this off?" he asked.

I shrugged with all the confidence of a one-armed pole vaulter. "You mean, plan one of the greatest art heists of all time in less than two days? Sure," I said. "I don't see why not."

BOOK FOUR

THE MASTERPIECE

CHAPTER 73

CARLOS FROM QUEENS HAD an Uber driver rating of 4.75. What prevented him from having a perfect five-star rating was probably the fact that he liked to chat up his passengers, not all of whom were necessarily in the mood to talk. But Carlos couldn't help it. He was a people person. Plus, driving around New York City all day long in an old Toyota Corolla for an average of $17.46 an hour was nothing short of monotonous. A little conversation went a long way in helping to pass the time.

"What line of work you in?" Carlos asked, shooting a quick glance over his right shoulder.

Usually, Carlos would wait until he made eye contact with a passenger via his rearview mirror before breaking the ice, but the guy he picked up in front of the Dominick Hotel in SoHo was wearing mirrored sunglasses. He also wasn't answering.

"Hey, Hans, you awake back there?" asked Carlos. "There's a Poland Spring there in the cooler by your feet, if you want."

"Hans" had a perfect five-star passenger rating. What's more, TipOff, the underground app crowdsourced by Uber and Lyft drivers to rate how generous frequent riders were, labeled him a

"Blue Chip." That meant Hans routinely tipped at least 20 percent. With some pleasant banter and the offer of bottled water, nicely chilled, Carlos was angling for even more.

"No, thank you, on the beverage," said Hans.

"I'm going to guess real estate. You look like maybe that's what you do," said Carlos. "Am I right? Commercial? Residential?"

"No. I'm not in real estate."

Carlos waited for Hans to tell him his profession. They always did when he first guessed wrong. He almost always guessed wrong. That was the icebreaker.

But Hans wasn't saying.

"Okay, I give up. You got me," said Carlos. "What do you do for a living?"

"You really want to know?" asked Hans.

"Of course. That's why I'm asking."

Hans adjusted his sunglasses, pushing them up a little higher over his chiseled features. "I'm a contract killer," he said.

"A what?"

"A contract killer," Hans repeated slowly. "People pay me to kill other people."

Carlos laughed hard. He got the joke. "Yeah, I saw that movie. *Collateral,* right? Tom Cruise?" He glanced again at his rearview mirror. "Ha! You kind of look like him a bit with your shades on. Good one. I've never gotten that before. You're the first."

"That's because there's so few of us," said Hans.

Carlos was more than content to play along. This was fun. Best ride of the day, so far. "Oh, yeah? Not a lot of you contract killers out there, huh? People would think otherwise."

"Your Hollywood loves to make movies about us."

"But you're a rare breed."

"The rarest," said Hans. "More men have walked on the moon than do what I do."

Carlos was loving every second of this. "Oh, yeah? And how many's that?"

"Men who have walked on the moon? The number's twelve."

"A dozen. Is that really true?"

"I never lie."

Carlos laughed again. "Yeah, me neither."

Hans reached for the cooler by his feet, helping himself to a cold bottle of Poland Spring. He twisted the cap. "Neil Armstrong, Buzz Aldrin, Pete Conrad, Alan Bean, Alan Shepard, Edgar Mitchell, David Scott, James Irwin, John Young, Charles Duke, Eugene Cernan, and Harrison Schmitt," he said. He took a long sip.

"Holy shit, you actually know that? All their names?"

"And not one of them ever did it twice."

"What about you?" asked Carlos.

"What about me?"

"You're a contract killer, right? What's your number? How many have you killed?"

"Twenty-nine," said Hans, without a hint of hesitation. He edged forward in his seat. "Although the number's about to change. That's where you're taking me right now. To see about number thirty."

"Ha! Just like *Collateral*," said Carlos, playfully jabbing a finger at his rearview mirror. "So I'm your Jamie Foxx, huh? Is that what I—"

Carlos's finger suddenly froze, his last words left dangling.

Hans had leaned back against his seat, stretching his arms out wide to expose the Glock 19 holstered underneath the shoulder of his suit jacket. "You never know in life, Carlos," he said. "You just never know."

The two rode in complete silence for the remainder of the trip.

CHAPTER 74

ALWAYS ACT LIKE YOU have a tail even when you think you don't...

Hans got out at the corner of West 12th Street and Seventh Avenue, walking two blocks north while taking advantage of a Don't Walk sign along the way to check his six. Making a left on West 14th, he continued three-quarters of the way down the block toward Eighth Avenue. After stopping to tie the laces of a wingtip shoe that didn't need tying, he arrived at the small boutique luggage shop that was nestled in between a bank and a Walgreens drugstore. Blink and you'd miss it.

Elder & Sons sold all the major brands—Samsonite, Travelpro, Hartmann, American Tourister—and had been in business for more than thirty years, somehow managing to stay afloat despite increasing competition from major chains like Macy's and Target, not to mention the endless array of online options. Amazon alone would seemingly have spelled doom for an independent shop that could never win, or even compete in, a price war.

And, yet, Elder & Sons endured.

Perhaps it was the personalized service. The name didn't lie. Elder & Sons was indeed a family business. A father and his two boys, now in their twenties, neither of whom ever entertained any other pursuit while growing up besides luggage. For all the Elders, luggage was their life. Their public lives, at least.

"Can I help you?"

Hans removed his sunglasses, smiling at the younger of the two brothers behind the counter. The older brother was tending to a customer over by the display wall. "Yes, I'm here to pick up a delivery," said Hans. "It was special ordered for me."

"Of course. Wait one second, I'll be right back." The younger son of Elder & Sons disappeared behind a thick curtain, returning within a matter of seconds. "If you could come this way, please."

Hans followed him back behind the curtain, through a small office, and down a set of rickety wood stairs to a stockroom. The man waiting for him there needed no introduction.

Richard Elder handled all the money for the syndicate, although no one in the very small group actually referred to themselves as a syndicate. Just like no one in the group referred to Richard Elder by name. He was known only as the Bookkeeper.

After a nod to his son, who quickly turned to climb the stairs back to the showroom floor, the Bookkeeper and Hans were alone.

"It's been a while," said Hans.

"Perhaps you should lower your rates," said the Bookkeeper.

"If you actually believed that, I wouldn't be here right now, would I?"

It was a very good point. The best don't come cheap, and the Bookkeeper knew it. He admitted as much by letting Hans's retort linger in the air a moment before getting down to business. He opened the hard-shell briefcase that was resting on the workbench against the wall. Hans walked over to take a look. He knew immediately.

"That's too much," he said, staring at the neatly stacked and wrapped bricks of fifty-dollar bills.

"You're right. It's exactly twice as much as what was agreed to," said the Bookkeeper, handing Hans a manila envelope. "There's been a slight change in plans."

Hans removed the photo, which was attached to what was called a leg sheet. It detailed the comings and goings of the additional mark, possible venues for a clean hit.

"Two for the price of two?" asked Hans.

"We wouldn't expect a discount." The Bookkeeper pointed at the photo. "Do you know who he is?"

"Better yet," said Hans, "do *you* know who he is?"

There was a lot to unpack in that rhetorical question, beginning with the fact that this additional mark was far from your average target. Of all the people on this planet, 99.9 percent can be eliminated, if handled correctly, without any real fear of retribution. For the remaining one-tenth of 1 percent, the stakes are much different. Their connections run extremely deep, their circles tight. Government. Intelligence. Military. Royalty, and other select families with a similar degree of power and influence. Those loyal to them will stop at almost nothing to get revenge.

"It turns out he's working with von Oehson," said the Bookkeeper.

Contract killers get paid to do two things. Kill, and not ask too many questions. But you're not long for the business if you don't know when to make exceptions. Sometimes you have to know more.

"Are you sure?" Hans asked slowly. What he was really asking was whether the Bookkeeper was giving him firsthand information. Claiming "I have it on good authority" wasn't going to cut it. Neither was the offer on the table.

"Yes. I'm sure," said the Bookkeeper. "And I also understand."

As with contract killers, the luggage business also had a secret to longevity: always know what it takes to satisfy whoever walks through the door.

The Bookkeeper reached underneath the workbench, grabbing another briefcase. It was identical to the first one in every way, including its contents. He popped the latches.

"Two for the price of four," said the Bookkeeper. A total of one million dollars.

Hans nodded. "That looks about right," he said.

CHAPTER 75

THERE WERE COUNTLESS CALLS I needed to make—planning, logistics, leveraging past relationships, and asking straight-up favors—but the most important call was the one I wouldn't be making. It was the one I'd be getting. I was sure of it. It was never a matter of if, only when.

What happens when you take a field trip without getting your permission slip signed? You get called into the principal's office.

The Foxx rarely texted or emailed. That would mean putting it in writing, and writing meant admissible evidence. For the same reason, he never left voice messages. Then again, pity the operative who didn't answer right away when Landon Foxx was calling.

Shortly after reading *Goodnight Moon* to Annabelle and tucking her in, my cell lit up with his initials. I ducked into my office down the hall and answered.

"What have you been up to?" he asked.

"Not much," I said.

"Liar."

"Okay, where and when?"

"The diner. Five o'clock," he said, before hanging up.

Foxx didn't need to specify which diner or whether he meant

a.m. or p.m. The CIA's New York section chief and I had the kind of history that made shorthand our official language. I knew exactly where I was going and at what time.

At exactly 5 a.m., after leaving a note for Tracy on the off chance he woke up to find me gone, I walked into the twenty-four-hour Greek diner in Brooklyn that was a few blocks away from a safe house that Foxx used as an auxiliary office. If something was official agency business, it ran through his "official" office in Manhattan. Anything off the books, meaning anything that needed to be kept from the prying eyes of congressional oversight, was run through Brooklyn.

And as for the occasional thing that "never happened at all," that was reserved for the back booth of the Greek diner at a time of day when there were more pictures of Anthony Quinn on the wall than there were other customers.

"You're late," said Foxx as I slid into the booth, lining up across from him.

"No, I'm not," I said.

"Don't start with me." He took a bite of his egg white omelet, hold the hash browns. Two slices of rye toast hung off the side of the plate. A waitress came over with a menu for me and he promptly waved her off. "He's not staying long," he announced.

I'd figured there was a 90 percent chance that Hungarian intelligence officials weren't the only ones listening in on Dorian Laszlo's office and the rest of their consulate in Manhattan. Given the warmth Foxx was showing me, I was now 100 percent sure. The CIA definitely had ears in the building, as well.

"I was going to give you the heads-up," I said.

"No, you weren't."

Foxx leaned back, straightening his broad shoulders. He was a couple of years shy of sixty, but you'd only know it by looking at his birth certificate. The guy was still running marathons, had seemingly zero body fat, and somehow managed to avoid the weathered face and beaten-down soul of someone who'd spent more than three decades with the agency, and half that time in Israel, Cairo, and then Istanbul. Not exactly easy gigs.

"Fair enough," I said. "What would you like to know?"

"The beginning, the middle, and, most important, your endgame," he said.

"Is that all?"

"Or I could just have you killed."

He was kidding. But he'd made his point. I started talking, telling him what he'd asked for—the beginning, the middle, and, most important, my endgame. "I got approached by Mathias von Oehson," I began.

When I was done explaining, Foxx was taking the last bite of his rye toast. The crunch practically echoed in the otherwise empty diner.

"You really think you can pull that off?" he asked.

"What? You're saying I can't?"

Foxx cracked a smile. He never liked me much, but he trusted me. "'Modest doubt is called the beacon of the wise,'" he said.

"Of all the Shakespeare to quote, you pick *Troilus and Cressida*?"

"That's because it would be wasted on anyone else, Reinhart."

"Careful," I said. "That sounds dangerously close to a compliment."

He pushed his empty plate to the edge of the table. "You've told me the who, what, when, and where," he said. "What I want to know now is the why."

One good Shakespeare quote deserved another. "I see your *Troilus and Cressida* and raise you *The Merchant of Venice*. 'To do a great right, do a little wrong,'" I said.

Foxx could understand my wanting to protect Carter von Oehson from the outset, but now I was potentially putting the agency at risk. He wasn't asking me about my motivations. He was ascertaining *his*. Why should he let me do this?

We both knew why. A student of history, especially wars, Foxx hated Nazis more than Quentin Tarantino did. Moreover, Viktor Orbán's tenure as prime minister of Hungary since 2010 had been a major headache for US intelligence. What I was proposing was the daily double of payback. It was worth the gamble.

Foxx folded his arms. "You know I can't give you my blessing, right?"

"I don't want your blessing," I said. "I just want your blind eye."

In some corners of government, where words like *protocol* and *transparency* are still said with a straight face, there's no difference between getting a blessing and turning a blind eye. But for the likes of Landon Foxx—those intel players who will take to the grave more secrets than a Park Avenue psychiatrist—the difference is night and day. Because it's never what you know. It's what someone else can prove that you know.

"Get out of my face," he said. It was all I needed to hear as I quickly slid out of the booth with a satisfied grin.

My permission slip had been signed.

CHAPTER 76

AS SOON AS TRACY clicked his seat belt I handed him a blindfold, otherwise known as the sleep mask I use when flying. "Here," I said. "Put this on."

"You can't be serious," he said, giving me the Look.

I usually didn't fare very well against the Look, but there was no backing down on this one. I didn't even flinch. "Trust me," I said. "It's the only way."

"Who is this guy again?" asked Tracy.

"I told you. He's a friend."

"And why can't I know where he lives?"

"You'll see," I said.

Tracy held up his blindfold. "Was that supposed to be funny?"

I hit him with my Robert De Niro impression from *Goodfellas*, the "Get your shine box" scene. "Lil' bit," I said, scrunching my face. "Lil' bit."

Tracy rolled his eyes before putting on the mask. He wasn't a fan of my De Niro impressions. "You got any earplugs, as well?"

We started the drive out to Fort Lee, New Jersey, in our old Jeep Cherokee that we always talk about replacing but never do. By the time we crossed the George Washington Bridge, Tracy stopped muttering how "silly this all is" and seemed content to lean back and listen to the Tom Petty channel on the radio. Finally, after an excellent back-to-back set of "Free Fallin'" and "American Girl," I pulled into an empty parking lot near a warehouse for a medical supply company that no one has ever heard of, primarily because it doesn't actually exist.

Tracy reached for his blindfold as soon as I cut the engine. He couldn't wait to get the damn thing off.

"Hold on, not yet," I said.

"But we're here, right? *The Batcave?*"

"Almost."

I came around to get him from the other side of the Jeep, guiding him by the arm across the vacant lot to the security gate near the warehouse entrance. I knew the code for the gate, but there was no code for the steel door ten feet behind it, and definitely not one for the second steel door waiting for us after that.

Julian liked his privacy. For good reason.

"Okay, we're good," I said, once we were all the way inside. Tracy took off the blindfold, his eyes slowly adjusting in the low light.

"Hi, Tracy. I'm Julian."

Even if Tracy still had the blindfold on he would've made the connection based on the British accent alone. "Wait. You're the guy from the bar at Frankie's, the one who gave me his seat."

"Yes. That was me," said Julian. "The one and only."

"Only a little less drunk," said Tracy, realizing it was all an act.

"Not as less as you might think," Julian assured him. He motioned for us to follow. "I've got a seventeen-year-old Nikka Taketsuru opened. Who's joining me?"

"We'll pass," I said as we fell in line behind him. "I'm driving, and Tracy needs to focus."

"Speak for yourself," said Tracy.

252 • JAMES PATTERSON

"Actually, as much as I hate to deprive a chap of a good Japanese pure malt, Dylan might have a point," said Julian. "We have a lot to cover."

Any further objection from Tracy ended the second we turned the corner into Julian's office. Tracy looked around, mouth agape, at the mainframe computers, three-dimensional printers, and other gadgets along with Julian's giant desk configured from the wing of an old Fokker Eindecker, the first German fighter plane. And surrounding it all were walls that doubled as seamless projection screens carrying a live feed from Julian's latest hacking conquest — the newest Mars rover, *Perseverance.* It was as if we were standing on the red planet with a three-hundred-sixty-degree view.

"Holy shit," said Tracy.

"Yeah, I get that a lot," said Julian. He scratched his beard. "Come to think of it, that's not true. You're only the seventh person ever to see the inside of this place. Our friend, Agent Needham, was actually the sixth. Where is she, by the way?"

"Watching Annabelle," I said.

"That's one overqualified babysitter," said Julian.

Tracy was taking it all in. Everything. He turned to Julian. "So you were, what, my backup at Frankie's? Protection? A little George and Ira Gershwin?"

That's what I get for telling Tracy about Vladimir Grigoryev's serenading me instead of killing me. Meanwhile, Julian, who had an IQ higher than the 145-degree melting point of palmitic acid, looked at me without a clue. *George and Ira Gershwin?*

"'Someone to Watch Over Me,'" I said. "A song from one of their musicals."

"Clever," said Julian. "A bit on the nose in terms of gay men stereotypes, but still very clever." He poured himself two knuckles of his six-hundred-dollar Japanese whiskey. "Shall we get started?"

If we were truly going to pull this off, Tracy needed an extra pair of eyes and ears. But we could only get so close to him when the exchange happened. Julian's job was to bridge the gap. He went over to his desk, reaching for the already opened FedEx package.

"Do they work?" I asked.

"That's why you guys are here," he said. "We're about to find out."

CHAPTER 77

JULIAN HANDED TRACY THE package, leaving it to him to remove the slender rectangular case inside. The lid was on a tight spring-loaded hinge. The lining inside was padded for extra protection. CIA labs often make duplicates of their experimental spyware, but rarely when given such short notice. This was a one and only.

Tracy stared at the thick black frames. "What are these, like, special Dick Tracy glasses?" he asked.

"You're thinking of his wristwatch," I said.

"But Dick Tracy wore glasses like this, too, right?"

"He did, but it was the watch that was special. It doubled as a two-way radio."

"Are you sure his glasses didn't do anything?"

"I assume they helped him see better."

"Ha. Very funny," said Tracy. "You always make lame jokes when you're not sure about something."

"No, I don't."

"Yes, you do."

Julian stared in disbelief at both of us. "Bloody hell, you two really are married," he said. "If it's any consolation, Tracy, these particular glasses happen to be very special. Go ahead. Give 'em a try."

Tracy put on the glasses slowly, as if waiting for some big reveal. There wasn't one. "I think your definition of *special* might be different from mine," he said.

Julian moved to the laptop behind his desk, pressing a couple of keys. "Reach up to the frame around the left lens," he said. "Use your thumb and forefinger to adjust how the glasses are resting on your nose. You know, like people do. Make it look natural."

Boom. The second Tracy adjusted the frames, the walls of Julian's office changed. We were no longer on Mars. We were now looking through Tracy's eyes. Everything he was seeing, we were seeing.

"*Whoa*," said Tracy, only to hear an echo of himself. We could also hear everything he could.

"That tiny hole on the frame by the left lens, where the little screw for the hinge would normally go—that's your first camera," said Julian. "When it's on, it activates a microphone on the bridge of your nose."

"So I'm wearing a wire without having to wear a wire," said Tracy.

"Exactly. Better yet, we can also communicate with you." Julian grabbed a headset from off his desk, covering his mouth as he whispered something into the mic. I couldn't hear him.

But Tracy could. "Maxwell," he answered.

"No kidding," said Julian. He'd obviously asked what my middle name was. "All these years, and I never knew that. Dylan Maxwell Reinhart."

"Wait, how is that happening? How am I hearing you?" asked Tracy. "There's nothing in my ear."

"Bone conduction," said Julian. "The sound waves are emitted through both temples in the frames. They bypass the eardrum via your cheekbones and directly stimulate the inner ear."

"You lost me at bone conduction," said Tracy, "but very cool nonetheless."

"You ain't seen nothing yet," said Julian. "Now reach for the rim around the right lens, just like you did with the left. Real casual."

Tracy adjusted the frames again. We'd already left Mars but it was now shades of the red planet again. *What the...?*

"That's the second camera, on the right side," said Julian. "Thermal imaging."

That one even took me by surprise. I leaned over, staring into the frames. "All in that tiny hole?"

"Yep." Julian stepped out from behind his desk. "See anything interesting, Tracy?"

I spotted it right away amid the red-tinted outline of Julian projected on the wall. Tracy wasn't too far behind. He pointed at Julian's waist. "You've got a gun tucked underneath your shirt," he said.

Julian lifted his shirt, removing his Glock. "The metal obstructs your body heat so you're able to see it underneath clothing."

Tracy didn't seem as impressed as he should've been. He'd already jumped ahead. The ramifications. "Wait. If someone in that room has a gun and I don't, how does this really help me?"

"Because it helps *us*," said Julian. "It lets Dylan and me know who's carrying in case you need to hit the panic button."

"What panic button?" asked Tracy.

"It's actually not a button. The second you take those glasses off is the second we're bursting into the room," said Julian. "That's your SOS."

"Won't you already be able to see everything I can see?"

"Yes. We can see and we can hear. But we can't feel."

"Feel what?"

"Never mind. It's not a big deal," said Julian. "Forget I said anything."

As if that answer would ever satisfy Tracy.

CHAPTER 78

JULIAN LOOKED AT ME. His winking would've been redundant. Better that I be the one to scare the crap out of Tracy.

"*Feel what?*" Tracy repeated.

"For instance, and this is just an extreme example to illustrate a point," I said. "Let's say, if a gun happened to be pressed against the back of your head." I quickly raised my palms. "Not that that would ever happen."

"No, that's definitely not going to happen," added Julian quickly. "Because when you're in that room, you're going to keep everything in front of you."

This was Julian at his finest. I may have earned a PhD in psychology, but he was born with one. When you really want people to take your advice, don't merely tell them what to do. Instead, make them fully understand why they need to do it. Make them *feel* it. Down to their core.

Rest assured, Tracy now fully understood. *I need to keep everything in front of me.*

"Now let's talk about the exchange," said Julian. It was the perfect segue. "We've got a mob boss, a Monet, and a fifty-million-dollar transfer on the sly from a foreign government. What could possibly go wrong?"

The arrangements were set. Tracy had gone back and forth on the phone with Brunetti and Laszlo multiple times. Brunetti wanted the exchange to happen in a place of his choosing, namely, someplace he controlled. Fittingly, Laszlo wanted it to happen at the Hungarian consulate. The compromise that Tracy pushed for was "Switzerland," someplace neutral. He'd suggested the Roxy Hotel, which we knew would work for Brunetti since it was right across the street from his restaurant. Still, Brunetti insisted that he be the one to book the room. He'd clearly seen enough footage of hotel sting operations over the years.

Lastly, Brunetti and Laszlo were each allowed a plus one. But only one.

"The guy that Laszlo brings to authenticate the painting," said Tracy. "Should I be worried about him?"

"In what sense?" asked Julian.

"It's one thing to google the name 'William D'Alexander,' it's another if this authenticator goes asking around about him. Obviously no one in the art world has met me, let alone heard of me."

"You're right, and normally that could be a problem," said Julian. "But it won't be, not tomorrow."

"Why not?"

"Because the supposed expert accompanying Laszlo probably wouldn't know a Picasso from a pizza, let alone whether a Monet is real or fake."

"What he means is that the guy's not an art expert," I said. "He's Hungarian intelligence. He'll be there to protect Laszlo, the painting, the whole deal itself."

Tracy nodded. He got it. He knew we could hear the calls on both her cell and office phone, but still. "Why did you wait until now to tell me?" he asked.

"I figured it was better to show you the special Dick Tracy

glasses first," said Julian. "You know, to make you feel better about there being more than one guy in the room with a gun."

"Great. How'd that work out for me?" asked Tracy. It clearly hadn't.

"Not as well as I had hoped," said Julian.

"Any other surprises you want to share?"

I was about to chime in with a definitive *no* when the phone rang. We all froze for a moment. It wasn't any of our phones.

Julian swung back around his desk, looking at one of his monitors. "Damn," he said. "I was afraid this might happen."

I knew he could see her caller ID. At the eleventh hour, literally, Laszlo was getting a call from the powers that be. Not the ambassador. Not anyone here in the states. The *true* powers that be. The head of Hungarian intelligence. He wasn't calling simply to wish her good luck.

Julian put the conversation on speaker so we could all listen in. Laszlo hardly did any of the talking.

Their plan had changed. The Hungarian ambassador was no longer taking the Monet back to Budapest with him. Laszlo was now to personally escort the Monet back on a private jet that had already been arranged out of JFK. She was not to let the painting out of her sight at any time.

"I understand," said Laszlo, not questioning anything. She was given the time of the flight, which terminal, the full details.

If she wasn't happy about this new development, she sure wasn't letting on. She was a good soldier. Or maybe she simply understood the extra precaution. They'd come so far in finally getting the damn painting back, why leave anything to chance? Laszlo would simply go a little farther in making sure it arrived back to Hungary safely. It made sense.

And it completely screwed up our plan.

No one said the words out loud after the call ended, but

all three of us were thinking the same thing. *What the hell do we do now?*

"We postpone a day, give us some extra time to figure out another option," said Julian.

"Too risky. Postponing will spook both sides," I said.

"Dylan's right. It's now or never," said Tracy.

Julian folded his arms, nodding. Whatever blind spot he had for American musical theater he more than made up for with British playwrights. "Noël Coward, it is," he said. "The show must go on."

I reached for my phone, hitting speed dial. It was just the spark of an idea, far from fully formed. But if it was going to work, I knew one thing for certain. We needed more help.

"What are you doing?" asked Tracy.

"Expanding the cast," I answered.

CHAPTER 79

THE BEGINNING OF MY years with the CIA intersected with the final months of a paramilitary operations officer who was just about to retire. Julian had introduced us in the back room of a London pub. The room, which was closed off to the public, was basically a private bar hidden within a bar, a safe refuge for US and British intelligence officials and the occasional operative.

The CIA officer's name was Charles, but he was a "call me Charlie" kind of guy. At least around alcohol. After my first night of drinking with him, I was no longer Dylan. I was Dill.

Charlie liked to tell stories. Mostly great ones. Some surely embellished. He'd spent years in Honduras, training rebel forces to fight the Sandinista government. He'd seen a lot of messed-up stuff. *Done* a lot of messed-up stuff, too. All in the name of a philosophy as old as the Roman empire. Victory always comes at a cost.

I remember the last time I saw Charlie, not that I realized in the moment that it would be my last time with him. I think maybe he knew, though. That's why at the end of the night he pulled me aside for something other than another one of his stories. It was advice. Except when someone tells you something that you can remember word for word more than twenty years later, it's no longer merely advice. It's a mantra.

Charlie wasn't privy to the specifics of my mission in London at the time, but he knew I was young. Untested. And perhaps a bit unnerved by the inherent risk of my newfound profession.

"To doubt is human," he told me, with a heavy arm around my shoulder. "Doubting is healthy. But only before the beginning of a mission and after the very end. Anytime in between, doubt is your worst enemy. It's a trap. A Trojan horse. A self-inflicted fatal wound. In the middle of a mission, doubt only belongs to the dead."

Charlie was at least six bourbons deep when he told me that, but he spoke every syllable crystal clear. "Whatever happened to Charlie?" I asked Julian, years later.

Julian didn't know. No one did. I suspect that was by design. Charlie and his pension disappeared off the grid. In a related story, there are more than one hundred thousand islands in the world.

"Wish me luck," whispered Tracy as he approached room 1106 of the Roxy Hotel. From the stairwell by the eleventh floor, I could hear him perfectly through my headset. The stairwell door didn't have a window, but I had the visual feed on my cell courtesy of Tracy's glasses.

"You don't need luck. You've got this," I told him. "No doubt."

The bearded businessman sitting in the lobby with his laptop, otherwise known as Julian, was our spotter. He was the only one of us that neither Brunetti nor Laszlo would recognize.

Brunetti had arrived first with his plus-one per the arrangement, although he of course was cheating and actually brought two henchmen with him. The second one remained in the lobby and tried to look as inconspicuous as a six-foot-four, three-hundred-pound man possibly can. In other words, not very well.

Anyone else would've panicked on seeing Brunetti show up

without the painting, but not Julian. He assumed as much. Only after Brunetti checked in and went to his randomly assigned room to make sure there was no surprise waiting for him did his first henchman reappear in the lobby, exit the hotel briefly, and return with an oversized portfolio case.

Minutes later, Brunetti gave the signal to Tracy by texting him with the room number. Tracy then texted Laszlo. To keep his "Switzerland" efforts intact, Tracy was to arrive second, in the middle, before the Hungarian delegation.

"It's Bill D'Alexander," said Tracy, immediately announcing himself after knocking on room 1106.

Brunetti's guy let him in. Tracy had switched to thermal mode on the glasses before the door opened so we knew immediately.

"Pistol, right hip," whispered Julian.

"I see it," I said.

Tracy walked through a foyer, past a dining area, and into a spacious living room. Brunetti was about to pocket fifty million, so the least he could do was spring for a suite.

"Hello, Bill," said Brunetti. "How are you?"

"That depends," answered Tracy. "Are you going to make me strip again?"

"That won't be necessary."

"Are you sure? I wore nicer boxers just for the occasion."

"What you can do for me," said Brunetti, "is spread your arms out wide so Matthew here can see if you're ticklish."

Tracy obliged, allowing a guy who seemed way too big for the name *Matthew* to give him a good old-fashioned pat down. Matthew gave his boss a nod. *Clean.*

Except Brunetti was now giving Tracy a strange sort of stare. "There's something different about you," he said.

Tracy didn't hesitate. "I already told you about the boxers," he joked.

It was as if Brunetti couldn't hear him. Or didn't want to. "Your face," he said. "What's different?"

"I got a haircut yesterday?"

"No. That's not it." Brunetti snapped his fingers, the reason coming to him. He pointed at Tracy. "Glasses. You weren't wearing glasses when we met."

"*Easy now,*" I whispered to Tracy.

"I wasn't wearing these? Are you sure?" asked Tracy.

"I'm positive."

"Then I was wearing my contacts. No need for glasses."

Brunetti nodded. "They're nice," he said. "Those frames. Who makes them?"

Oh, shit.

"*Don't lie,*" I whispered. "*Tell him you don't know.*"

I'd already done the math in my head. Four seconds to reach the door of the suite. One second to shoot the lock. Another second to take down left-handed Matthew before he can reach for the holster on his right hip.

Julian was suddenly in my ear. He could isolate his channel so it was just me who could hear him. "I know what you're thinking, mate, but not yet," he said. "Hold tight."

I watched as Tracy glanced at Matthew before answering Brunetti. "I don't know who makes them," he said. "I barely even remember where I got them. I think it was one of those chains, like Pearle Vision, or something."

"They usually put the name of the maker on the inside of one of the arms," said Brunetti. He reached his hand out. "Here, let me see them for a second."

CHAPTER 80

MY GUN WAS OUT. I was going in.

I was just about to push through the stairwell door and bolt into the hallway when through my earpiece came the sound of knuckles on another door. Someone was knocking on Brunetti's suite.

It couldn't be Laszlo. There was no way Julian missed her coming into the hotel. That was his main job at that point, spotting her. But if it wasn't her?

Whoever it was, the knock immediately changed the topic of conversation in the suite. There was no more talk of Tracy's frames. I looked back down at the camera feed on my phone. The glasses were still on his head. Tracy was watching Brunetti's man, Matthew, walk to the door. The guy's hand was hovering over the pistol on his right hip. He disappeared from the living room of the suite, only to reappear seconds later.

"It's not her," Matthew announced to his boss, keeping a low voice. He'd obviously looked through the peephole. "It's a guy."

The ire on Brunetti's face when Tracy turned to him. *You better explain fast. Real fast.*

"The authenticator," Tracy offered. "He and Laszlo, maybe they're arriving separately."

"Or maybe something else entirely," said Brunetti, beginning to pace. He wasn't liking this.

Julian was our eyes in the lobby. Tracy was our eyes in the suite. The only one with a view of the hallway was me—that is, if I was willing to risk opening the stairwell door to take a peek.

Tracy beat me to the punch. He was on the move before I could decide, walking past Matthew to the entrance of the suite. Damn, Matthew's trigger finger looked twitchy. Tracy leaned in, looking through the peephole. He was too close to it for me to see what he could see.

"Can I help you?" he asked through the door.

"I work with Dorian Laszlo," came the man's voice.

"Where is she? Why isn't she with you?"

"Think of me as the advance scout team."

"Do you have a name?" asked Tracy.

"I'll give you one better."

As soon as he said that I knew who he was. What he was. And what he was about to hold out in front of him to show Tracy. His ID and badge.

Expect the unexpected.

Julian and I were right about Hungarian intelligence. We just didn't expect him to arrive in advance of Laszlo. He wasn't posing as the authenticator.

Tracy could only be thinking one thing: *What do I do now?*

"Ask him if he's carrying a weapon. He's going to say no," I whispered. I waited and listened to the exchange.

"I'm clean," said the agent.

It was plausible. Advance teams are often just a fancy way of saying guinea pigs. This was about Laszlo's safety, not his. Most important, it was about the deal going through.

I continued in Tracy's ear. "Now go outside into the hallway. Don't look back at Brunetti for approval. Just do it. I'm right here if something goes wrong."

Thinking this agent wasn't carrying and knowing it were two different things. As soon as Tracy stepped into the hallway and hit him with the thermal camera, both Julian and I could see that the guy was telling the truth.

"Ask him where his partner is," I said.

It was like that scene with William Hurt and Holly Hunter in the movie *Broadcast News*. I'd say the words into Tracy's ear and out his mouth they would come.

"What makes you think I'm not alone?" the agent asked.

"Don't answer, just stare at him," I said. The guy, of course, had a partner. He was simply weighing the pros and cons of admitting as much. The pros won out.

"He's outside the hotel," the agent said finally.

Tracy knew the next question. He asked it before I could even tell it to him. "And you're here to do what, exactly?"

"One, check the room. Two, make sure there's only two people in that room when Ms. Laszlo arrives. You and the seller," said the agent. "As was agreed to."

Again, Tracy was ahead of me. There was no hesitation. "Wait here," he said.

With that, Tracy had officially taken the reins. He'd been our eyes and ears. Now he was also the brains. He'd gained a true sense of Brunetti by this point, namely, that the guy spoke only one language. Leverage.

Tracy went back into the suite, marching straight up to him. "Here's the deal. That is, if you want this deal to happen. The guy outside is a Hungarian intelligence agent. He's doing the same thing you wanted to do, making sure this room is safe."

"So what did you tell him?" asked Brunetti.

"The same thing I'm telling you. He's not coming in. That's because your man Matthew here is leaving. He'll be waiting for you in the lobby."

"And if I say no to that?"

"Then you can have this room all to yourself," said Tracy. "Also, you'll be out fifty million dollars and own a pretty painting that you'll never be able to sell to anyone else. The Hungarians will make sure of it."

George Burns said it best. *Acting is all about honesty. If you can fake that, you've got it made.*

I watched. We all watched—Tracy, Julian, and me—as Brunetti bobbed his head for a few seconds, making up his mind. He may have looked undecided, but I was convinced it was all just for show. Brunetti had already made his decision. In that moment it was Tracy who had all the leverage.

Brunetti turned to Matthew, all three hundred pounds of him. "Go wait in the lobby," he said.

CHAPTER 81

TRACY HAD MOVED EVERYONE around like chess pieces, clearing a path for Dorian Laszlo to arrive at Brunetti's suite. "She's here," said Julian. "She just walked in."

With her was a guy who, now fittingly, would never be mistaken for Hungarian intelligence. His look screamed one of two professions, art authenticator or eighth-grade science teacher. Either way, his wearing a bow tie seemed utterly redundant.

Tracy handled the introductions once everyone was face-to-face. This was the very definition of a private sale, but there was no way to keep the players a secret. As long as the transaction itself remained a secret, neither Brunetti nor Laszlo cared. There was even some polite small talk. Brunetti said he'd never been to Budapest. Laszlo assured him it was worth the trip. "Try our nokedli," she said. "They're almost as good as the gnocchi at Frankie's."

Brunetti wasn't entirely immune to flattery. He beamed. "You've been to my restaurant, huh?"

"Who hasn't? It's one of my favorites," said Laszlo.

So far, so good. I knew exactly what Tracy was thinking. *Harness this.* It was time to segue.

"So who wants to look at some art?" asked Tracy.

The authenticator, who'd barely spoken a word up until this point, couldn't help himself. "I do," he said. You couldn't blame him. He was about to see the painting equivalent of a unicorn, a stunning and storied Monet that had disappeared years ago—*poof*—and hadn't been seen since by anyone in his field. Until now.

All eyes were on Brunetti as he reached for the portfolio case that was leaning up against the front of an armchair. The sound of his unzipping the case might as well have been a jet engine, it was so quiet in the room.

"Here," said Brunetti, stepping aside. "I'll let you do the honors."

The authenticator approached the case, or at least I assumed he did. Tracy had kept staring at Brunetti. Julian and I had warned him repeatedly about keeping an eye on him. Still, the biggest threat to the deal at that moment was the guy whose job it was to declare that the painting in the case, *Woman by the Seine*, was genuine. The real thing.

It didn't matter how much I was sure that it was. What mattered was what the man wearing the bow tie thought.

I whispered once more in Tracy's ear. A verbal nudging so Julian and I could see what was happening. *"The painting."*

Tracy's head swiveled to the authenticator, who was unwrapping the Monet from a moving blanket, presumably the one that von Oehson had kept it in. That was a good sign.

I waited for the authenticator to take out a loupe or a black light or some other tool of his trade. Good thing I wasn't holding my breath. *Are you really just going to naked eye this thing, buddy?*

Apparently. After propping it up on the arms of the armchair, he stared intently for a silent minute, his eyes darting left and right, up and down, all over the painting. Seemingly satisfied, he then turned it around to look at the back. He stared with the same intensity, only for less time. Mere seconds, in fact. The way he nodded to himself it was almost as if he were looking for something.

Or maybe that's just revisionist history on my part.

Truth was, I didn't see the red flag coming until it was waved right in front of my face.

CHAPTER 82

THE GUY AND HIS bow tie didn't say anything while examining the painting, not a word about what he was thinking. His verdict came after he stepped back, turned to Laszlo, and gave her all she needed to know. A simple nod.

Although it's debatable whether a nod that triggers a fifty-million-dollar transaction can really qualify as simple.

Julian and I were beholden to Tracy and wherever he was looking, but as he took turns gauging the reactions of both Brunetti and Laszlo, it was Laszlo's expression that clearly stood out. She was elated, and as much as she surely wanted to play it cool, she couldn't. Ms. Prim and Proper, measured and exacting, even managed to flash a spot of dry wit, as Julian might say.

"Cash or check?" she asked, turning to Brunetti.

The answer was, of course, neither. The details of the payment were prearranged, a negotiation that Tracy oversaw and mediated as any art broker would. Laszlo, on behalf of her government, was insistent that there could be no paper trail—nothing spelled out or signed or codified in any way. That wasn't a problem for Brunetti. He wasn't exactly intending to give her a receipt.

No, there was easy agreement on the lack of documentation.

No one wanted to deal with a printed form of payment. Buyer and seller agreed on a wire transfer. They even agreed on the currency. US dollars. What had to be negotiated, however, was the banks that would carry out the transaction. Laszlo needed their payment to land offshore, meaning not on US territory. In return, Brunetti demanded that no third-party bank be involved. He needed to be paid directly from the Magyar Nemzeti Bank, otherwise known as the central bank of Hungary. It was the only way he could know for sure that he was selling the painting to the one buyer who truly had more to lose than he did if the sale was to somehow be made public.

"Deal," said both sides.

Brunetti reached into a side pocket of the portfolio case, removing a laptop. No one else could see the screen, but he presumably had it in sleep mode, having already accessed the hotel's internet. He needed to make only a few keystrokes before handing the laptop over to Laszlo.

It was her turn. Her government's turn. She was the only one who could see the screen now, but there was little mystery as to where we were in the process. Brunetti's offshore account required a bank routing number and an authorization code for the transfer of the fifty million. Laszlo pecked at the keyboard, slowly and deliberately, as if each number were being written in stone.

No more than thirty seconds later, it was done. The money had been moved. She handed the laptop back to Brunetti so he could see the confirmation. He nodded, smiling.

"Enjoy your painting," he said. "I'll even throw in the carrying case for free."

And that was that. Only it wasn't. It couldn't be. There was something that wasn't right, something we weren't seeing. But what? What was the problem?

There wasn't one. That was it. After all the planning, all the maneuvering to bring Laszlo and Brunetti together, I couldn't help this nagging feeling that the transaction had gone *too* smoothly. Sometimes the only thing more troubling than failure is success.

Still, I couldn't put my finger on it. There was nothing I could whisper in Tracy's ear, no advice. While I did have one question, it was the equivalent of opening Pandora's box. This deal was closed. Sealed. I wasn't about to do anything that might unseal it. Merely asking the question would risk Brunetti's wrath. I was convinced it wasn't worth it.

That's when I noticed what had caught Tracy's eyeline.

He was no longer looking at Brunetti or Laszlo. His focus was on the authenticator, who was about to wrap up the Monet with the moving blanket.

"I'm just curious," said Tracy. "How did you know so quickly that the painting is real?"

I could only guess the expression on Brunetti's face. If looks could kill. Tracy didn't even glance at him, though. He knew better. If only Tracy also knew better than to have asked the question. That was my immediate thought...right up until the moment the authenticator hesitated before finally answering. It was as if he were deciding whether to share a secret.

"Truth be told, I didn't even have to look at the front of the painting," he said, picking it up. He turned it around, holding up the back. "Do you see it?"

"That depends," said Tracy. "What am I looking for?"

Whatever it was, I couldn't see it, either. Tracy leaned in. "Oh," he said finally. "I see what you mean."

I saw it, too. So did Julian.

Shit. We were screwed.

CHAPTER 83

WE SHOULD'VE KNOWN. THE Nazis had a thing for numbering.

If they could tattoo people as if they were objects instead of human beings, further depriving them of any last shred of dignity before being slaughtered, then numbering the things they plundered from them—particularly works of art—would hardly seem out of the realm of possibility.

I cut my audio with Tracy so only Julian could hear me. "What the hell do we do?"

"Panic, for starters," replied Julian.

"Did you get the numbers?"

"Nine, one, five, two."

"Do you think it's a grease pen?" I asked.

"That or charcoal."

Not that it really made a difference. It wasn't as if they were selling art supplies in the hotel gift shop.

I kept staring at my screen, Tracy's POV. The Monet was wrapped up and back in the portfolio case. Brunetti was on his phone. Laszlo was on hers. She was out of earshot for Tracy, but not Julian. We still had the tap on her cell. He was wired in.

"She's letting her driver know that she's coming down," he said in my ear. "Sounds like it's the same agent who first came to the room."

That made sense. We knew that someone would be driving her. Now we knew who.

As for where they'd be heading, it had been all mapped out in advance. Laszlo was first stopping at Axion Partners on the grounds of Kennedy Airport, a top-of-the-line air-freight packager used by museums and the highest of high-end collectors. They were the most respected in the industry. More important, they were the most discreet. Because they were headquartered in Brussels, they had no legal obligation to report anything they packaged to the IRS or any other US legal authority, so long as it wasn't drugs or weapons.

I was back to my original question to Julian. "So what the hell do you want to do?" The only difference being that we'd both had a minute to think about it.

Sometimes a minute is nothing more than sixty quick seconds ticking by. Other times, it can feel like a lifetime.

In Julian's case, his lifetime had been spent never letting a problem get the better of him. "Are you thinking what I'm thinking?" he asked.

"Hopefully not," I said. "Because I'm thinking we're screwed."

"Not quite yet. There still might be one way to get this done," said Julian.

And her name was Elizabeth.

CHAPTER 84

THE ART OF MANIPULATION begins with convincing someone that you know something about him you're not supposed to know.

"Can I help you?" asked the man behind the counter at Axion Partners. He was nattily dressed in a gray herringbone three-piece suit with a double Windsor knot against a spread collar. He was also clearly proud of the whole ensemble.

"Yes, you absolutely can help me," answered the woman in the long black coat and dark sunglasses. She was towing a rectangular object, about waist high, strapped to a hand truck. It was covered by a black oversized blanket. "I believe you have an appointment with a customer who will be arriving here shortly. Her name is Dorian Laszlo."

The man behind the counter stared at the woman, waiting for her to continue. She didn't. After five seconds of awkward silence, he cleared his throat. "Are you asking me to confirm that?"

The art of manipulation progresses by establishing a power imbalance.

Elizabeth whipped out her badge. "Yes, that's exactly what I'm asking."

The man spent a little more time studying her ID from the Joint

Terrorism Task Force than most others normally do, but the result was the same. Compliance. "Let me check that for you, Agent Needham," he said, reaching for a leather-bound appointment book on a table behind him.

"I appreciate it," said Elizabeth. "Now that you know my name, what's yours?"

"Stuart," he said. He opened the book, his forefinger scrolling midway down the page before stopping. "Yes. Here it is. Dorian Laszlo. Artwork packaging."

"I'm going to guess that there's also an asterisk or some notation for it being a rush job." Of course this wasn't a guess at all.

Stuart nodded. "Yes. For a premium we offer customers a pack-while-you-wait option. That's what Ms. Laszlo specified."

"Do you know what it is that she wants packaged?"

He glanced again at the appointment book. "Like I mentioned, it's artwork. Beyond that I don't know specifics."

"I do," said Elizabeth. "Ms. Laszlo will be asking you to box up a Claude Monet, entitled *Woman by the Seine*. It has an estimated value of a hundred million dollars. There's just one problem, though."

"What's that?"

Elizabeth leaned in, her voice dropping to a whisper. "It's a fake."

Stuart blinked a few times while adjusting the vest of his three-piece suit, giving it a tug. He was processing what he'd been told, filtering it through the purest form of Darwinism. Self-preservation.

"Even if what you're telling me is true, Agent Needham, how is that a problem for me?" he asked.

"It's only a problem for you if you don't help us. And when I say us, I want you to think in capital letters. Capital U, period. Capital S, period. The United States," said Elizabeth. "You do want to help your country, don't you?"

"Of course I'd like to help," said Stuart. "It's just that I don't know what you want me to do. It's not anything that can get me fired, is it? Or anything illegal?"

At a critical juncture, make him think that you're taking him into your confidence.

"No. We're the good guys, Stuart. This is about the bad guys. What I need to know, right now, is whether I can trust you. I'm not supposed to tell you what I'm about to tell you. I'm the one who could get fired. *So can I trust you?*"

CHAPTER 85

"GOOD," SAID ELIZABETH, OFF Stuart's nod. She edged even closer to the counter, removing her sunglasses. "You see, the only people in this world harder to find than terrorists are the ones who fund them. They're rich and they're powerful, and they use both those advantages to help keep what they do extremely well hidden. They cover their tracks. They're very good at it. But from time to time, we've discovered, they still make mistakes."

"What kind of mistakes?" asked Stuart. He was glued to every word.

"Expensive women and paintings, mainly. Prostitutes and priceless art—they can't get enough of them, although they sure as hell try. And that's how we flush them out. Of course, when it comes to art, our government can't sell them actual Monets or Picassos or van Goghs, but we can make them think that's what they're buying. So that's what we do."

Elizabeth paused, watching Stuart tug on his vest again as he took all of this in. He wasn't quite there yet, though. He wasn't supposed to be. "I'm not sure I'm following," he said.

"Funny you should say follow. These fake paintings that we

sell them have tracking devices built into the frames. That's how we find these guys."

Ahhh, said Stuart's face. "So Dorian Laszlo works for a terrorist?"

"She's actually an unwitting accomplice," said Elizabeth. "She's a go-between. She doesn't know the truth about who bought this Monet on the black market. The problem, and why I'm here, is that we just got reliable intelligence that the buyer suspects something. In short, he's onto us."

"How?"

"We needed a quick and easy way to identify our forgeries out in the wild, so we came up with a numbering system. In fact, that's how you're going to know that everything I'm telling you is true. On the back of the supposed Monet that Dorian Laszlo is bringing here you'll see four little numbers scribbled in black. Nine, one, five, two."

The art of manipulation is complete once you've convinced him that acting in your best interest is also in his best interest.

"So what is it that you want me to do? Tell me. I want to help," said Stuart.

Elizabeth unstrapped the item on the hand truck. She lifted it to the counter, turning back the corners of the black blanket it was wrapped in. "Do you recognize the packaging?" she asked.

"Of course," said Stuart. "It's ours. When did we do it for you?"

"You didn't." Elizabeth took a step back, as if admiring it. "But you could have fooled me, right?"

Stuart stared at all the Axion logos and markings on the slender wooden crate. The shipping label, too. Everything was a perfect match. "Fooled both of us, I would say. How were you able to do this?" he asked.

"If we can create a convincing forgery of a hundred-million-dollar painting, we're not about to let the damn box it arrives in get in the way," said Elizabeth. "The only thing missing are those wire thingamajigs that you guys use for security on the seal."

"I call them the no-tamper ties," said Stuart. He looked again at the crate. "So what's inside?"

"A better forgery, that's what. The buyer, like I said, somehow got wise to our numbering system. Or so we believe. That's why we need to make sure *this* is what Dorian Laszlo leaves with."

Elizabeth liked that she didn't have to lie to Stuart about what was inside. It was indeed a better forgery—certainly better than the one that Julian and his forger had intended to send to Budapest. Elizabeth had been on her way to the restricted cargo area of JFK to make the switch with the real Monet when she got the call from Dylan. "Change of plans," he told her.

First, she had to get her hands on a black grease pen.

Second, she had to open the crate so she could write the four numbers on the back of the painting. Nine, one, five, two. Dylan had sent her a screenshot from Tracy's glasses so she could copy the handwriting style as best she could. The only problem was those wire thingamajigs. The no-tamper ties. She didn't have any extras. Who would've thought she needed any? She had to get new ones now before making the switch, which meant her racing to Axion and engaging with her new best friend, Stuart.

"So what exactly am I supposed to do?" he asked, glancing at a clock on the wall behind him. It was the old-school variety, with a spring-loaded second hand that clicked with each movement. "Ms. Laszlo is scheduled to be here in about ten minutes."

This was the one part of the new plan for which neither Dylan nor Julian had an answer. Elizabeth was on her own. She couldn't let Dorian Laszlo see her since they'd already met, and if there was one takeaway from that meeting, it was that Laszlo wasn't about to let her country's newly reclaimed Monet out of her sight while it was being packaged.

"Do you have a coffee maker here?" asked Elizabeth.

Stuart looked at her as if she were crazy. The clock was literally ticking away over his shoulder. Laszlo could walk through the door at any moment. *"You're asking me for a cup of coffee?"*

"It's not for me, it's for you."

"I don't drink coffee."

"I don't need you to drink it. I need you to spill it," said Elizabeth. "At just the right moment."

CHAPTER 86

"WHAT WAS THE GUY'S name again?" I asked.

"Stuart," said Elizabeth. "Clumsy, clumsy Stuart."

Timing is everything, and having Stuart spill coffee on Dorian Laszlo was everything Elizabeth needed to make the switch. The second Laszlo scurried off to the bathroom at Axion Partners to assess the damage to her blouse, Elizabeth appeared from the storage closet with the fake Monet in hand.

"You should've heard the way Laszlo cursed him out. She was so ticked off," Elizabeth told me over the phone, chuckling. "Oh, and regards from Richard Landau. He said he hopes to see you again soon at the Yale Club."

"He probably shouldn't hold his breath on that," I said. Fittingly, von Oehson had his old chum pick up the painting from Elizabeth.

"So did you hear from him yet? Von Oehson?" she asked.

"Not only that, I'm going to see him this weekend."

"Why?"

"He made me another offer I couldn't refuse."

Normally, I'd never allow my students to be used as pawns in a rich man's game, but if they ever found out the alternative—my turning down the offer and saying no—I'd never be forgiven. Not by a single one of them.

It was finally safe for Carter von Oehson to return to school. All the same, his father wanted to "ease" the transition, and I agreed to cooperate. Mine would be Carter's first class back. Of course, postponing that class until the weekend, especially leading into the reading period before finals, would hardly be popular unto itself. I never would've done it were it not for the sweetener, the offer made to me by Mathias von Oehson.

The plan was another field trip. This one beyond Woolsey Rotunda and the confines of the Yale campus. The entire class, one hundred twenty to be exact, boarded two luxury buses in New Haven on Saturday afternoon and headed into Manhattan. In the process they amended one of the great punch lines of all time. How do you get to Carnegie Hall? *Practice.* (Or, if you're lucky, be the guest of an insanely rich multibillionaire who happens to sit on the board.)

I was the warm-up act. No one knew who the headliner was, only that it would be "worth their while." Even at that it was an undersell.

I gave my lecture from the stage of Carnegie Hall, which was admittedly a thrill. The students were spread out among the first ten rows, trying their best—most of them, at least—to pay attention. This was the last class before the final, and as any Yale undergrad not living under a rock knows, my finals are nothing you can study for. You simply have to hope that all my blabbering during the semester somehow resonated in one way or another. If so, I always assure them, "You'll do just fine and dandy on the test."

At the end of my lecture, I asked whether there were any questions. One hand immediately shot up. "Yes, Carter," I said. "What's your question?"

We hadn't spoken in the days since his miraculous return at St. Sebastian's church. I didn't want him knowing that I was working for his father. His father didn't want him knowing, either. It was better that I not even give him the opportunity to ask me again about my being at his funeral. Hence, I'd kept my distance.

Carter stood. "It's not actually a question, it's something I wanted to say," he began, before taking a deep breath. "I haven't been able to talk to each one of you yet, so with all of us here... I just... you know, feel bad about what happened. It's a crazy story, and I think in time I'll be able to talk about it more, but until then I'm really sorry that I made so many people sad and angry and frustrated and... well, probably a little pissed off. I heard about that primal scream you all did." He then flashed his signature smile, which made everyone laugh. "Okay, a lot pissed off!"

His classmates laughed some more. A few clapped and hollered.

"Thank you, Carter. I think that was a stand-up thing to do," I said. I figured that was the perfect segue. "And speaking of stand up..."

They all would've groaned had they known yet who I was about to introduce.

I first gave thanks to Carter's father for inviting our special guest. Then, without further ado, I made way for one of my true favorites. This was the guy who so brilliantly captured the reality of what it means to be Black in America years before anyone even uttered the phrase *Black Lives Matter*. And he did it with one single line in a live comedy show.

"There ain't a white man in this room that would trade places with me."

I exited stage left, and from stage right came Chris Rock to do an hour-long set in front of one hundred twenty kids who suddenly sounded like twenty thousand. To hear my students scream so loudly again, this time out of excitement, was the best bookend I could think of to the saga of Carter von Oehson and his suicide that wasn't.

No one else needed to know the truth. The whole truth. Because that's the way the world works. Some secrets are better left in the dark—much like the man who had arranged all of this, now standing in the shadows, waiting for me once I walked off the stage.

CHAPTER 87

I STOOD NEXT TO Mathias von Oehson, and we both listened and laughed for a few minutes as Chris Rock absolutely killed it. Playing to a small crowd, albeit in Carnegie Hall, surely brought him back to his club days.

Eventually, there was an exchange to be had. I figured the faster we got to it, the sooner I could get back to enjoying the show.

"So are you at least hanging it on a wall this time?" I asked.

"I'm not sure yet," said von Oehson. "I'll wait for the satisfaction of having it back to level off, and then see how I feel. I doubt it, though." He paused. "That still strikes you as odd, huh?"

"No, not really. To each their own." Although that wasn't really the truth. It did seem a bit strange that he would keep this beautiful Monet wrapped in a blanket, stuffed away in a closet. Sure, he couldn't let others know he had it, but that didn't prevent him from hanging it somewhere in private, if only for his own satisfaction. Could a man like him ever possess a greater trophy?

It was as if he could read my mind. "Have you ever been big-game hunting, Dylan?" he asked.

"I've been hunting, plenty of times. But never for what qualifies as big game," I said. "Never felt the need."

"You're lucky."

"Or maybe just not that wealthy."

"You know that's not it. Given your field of expertise, or at least one of them, you probably understand the psychology behind it," he said. "Or better put, the abnormal psychology."

"Heads and horns," I said. "Try as some men might, you can't hang true satisfaction on a wall."

Von Oehson nodded his approval. "I told you from the beginning you were the right man for the job." With that, he reached for the inside breast pocket of his suit, removing an envelope. "My thanks again. It was always about my son, but you went above and beyond with the painting. Merry Christmas."

I took the envelope, and this time I kept it. It wasn't sealed, but I didn't bother looking at the check. Von Oehson watched as I tucked it away in my pocket. "What's with the smirk?" I asked.

"The smirk is for the pleasant irony."

"How do you mean?"

"You don't want to at least look at it? Confirm the amount?"

"Why? Did you shortchange me?"

Again, he smirked. *Okay, fine.* I peeked inside the envelope. Lo and behold, von Oehson had tacked on an extra $500,000 to the back-end payment. The check was for $1.5 million.

"I added a 1 percent bonus off the sale of the Monet," he said. "It seemed about right. Even more so now. That's the pleasant irony. You returned the painting to me without first collecting what I still owed you. You trusted a guy to make good on a deal that was struck on anything but trust. That's impressive."

"Or maybe I just know where you live," I said. "Some of your homes, at least."

"Funny." He motioned to the stage. "Maybe you should be out there."

"No. That's my greatest expertise of all," I said. "Knowing my limitations."

"Interesting," said von Oehson. "Now ask me what's mine."

I played along. The guy did just give me the biggest check I'd ever been handed. What was that I said about being a pawn in a rich man's game?

"Okay, what's yours?" I asked. "What's your greatest expertise of all?"

He smiled. A devilish grin. "Knowing the limitations of everyone else," he said.

CHAPTER 88

THE SINGLE BIGGEST DECISION Tracy and I ever made together was adopting a baby. Next to that, everything else—including our decision to get married—will always feel like a distant second.

As for our most *contentious* decision, the one over which we're diametrically opposed and have spent countless hours heatedly debating, and are still debating on an annual basis... well, that can only be a matter of the utmost seriousness, right?

That's right. The all-important matter? *When are we putting up the Christmas tree?*

For years and years, I've given in to Tracy's fairy-tale New England, gag-me-with-an-L.L.Bean-catalogue tradition that's been carried down through generations of his family, which is to wait until Christmas Eve to buy and decorate the tree. Never mind that Tracy is actually the son of two born-and-bred Iowans. Somewhere in that McKay family tree, undoubtedly being tapped for maple syrup, must have been some Mainers.

But this year was going to be different. I was making an executive decision, a unilateral overturn of my annual concession. It's amazing what outsmarting an entire European country refusing to fully come to terms with its Nazi sympathizing past can do for one's self-esteem.

Or maybe it was the $1.5 million check burning a hole in my

pocket since yesterday and that I was going to hand it over to Tracy for Harlem Legal House the second he tried to object.

"Ho! Ho! Ho!" I hollered, coming through the door of our apartment with a six-foot Douglas fir wrapped in netting, courtesy of the Christmas tree store, otherwise known as the corner deli down the street.

I waited for the pitter-patter of Annabelle's feet as she ran to greet me, her laughter growing louder and louder with each advancing step. Instead all I got was silence.

"Hello?" I called out. They were supposed to be home. Tracy had told me as much before I left for Carnegie Hall. He was eager to hear about whatever conversation I'd had with von Oehson. I was eager to now tell him.

They must have gone out for something, I thought. A last-minute trip to the market for dinner fixings. Since Tracy hadn't texted, he had probably left a note for me in the kitchen.

But there was no note.

I turned the corner of our foyer and put the tree in its stand. Someone was waiting for me on the couch in our living room. Legs crossed, arms folded, teeth gnashed. The ligaments around his jawbone were rippling up and down.

"You're not supposed to be here," I said. It wasn't so much a rude thing for me to say as it was an observation laden with implications, none of them good.

"Sit down, Reinhart," said Landon Foxx.

This was my home. My castle. I could do whatever I wanted. Of course, so could Foxx. It was one of the perks of his being the CIA's New York section chief. He could do whatever he wanted almost anywhere he wanted, including my home.

I sat down. As my knees bent I could feel them begin to weaken. First things first. "Where are Tracy and Annabelle?" I asked. I'd already crossed off their going to the market. Now I was just fighting back the looming wave of panic.

"They're fine," said Foxx. "They've been taken to a safe house."

"Brooklyn?" That was the one he used as his external, off-the-record office.

"No. Different location. I took them there personally."

That was even worse. It meant he wanted to make sure no one else could expose their whereabouts, *including me*.

It was right about then I noticed the folder sitting on the cushion next to him.

"What the hell's going on?" I asked.

"You obviously have no idea, do you? Of course you don't. When you screw up this goddamn royally, you're always the last to know."

"What are you talking about? Everything went according to plan," I said.

"You're right," said Foxx. "Only it wasn't your plan. It was never your plan. It was always von Oehson's, right from the start. He was pulling all the strings and you got played, Reinhart. Plucked like a fiddle."

"No. You're wrong," I said. I was quickly running everything over in my head, every detail, each move, the end result. "The Hungarians are proud owners of a fake Monet they'll never know isn't the original. I told you that, as well as Brunetti's role in making it happen. Who cares if he netted fifty million in the process?"

"Fifty million? Try fifty *billion*," said Foxx.

"*What?*"

"Although I suspect Brunetti's cut truly was the fifty million. Von Oehson always makes money for those who invest with him."

Foxx hadn't explained anything yet, not a word to make me begin to understand, but there was no stopping the feeling of dread that had joined in the panic that was no longer merely looming. It was crashing over me. Crushing me. Swallowing me whole. I was drowning.

I had screwed up, all right. Goddamn royally.

CHAPTER 89

EVERYTHING WAS A BLUR, including the ride out to Connect-icut. I didn't ring the bell at von Oehson's house in Darien, I pounded on the door until my fist nearly bled. All the rage I had for him, the anger—it was beyond anything I'd ever felt, with only one exception. The fury I now felt for myself. *How could I have let this happen?*

I didn't think about who might answer the door. I didn't care. I was too busy thinking everything else through, how von Oehson had pulled it off. Foxx had the endgame down, but there were still dots to connect. One of them was Brunetti. For sure, he was in on it.

The mob boss, who had more security tech on his gambling boat alone than most maximum-security prisons, used a remote keystroke-logging software program. It was able to track and record every letter and number that Dorian Laszlo had input to initiate the transfer of the fifty million to him. That was their back door. That's why he had insisted up front that there be no third-party institution involved, no shell company or phantom investment fund. Brunetti needed to be paid directly from the central bank of Hungary.

But the software he used, sophisticated as it is, only gets you to that back door. It doesn't get you in. The Magyar Nemzeti Bank isn't like an ordinary bank, with savings and checking accounts that you can simply withdraw from as you would an ATM, if you happened to know the password. The only money that goes out has to be allocated. In other words, Laszlo was able to transfer the fifty million to Brunetti because the amount had already been set aside for her by the bank.

So how did Brunetti—or, I should say, von Oehson—turn fifty million into fifty billion?

And if that was his plan all along, there was an even bigger question.

What kind of a man kidnaps his own son?

The door opened, and I was suddenly face-to-face with the one person who could tell me.

"What are you doing here?" asked von Oehson. "Did I not pay you enough?"

He was still smiling, but it was forced. Very forced. The person-ification of cool and collected knew he had a problem at the mere sight of me. Damage control among the very wealthy has a certain look to it. You might say it looks a lot like a very forced smile.

I didn't wait for the invite to step inside. I didn't wait for anything. *"You'd like that, wouldn't you?"* he'd said the first day we met. *"Taking a swing at me?"*

My fist, still balled from banging on the door, connected all four knuckles flat against his chin, the force dropping him like a house of cards. He landed with an echoing thud inside his cavernous foyer, his head smacking hard against the shiny white marble. For a few seconds, I stood and watched as blood trickled slowly from the side of his mouth. The plum-red drool was the only thing moving on him.

"Get up," I said, stepping over him and into the house. "You and I are just getting started."

CHAPTER 90

VON OEHSON TRIED TO stand. He couldn't. Not yet. Best he could do was push himself up with his arms just enough so he could sit. The front door, which I'd closed behind me, was now keeping him propped up. If it wasn't there he'd still be flat on his back.

"Who else is here?" I asked.

His head was down, his chin like a leaky faucet. *Plop...plop...plop...* the blood was dripping. He wasn't answering.

"*Who else is here?*" I repeated.

"It's just me," he said finally. "Carter's up at school...the wife's in Palm Beach." He lifted his head. For the first time I saw the eyes of a man who maybe didn't have all the answers. "How'd you know I wasn't in the city?"

"The same way I'm holding this," I said, raising the folder that Foxx had given me. "But we'll get to that in a moment."

"Ten million," he said.

The guy had no shame. "Do you really think you can buy your way out of this?"

"Twenty."

"Insult me one more time and I swear I'll kill you."

"What do you want, then?"

"The truth," I said. "From the beginning."

"Carter was never in danger."

"Gee, I feel so much better now."

"Do you want to hear this or not?"

"You stole your painting back years ago. That wasn't enough?"

"No. The painting was about justice," he said. "What I wanted was revenge."

"No matter what the risk?"

"Controlling risk is what I do."

"How's that working out for you right about now?"

"I'm still going to get away with it," he said, "no matter how much you know."

"*Get away with it?* You arranged for the kidnapping of your son, and let the world think that he had killed himself."

"Stop with the morality play, will you? It's not your department."

"What about the gambling problem? Carter and those bets? Was that all made up, too?" I asked.

"Not all of it. In fact, that's what gave me the idea, the chance to finally pull this off after all these years. Carter forged that check from his mother, all right. Everything after that was my creation."

"You mean, your masterpiece."

"You gotta admit," he said. "It was no ordinary plan."

"So Carter, the painting—"

"He knew nothing about it. He still doesn't. But, yeah, his little gambling problem was real. He was reckless. Spoiled. A little kidnapping wasn't such a bad thing for him. A good wake-up call. Good for his character. Nice touch staging his return at his own funeral, don't you think?"

"You're sick."

"And you're just pissed because you got played," he said, rising to his feet.

I could feel my fist balling up again but there was no point. No matter how many times you knocked a guy like von Oehson on his ass, you could never knock the asshole out of him.

He was even cracking a smile as he continued. "*Pawn* really isn't the right word for you, though, is it? You were more like a very predictable bishop. Or maybe a knight. To be honest, I haven't played chess in years."

"Not with pieces, you mean."

"Hey, you made all your own moves," he said. "Each and every one was your decision. All I did was set up the board in just the right way."

"No. What you did is use me," I said.

"I use everybody, Dylan. That's what rich guys do. Welcome to planet Earth."

I stood there, staring at him. Glaring at him. Thinking about why he'd chosen me, how I truly was the right man for the job. He knew I'd say no when we first met, that I'd turn down his offer, so he made sure in advance that I'd end up saying yes.

He fed me just enough information, but never so much that I would catch on that he was leading me. I had to believe that I was always the smartest guy in the room. I'm the one, after all, who figured out the clue Carter had left in his father's office. I spotted the telescope facing inward toward the bookcase, which gave us Jade's fingerprint on the glass. How clever Carter had been, I thought, his putting it behind *The Glass Menagerie*.

But it wasn't Carter. It was never Carter. It was always his father.

Von Oehson knew I'd bring all my skills to bear and begin connecting those dots, one after the other.

But wait. One dot didn't make sense. Unless...

"Don't tell me that Grigoryev was in on this, too," I said. It didn't seem possible.

"Hell, no," said von Oehson. "I didn't know he was the one who ran the escort service. You weren't supposed to know, either. Or, at least, you weren't supposed to *need* to know. You moved even faster than I thought. Before I could point you in the direction of Brunetti, you got tangled up with a mad Russian."

I had a comeback for him, and I had more questions. A lot more questions. But it was late. Later than von Oehson even realized. There was more to this visit than telling him the jig was up.

So I cut to the end and the purpose of his elaborate plan, a payback that he had waited years to extract from the Hungarian government. Everything had to be just right, and it started with his finding the guy who could solve this mystery of his making. The disappearance of his son was the smokescreen. This was only about getting the Hungarians to buy back the Monet so he could not only hack their central bank to the tune of fifty billion dollars, but also conceal the transaction so it couldn't be traced. He even knew I'd figure out a way to switch the real Monet with a fake.

All in all, Mathias von Oehson had indeed painted a true masterpiece. And all in the name of revenge.

"Where's the money?" I asked.

He cracked another smile. It didn't matter that he was still bleeding and bruising right before my eyes. *"What money?"*

"Seriously? That's your answer?"

"Oh, relax, will you? Everyone made out who deserved to, including your husband's legal aid center. You know your world history. Are you really going to cry for Hungary? The only ones who got hurt were the ones who had it coming to them," he said.

"Funny you should say that."

"What does that mean?"

The time had come to wipe that smugness off his face.

It was time to show him the folder.

CHAPTER 91

"YOU HID THE MONEY once you stole it from them, but you couldn't hide the fact that it was gone," I said. "There's no way. We're talking fifty billion dollars."

"Or roughly the sum total of all their foreign investments," said von Oehson.

"What did you think was going to happen?"

"I'll tell you what *isn't* going to happen. There'll be no lawsuit, no police investigation, no going public with it. Nothing. They can't pin it on me."

"What about Brunetti?"

"First, the Hungarians would have to admit what they were engaged in. Last I checked, the EU and the rest of the world haven't changed their minds about the Nazis. Second, as far as wars go, do you really think they want one with a New York crime boss? If our own government has never been able to take him down, what makes you think that—"

Von Oehson's voice didn't merely taper off. It had stopped dead in its tracks.

Just like Frank Brunetti.

"Long-range rifle, one round, approximately a hundred yards as he walked out of his beloved restaurant to get into a limo this afternoon," I said, thrusting the eight-by-ten photo in front of von Oehson's face. It was a still frame—a screen grab, to be more precise—from the recording of the hit filmed through the scope of the gunman. That's how paid assassins verify their kills these days, by sending an encrypted video file. Just not encrypted enough, in this case. It was intercepted by MI6, who happened to be tracking large financial transfers between an arms dealer in Bahrain and a suspected terrorist cell in London. Collateral intelligence, as it's often called.

"This can't be real," said von Oehson. "It would've been all over the news. My phone would've lit up. I manage most of Frank's money."

"That explains the connection between the two of you."

He kept shaking his head. "You're trying to gaslight me."

Some people just don't trust anyone.

I reached into the folder, removing what amounted to a printed contact sheet from the intercepted recording. There it was, Brunetti's murder, frame by frame, the side of his head exploding and his beginning to fall to the pavement. The reason he never fell all the way was the same reason that the story had yet to break. One of his two henchmen caught him on his way down and shoved him into the limo, which immediately sped off.

Von Oehson grabbed the sheet from my hand, his eyes scanning left to right, back and forth. *Plop.* Another drop of blood rolled off his chin, catching one of the corners. "So there's a chance Frank's still alive," he said.

"No. The reason the world doesn't know yet about his death is that those under him know the repercussions. They're protecting their wallets. More important, they're trying to save their own asses. If anyone wanted to kill them, now would be the time. They've never been more vulnerable, which means they've also never been more dangerous."

"What are you saying?"

"It's what I'm asking," I said. "Who else in Frank's inner circle knew about your being involved?"

"No one."

"You can't know that for sure."

He understood what I meant. He could never be certain that Brunetti didn't tell anyone. "No one was ever in the room besides us," he said.

"What about calls?"

"What about them?"

"Did you ever discuss it over the phone?" I asked.

"Do I look that stupid?"

I pointed at the eight-by-ten of Brunetti getting his head blown off. "Funny. Frank once asked me that same question."

Point taken. "No. The few times it came up in a call we always talked in code," said von Oehson. "Anything important was discussed in person and in private. But, yeah, it's not impossible that he told someone."

"Which means it's possible they think it was you."

"*Who killed him?*"

"More like arranged to have him killed," I said. "Either way, same difference."

"Wait. You don't actually think that I—"

"No. We know it wasn't you. You clearly draw the line at kidnapping and grand larceny. The question is, what do the Hungarians know?"

"They shouldn't know anything," he said. "Not about me."

"That's why I'm here. To keep it that way."

"How?"

"For starters, getting you out of here," I said.

"Why would you need to do that?"

I had a good answer for him. But suddenly, somebody had an even better one.

CHAPTER 92

EVERYTHING WENT DARK ALL at once. The chandelier over-head in the foyer, the sconces along the walls, every single bulb around us inside the house and out. The power had been cut.

I reached for my Glock. I had Foxx to thank for that. I wouldn't have been carrying were it not for him. That was a deal breaker, he'd said. If I insisted on bringing in von Oehson on my own, then I absolutely had to be armed.

Of course, guns aren't of much use if you can't see what you're shooting at.

Von Oehson had his phone out before I could grab mine. He hit the flashlight.

I repeat, guns aren't of much use if you can't see what you're shooting at.

My head whipped left and right, my eyes desperately trying to adjust enough to make out any window in my line of sight. It was like Michael Corleone in his bedroom, when Kay asked about the draperies. Only she wanted to know why they were open. I was confirming that they were all closed. That's why the gunman wanted darkness. So he could see his target light up.

"GET DOWN!"

I dove at von Oehson, decking him once again. This time to save his life. I was in the air, two bursts slicing past my ears overhead. Long-range ammo makes the most sinister sound. It's like the devil blowing out your candles.

We both hit the ground. I spun, lunging for von Oehson's phone, which I'd knocked out of his hand. I killed the flash, caught my breath, and proceeded to give him the most obvious set of instructions I'd ever given anyone. "Stay here. Don't move!"

"The generator," he said. "It's going to kick in in a few seconds."

"No. It's not," I told him. This wasn't amateur hour.

I pushed myself up, slinging my back against the wall alongside the front door. The shots were so clean, the product of steady hands, that there was no sound of broken glass to follow. I had a living room to my left, another living room to my right. The rich are so damn redundant.

I guessed left, edging my way to take a look outside. Kneeling at the first window I came to, I pushed the curtain an inch to see what I expected to see. Nothing. Pitch blackness, no movement. But someone was sure as hell out there. Maybe even a couple of someones.

The sucker's gambit, otherwise known as trying to elicit fire to locate a shooter, is like randomly checking the coin return on a vending machine. It rarely, if ever, pays off, but you still do it anyway.

I held out my phone just below the window, snapping a curtain selfie with the flash on. Maybe the guy had a twitchy trigger finger.

But not this guy. I listened to the silence. There was no shot, no sound of anything. It was my move again.

Whoever was outside, we needed to keep him there until we had a plan. I aimed, shooting out one of the windows on the far side of the room, then turned and fired across the foyer at a window in the other living room. Two blasts, one message. We're armed. Enter at your peril.

Maybe a neighbor would dial the police, but it wasn't going to be us making the call. Not yet. Only if we had to. Scaring this guy away wouldn't make the problem disappear. Whether it was today, tomorrow, next week, or next year, it was either him or von Oehson. As for me, I didn't have a choice. I was along for the ride.

I turned back, edging along the wall. I had the plan now, what we had to do. We needed a vantage point. A balcony, if there was one. Otherwise, the attic. As close as we could get to a three-hundred-sixty-degree view of the property, with only one way to reach us from inside the house.

I reached the entrance to the foyer, whispering to von Oehson. "We need to get upstairs," I said. "The higher up, the better."

Only he didn't respond.

He was gone.

CHAPTER 93

YOU'VE GOT TO BE kidding me...

It was bad enough that there was a guy outside who wanted to kill him. Now there was someone inside the house who wanted to kill him, too. Me. If I could only find him.

Where the hell are you, Mathias? Where did you go? And why?

I knew my way to the kitchen from my first trip out to the house. I highly doubted he was just getting a snack, but it was as good of a place to start as any.

Crawling on my hands and knees, I made my way across the foyer and down a wide hallway. Before I even reached the kitchen I heard it. A low rumbling beneath me. An engine starting up. *Shit.*

I scrambled to my feet, blindly turning every door handle I could see in my path. Bathroom. *Damn.* Coat closet. *Damn.* Finally, the winner—the stairs to the basement. I started down, phone out front, the light from the screen allowing me just enough vision to see the steps.

What the hell is this?

The "basement" was only another hallway. Narrower, like a tunnel. The sound of the engine was getting louder, revving. I started to run. A light hit me square in the eyes. Two beams. Headlights. Von Oehson was making his getaway.

Over my dead body.

I'd bolted out from the end of the tunnel directly in front of his path, the curled nose of a Ferrari screeching to a halt only inches from my knees. It was a standoff in the middle of a massive garage with a car collection that would make even Jay Leno jealous. They must have been worth a hundred million dollars, with each car more exotic than the next. At least the ones I could make out against the glare.

Von Oehson lowered his window. I lowered my Glock.

"We both know you're not going to shoot me, Dylan."

"Maybe I'll just shoot out your tires instead."

His smug face returned. "You're going to run out of bullets before I run out of cars."

I truly hated this guy.

But there was no time to dwell. The piercing sound of the home alarm system suddenly kicked in; it was the one thing the gunman couldn't cut the power to. He was in the house. Great. *Peachy keen.*

"Get in or get out of the way," barked von Oehson, hitting a button to open a double-wide garage door that was up a ramp after a quick right turn behind me.

I stood there, still blocking his way, trying to think of another move to make. If there was one, it wasn't coming to me. Von Oehson revved the engine, forcing my hand. The gunman was surely on his way down now.

I got in.

We sped off before I could even close the door behind me, the tires screaming against the polished pavement as we turned up the ramp.

"Hold on," he said, as we hit the lip of the driveway, the

front wheels going airborne. They landed with a jolt, my head banging against the back of the seat before I could turn to look behind us.

"Where were the keys?" I asked, as we skidded out onto the street.

"What?"

"The keys!" I shouted. "Where do you keep the keys?"

Von Oehson could hear me, although he hadn't arrived yet at why I was asking. Suddenly, he realized. "Fuck!"

Yeah, that's what I was afraid of.

CHAPTER 94

THE KEYS WEREN'T LOCKED up. Some were hanging on the wall, others were literally sitting in the driver's seat. I was pretty sure that's what von Oehson was saying. It was still hard to hear him over the engine as we redlined past a twenty-five miles per hour speed limit sign. The trees, other houses, everything was a blur as we approached the end of the street. His right foot was nowhere near the brake. Stop sign? What stop sign?

Also, where the hell are we going?

That question got pushed to the back burner as I leaned forward to catch the angle of my side view mirror. "Here he comes," I said.

Von Oehson glanced over his shoulder. "Damn."

"What?"

"He took the Stradale," he said.

I knew my cars, but not all of them. I gave another look back, staring mostly at high beams. "Is that also a Ferrari?"

"Yep."

"What model did you say?"

"An SF90 Stradale."

"What model is this?" I asked.

"An 812 Superfast."

"Tell me that means it's faster."

"Nope."

Seriously? Not only were we being chased by one of von Oehson's own cars, it was an even faster one. This wasn't Ford versus Ferrari. This was Ferrari versus Ferrari.

"Look out!" I yelled.

There were two SUVs crossing in front of us at a four-way intersection. Von Oehson swerved but never slowed, threading the needle as he zipped between them. The only thing louder than their horns blaring at us was the sound of our would-be assassin slamming on his brakes.

"Turns!"

"What?" he asked.

"Turns! Start making turns!"

We'd bought ourselves a gap, a few seconds of spacing. Now it was all about sight lines and geometry. Right and left angles were our friends. Any straightaway was our enemy.

Von Oehson nodded. He got it. He'd also ponied up for a few Skip Barber Racing School lessons, apparently, because his turns were near flawless. Trail brake, late apex, full throttle. One corner after another and then another. Lather, rinse, repeat.

We were losing the guy. But that wasn't the same as having lost him.

I looked at von Oehson when he bypassed the next turn, continuing straight. *"What are you doing?"*

"There's a road up ahead on the right that leads to I-95," he said, with another glance at his rearview mirror. "He's nowhere in sight."

"We need to keep it that way. Hold off on the turnpike."

"Why? Now's our chance. We can shake him for good."

Von Oehson was famous for being able to see around corners.

310 · JAMES PATTERSON

But it was only a figure of speech. Before I could explain, he took the right turn. It was definitely the wrong one.

"Shit!" he said immediately.

Exactly. What makes a professional killer good at his job? He thinks like his prey. Those same high beams that had been right on our tail were now staring us right in the face. He was about fifty yards away, idling right smack in the middle of the road. Waiting.

Von Oehson instinctively reached to put us in reverse but he was wrong again. I grabbed his wrist to stop him.

"What the hell are you doing?"

"It's what *you're* going to do," I said. "Gun it!"

CHAPTER 95

THIS WASN'T THE MOVIES. I wasn't Thelma. He wasn't Louise.
If this was a death pact, he needed a harder sell from me. And fast.

"The guy came here to kill you, but he's not going to kill
himself to do it," I said.

I watched the light flick on behind von Oehson's eyes. He
slapped both hands back on the wheel, squeezing them until his
knuckles flashed white. Then he gunned it.

They both gunned it.

We were two Ferraris barreling straight for each other, going
from zero to sixty in two-point-something seconds, which meant
I had approximately a millisecond to tell von Oehson the one
other thing he desperately needed to do. "Duck!"

I knew what was coming at us besides 986 horsepower. Bullets.
Lots of them. No sooner did we peel out than they started flying,
shards of glass from the windshield raining over us from where
our heads were supposed to be. I had one hand on the steering
wheel, making sure both of von Oehson's hands stayed the course.
The rest boiled down to an educated guess, a simple calculation
born from studying human psychology for more than half my life.
Left or right? In what direction was the guy going to bail at the last

possible second? Call it Reinhart's Rule for a Million-Dollar Game of Ferrari Chicken. *Steering wheel on the left, bail to the left.*

Which meant he was coming right by me.

Unless, of course, I was wrong about everything. It was known to happen from time to time. Maybe this game would have no winners. In which case, von Oehson's insurance premiums were about to seriously spike.

I powered down my window. Listen for a moment, I told myself. *Hear it. Feel it. Just react.*

The sound that a Ferrari SF90 Stradale makes when swerving on a dime at more than one hundred miles per hour turns out to be no sound at all. It's like a black hole, sucking in all the air around it so nothing gets out. A silent scream.

I turned and fired. There was little aiming. Just keep it low and keep 'em coming. I had thirteen rounds left in the fifteen-round KCI mag in my G19, and I was unloading as many as I could. They were 9mm lottery tickets. Only one had to hit. *C'mon!*

Turns out, the sound that a 315/30ZR20 rear tire spinning at twenty-two revolutions per second makes when blowing out is anything but silent. The blistering *pop!* was matched only by the violent twisting and smashing of metal, carbon fiber, and glass against the pavement as the Stradale rolled over and over until it landed on some other Darien rich guy's lawn.

Von Oehson straightened back up over the steering wheel. His body was shaking, probably from the relief and shock of still being alive. What he wasn't doing, however, was stopping.

"Brakes!" I yelled. They weren't locked, but he was. It was more like a daze. He wasn't blinking. "BRAKES!"

He snapped out of it. The car screeched to a halt, the smell of burning rubber rushing through my open window as I threw my hands against the dash lest I go flying through our shot-up windshield.

"Holy shit!" said von Oehson.

That about summed it up. "Yep. Holy shit," I said. I sounded calm but my heart was still beating out of my chest.

"Wait. What are you doing?" he asked.

I was opening the door. "What do you think I'm doing? Checking on him."

"*Checking on him?* The guy was trying to kill us."

"He was only trying to kill you," I said. "I was just collateral damage."

"What if he's still alive?"

"We keep him alive."

"Why the hell would you want to help him?" he asked.

"Because right now that's the only way to help you."

CHAPTER 96

THERE WAS NO TIME to explain why. That much, in the moment, von Oehson could figure out.

I had him quickly turn the car around but not get much closer. "Engine off, lights on," I said. "Not the brights, though."

"Got it."

"Now the keys."

"You serious?"

But we both knew he'd already tried to bail on me earlier. Fool me once. I held out my hand. "And keep the doors locked," I said.

He reluctantly surrendered the keys and hit the lock button behind me. Off I went, gun drawn, my eyes locked on the flipped-over Stradale as thick smoke, black as the night, billowed from its undercarriage. My lungs could feel the burn with every breath, every step. Damn, it was cold.

With von Oehson's lights at my back I was already playing this all out in my head. I'd be giving Landon Foxx an early Christmas present. The gift would be wrapped in gauze and bandages, and maybe even placed in a medically induced coma for twenty-four hours to prevent further swelling around his brain (or something like that), but he would still be alive. And if he remained alive, what was inside that brain would be the gift that kept on giving.

Dollars to donuts, the guy behind the wheel—now presumably *upside down* behind the wheel—was the one who killed Frank Brunetti. He was a contract killer, and clearly big-time if he'd been hired by a foreign government. There was no telling how many other hits he'd done or for whom. That is, until Foxx and some special guests fresh up from Langley got their hands on him. I could picture this guy turning Chatty Cathy real fast, telling the agency everything.

And all I'd be asking for in return from Foxx was a clean-up job rivaling the *Exxon Valdez*. No big deal. Just make the local police pretend as if this night never happened, put von Oehson and his family in protective custody, and then convince the prime minister of Hungary and his intelligence arm to let bygones be bygones once they get their fifty billion back from von Oehson. After all, it was Christmas. The season of giving. Why not some forgiving, as well?

I was twenty feet from the tail of the car. There was still no movement. I started to angle around, stepping sideways, my elbows locked. A few more steps and I'd have a view of him.

"If you can hear me, place your hands at ten and two on the steering wheel," I said. "You've got three seconds to do it."

Only I wasn't counting to three. The exact moment when someone is making up their mind is the exact moment they're most vulnerable.

Springing to my left, I ducked into a crouch and stared down the barrel of my Glock straight into the driver's-side window. There were no hands on the wheel.

"Can you hear me?" I repeated.

If he could, he wasn't saying. Dead, unconscious, or setting a trap—it was one of those three. I saw the car flip. I saw it flip again and again. The force of the impact. He wasn't answering because he couldn't. That was my bet. It just wasn't a sure bet.

I got up from my crouch, slowly walking toward the car. I'd given him his chance, twice over. If he could move, he could talk. In other words, I was shooting on first movement.

But there was no movement. I edged up close to the car, peering in through the smashed-out window on the driver's side.

He wasn't dead.

He wasn't unconscious.

He wasn't there.

My head whipped back up the street. I was staring into head-lights, but I could see just enough of the silhouette, as the panic shot through me like lightning.

He was heading right for von Oehson.

CHAPTER 97

HE WAS FIVE FEET from the car, and I was fifty yards away. I might as well have been on Jupiter.

I burst into a sprint, shouting as loud as I could. "DROP IT!" Over and over. "DROP IT! DROP IT!"

He was still just a silhouette, but the arm was outstretched, right at the window. Right at von Oehson. I was a split second from firing.

I was a split second from making the biggest mistake of my life.

Von Oehson's door suddenly opened. He was stepping out of the car. That silhouette, the other person, wasn't anyone who wanted to kill him.

"It's fine," von Oehson shouted back to me. "It's my neighbor. It's okay."

My relief lasted for roughly another split second.

"GET BACK IN THE CAR!" I yelled. Von Oehson was dead wrong. It wasn't okay. *He* wasn't okay.

He also wasn't listening to me. "It's my neighbor!" he shouted again.

Now I pulled the trigger. I aimed straight in the air over my head without breaking stride, an extra exclamation point on the fact that I didn't care if it was Jesus himself he was talking to. The gunman trying to kill von Oehson wasn't lying dead or dying in the other Ferrari. He'd either run off or taken cover nearby. If it was the latter, he was about to have another chance to get the job done.

My shot echoed up and down the street, scattering any and all neighbors—including the one with von Oehson—who had ventured outside their multimillion-dollar homes after the sound of the crash to see what the hell had happened. I was fine hearing their panicked screams so long as what I didn't hear was another shot in the wake of mine. Amid all the chaos, von Oehson had basically frozen. Confused. Bewildered.

But worst of all, a sitting duck.

I closed the gap between us, slowing down only enough so I wouldn't completely knock von Oehson over while shoving him back in his car. Slamming the door shut behind him, I nearly clipped a few of his fingers.

Now I was the sitting duck. Only it didn't feel like it.

You ran off, didn't you? Or, more like, limped off. There's no way you survived that crash unscathed.

I did a quick three-sixty, taking one last look around before jumping into the shotgun seat.

"What the fuck?" said von Oehson.

"DRIVE!"

He was finally listening to me. He popped the engine start and gunned it, shifting from first to third in a matter of seconds. By fourth gear, when we were at least a mile safely away, I told him to pull over. Then I enlightened him.

The guy who wanted him dead was alive. Maybe not alive *and* well, but alive. What's more, we had to get out of there before the police showed up. Von Oehson nodded. Never did a simple nod convey so much understanding. The man who never wanted to involve the police in the first place didn't need any further explanation.

"What did you tell your neighbor?" I asked.

"That I came home, heard a noise in the garage. Someone was stealing one of my cars so I was chasing him. Not bad, right?"

In my mind I gave him an A for effort and an F for relevance. As in, at this point it didn't matter what the ef he told his neighbor. "Perfect," I said. "Nicely done."

"Of course, he's no doubt wondering right now who the hell you were, why you were with me, and why you had a gun. I'm not sure how I'm going to explain that." Von Oehson blinked a few times as if rebooting his brain. "Shit. That's the least of our problems, isn't it?"

"Yep."

"So I take it we're not heading back to my house?"

"Nope."

"What if we just made a quick stop so I could—"

"Whatever you think you need or want to do there, you don't," I said.

"Where to, then?" he asked.

"You know that highway you wanted to get to so badly?"

"Are we heading south or north?"

"South," I said. Just like this entire night so far. "Also, you're done driving."

"Why?"

"Because you won't be able to reach the steering wheel."

He, of course, had no idea what I meant by that. I stepped out of the car and walked back to the trunk, waiting a few seconds for him to get the hint and meet me there. Once he did, all it took from me was the slightest tilt of my head.

"Oh, hell, no," he said.

"Hell, yes. And this isn't a negotiation."

"I'll freeze to death."

"No, you won't," I said. "Your own carbon dioxide will keep you nice and cozy."

"You mean, if it doesn't kill me first."

"Nah, that would take at least ninety minutes. Where we're heading, it should take only an hour."

Von Oehson hemmed and hawed but knew he had absolutely zero leverage in the moment. He climbed in his trunk, curling up to the size of a Ferrari 812 Superfast's maximum storage capacity. Roughly two golf bags.

"An hour. That's what you said, right?"

"Yep. One hour. That's what I said." I reached up, grabbing the lip of the trunk lid with both hands. "Now you just have to pray we don't hit any traffic."

Slam.

CHAPTER 98

IT WASN'T MUCH WARMER for me driving ninety on the highway with a shot-up windshield. The feeling was like being in an Arctic wind tunnel. So much for visibility, too. With the heat cranking I kept having to crane my neck to see around the shattered glass and bullet holes. Every oncoming headlight was like a blinding kaleidoscope.

As he'd done many times before, Julian greeted me at his "office" entrance, a.k.a. the steel door that was ten feet behind another steel door that was past the security gate to a warehouse for a medical supply company in Fort Lee, New Jersey, that didn't actually exist.

"Here you go," he said, tossing me the pillowcase that I'd asked for via text.

"And here *you* go," I said, tossing him the car keys.

"What's this?"

"Remember what you asked for when you met Annabelle and me at the zoo? How I could one day repay you for all your help?"

I watched as Julian stared at the iconic logo on the keys, the black stallion up on its hind legs against a bright-yellow backdrop. "*A Ferrari?*"

"Follow me," I said. We walked to the abandoned parking lot in front of the warehouse. "She's going to need a new windshield, as you can see. Other than that she's in great shape. Runs like a dream."

Julian scratched his beard, chuckling. "Okay, whose car is this really?"

"I told you, it's yours. But since you asked, allow me to introduce you to its previous owner," I said, popping the trunk. "Julian, meet Mathias von Oehson."

Von Oehson was curled up in the fetal position, shivering. This was the worst night of his life, and my job was to make him feel it to the bone. There was a lot to do and very little time to do it, which meant we needed his full cooperation. Sometimes you have to get mean to get someone else to play nice.

"Good to meet you," said Julian, extending a helping hand to hoist him out of the trunk.

"Mathias, this is Julian. Julian is the man who's not only going to keep you alive, but also keep you out of jail," I said. "In return, you're graciously giving him this Ferrari. Deal?"

"Deal," von Oehson answered, rather humbly.

He was out of the trunk but still shivering. Before he could look around I threw the pillowcase over his head. "It's only until we get inside," I assured him.

"What is this?" he asked. "Where are we?"

"We're nowhere," I said. "This place doesn't exist. Understand?"

"Yeah, I understand."

"Good answer. Because until this whole shit show of yours is finally resolved, nowhere is your new home."

CHAPTER 99

THE STRATEGY, ONCE INSIDE Julian's office, was divide and conquer. There's a reason why it's the most dog-eared chapter in Machiavelli's *Art of War*.

Julian was in charge of banking. He needed von Oehson for that. I was in charge of damage control. For that, I needed Landon Foxx.

"Call him on the blender," said Julian, pointing me toward his communications room.

The blender was how you reach the CIA's New York section chief on his personal cell in the middle of the night without ever having to worry that anyone was listening in. The dedicated satellite phone digitized the conversation on both ends, scrambling every word in transit more than a thousand times a second. Can't be hacked, Julian has always maintained. He ought to know. He invented it.

So the good news was that I was talking to Foxx on the most secure line in the world. The bad news was what I had to tell him: *the bad news.*

No one likes a cover-up, but at least the agency is uniquely qualified to do the job. Only this couldn't be the agency. Not officially. It had to be Foxx. He had to convince a local police chief in Darien that the Ferrari SF90 Stradale that was lying flipped over and totaled on one of his residents' front lawns was a matter of national security and should be treated as if it never happened. This in a town where everybody knows everybody's business. Also, never mind the report of gunshots. As for the neighbor—probably plural—who saw von Oehson on the scene, best if we stay with the stolen-car story that von Oehson already told. Planting an item in the police blotter of the local paper ought to do the trick.

You got all that? Good. Because that's the easy part…

I needed Foxx to move on from a small town in Connecticut to an entire European country. Hungary, clearly bent on revenge in the aftermath, had taken out a contract on both von Oehson and Frank Brunetti. They were currently batting one for two, and surely looking for another crack at von Oehson. That is, unless Foxx could convince our NATO ally that such a move was seriously not in their best interest. Giving him a better chance to do that was what Julian was working on in the next room.

"When will he be done?" asked Foxx.

"I'm not sure yet," I said. "I'll call you back as soon as he is, though."

"That won't be necessary."

"Why?"

"Because I'll already know by then," he said.

Of course. I'd originally gone to von Oehson's house to bring him in, but Foxx was hardly waiting for that to happen. Time was of the essence, and as much as it made sense for me to be the go-between, Foxx knew there was no scenario in which von Oehson could keep the fifty billion. Any negotiating with Hungarian intelligence was predicated on the country's getting its money back. Then, and only then, could Foxx focus on the only thing that mattered to him—keeping this whole clusterfuck from going public.

One way or the other, Landon Foxx was going to get Mathias von Oehson to cooperate. I was one way, and the other was any host of possibilities, although Foxx ultimately putting a gun to von Oehson's head was undoubtedly near the top of the list.

In short, Foxx was already neck-deep in talks with Hungarian intelligence. He'd just told me as much without having to say the words. Classic Foxx.

"I understand," I said.

"You always do, Reinhart."

I never liked when Foxx paid me a compliment, few and far between as they were. It almost always meant he was hiding something from me.

Sure enough, he was.

CHAPTER 100

MAYBE THE ONLY THING harder than stealing fifty billion dollars by way of a thousand different simultaneous transactions involving at least two dozen different currency conversions across five continents and a multitude of shell corporations is trying to do it all in reverse in one night. Even the man who masterminded the idea was at a loss.

"This is like trying to put the toothpaste back in the tube," said von Oehson.

Of course, being called a genius on the cover of *Fortune* magazine is one thing. Actually being a genius is another.

"You cut the tail end of the tube open, put the toothpaste in from there, and fold it back over a few times," said Julian, not even bothering to look up from his keyboard. He truly was one of a kind.

My laughing at Julian's response was the only sound I'd made in the hour since I took a seat on the couch along the wall in his office next to the wing of the old Fokker Eindecker airplane wing that doubled as his desk. Even von Oehson, a man who owned almost every toy imaginable, was in awe of it. Sitting in an armchair in front of it, he kept staring at the rows of rivets against the chrome-molybdenum steel with sheer envy.

So this was the banking side of things. I'd covered damage control with Foxx, including protection for Carter up at Yale. I figured von Oehson's wife was well out of harm's way down in Palm Beach. Foxx came through for Carter via an operative who happened to be at Naval Submarine Base New London for a training exercise. He was promptly dispatched to nearby New Haven and the Old Campus dorm where Carter lived on the second floor.

As for keeping Mathias alive, returning all the money didn't guarantee anything. The only thing for sure was that not returning the money meant Foxx would have no chance of getting Hungarian intelligence to call off the hit. If there was a perverse irony, it was that Foxx and the agency would be all too willing to overlook Frank Brunetti's assassination. The multiple attempts by the FBI and IRS to take out Brunetti legally in court for more than a decade had been a waste of time and human resources. No one with a badge was ever going to shed a tear for the guy.

The proposition boiled down to this. You got your money back, Hungary, as well as your Monet (or, at least, you think you do). We'll forgive you for Brunetti if you let things slide with von Oehson. Let the man and his family be. Do we have a deal, Budapest?

After going four pods deep on Julian's Keurig, and with the sun beginning to rise, I watched as the very last of the fifty billion made its way back to the balance sheet of the central bank of Hungary.

"Done and dusted," announced Julian.

"I'll let Foxx know," I said, standing.

I was about to head into the next room to call him on the blender. Von Oehson had long since fallen asleep in his chair.

I knew Foxx had told me that he'd find out courtesy of the Hungarians, but letting him know personally still felt like the right thing to do.

"No need to call him," said Julian.

I knew that, but how did he know that?

"Why not?" I asked.

"Because he'll be here in a couple of minutes."

CHAPTER 101

I DIDN'T NEED TO ask why. I knew why. I was sure of it.

Foxx couldn't yet guarantee von Oehson's safety. The Hungarians were getting their money back, but they weren't fully ready to give a pass to the man who so brazenly stole it from them. Maybe they were trying to leverage the situation, bargain for some other concession. Maybe the hard feelings needed a little more time to soften. Whatever the exact reason, they weren't officially calling off the hit just yet. International diplomacy always happens at the cross section of power and patience.

That was the reason for Foxx's visit. It was all about von Oehson. Like it or not—and for sure Foxx didn't like it—he'd inherited a billionaire for a day or two. This still wasn't official agency business. He wasn't about to arrange a pickup. There'd be no delegating in the dark of night. He would see to this personally. That's how Foxx rolled. That's why he was coming. Yep. I was sure of it, all right.

And I was wrong.

"Where is he?" asked Foxx, the second he walked through the last of Julian's security doors. Of course he'd been there before.

"He's in my office," answered Julian. At least, I think that's

330 · JAMES PATTERSON

what he said. I was too busy staring at the folder in Foxx's hand. Immediately I had a bad feeling. His folders hadn't been boding well for me.

"Let's talk anywhere but there, then," said Foxx. Whatever this was, it wasn't for von Oehson's ears.

We ended up in Julian's communications room, if for no other reason than the walls were lined with sound dampeners. Julian closed the door behind us.

"What's going on?" I asked. "They still want von Oehson dead?"

"I'm sure they still do, but it's not going to happen," said Foxx. "Contract halted."

The hit was off. "That's good news," I said.

"It is. Unfortunately, there's a hitch."

"What is it?" I asked.

"It's you," said Foxx.

Of all things, Julian laughed. He couldn't help it, and I couldn't blame him. It sounded crazy. It was crazy. It didn't make sense.

"You're saying the Hungarians have a contract out on me?"

"No, that's not it," said Foxx. "They're cooperating. In fact, they claimed they offered the hit man the back-end payment on von Oehson even though the job was botched."

Now it was starting to make sense. Contract killers can get a little touchy when someone tries to kill them. "So you're telling me it's personal," I said.

"Apparently very personal," answered Foxx. "This guy wants you dead. That's the prevailing theory."

"Based on?"

"He initially went dark, didn't respond to his handler. When he finally did, he turned down the back-end offer. A significant sum, I was told."

"You said it yourself, he botched the hit. He's a pro," I said. "He's not going to take the money."

"Exactly."

"So why the theory about me?"

"This is why," said Foxx, reaching into the folder.

The picture was a screen capture from a security camera. Black and white, a little grainy, but it was clear enough. The time stamp was only a couple of hours earlier. I didn't recognize the man, but I sure knew where he was standing. It was the lobby of my apartment building. As if I needed any more proof, there were cuts and bruises on his face. The car wreck variety. "How did you ID him?" I asked.

"I told you," said Foxx. "The Hungarians are cooperating."

"They sold the guy out?"

"They provided a photo but not a name. I ran him with facial rec through every intel file we have. Nothing. The guy's a ghost."

I stared again at the picture. "But at least with his face—"

"Right," said Foxx. Big Brother's always watching. "I was able to track most of his movements since he arrived in the country. He landed at JFK a couple of days ago, is staying at the Dominick downtown, and took a quick field trip upstate to procure the rifle and scope that killed Brunetti, as well as a few Glocks."

"A purchase?" I asked. Gun laws in this country have more loopholes than a piece of knitting, but buying with a fake ID still remains a stretch.

"No. A robbery. Scared the shit out of the gun shop owner, too. Toyed with him. He likes to play games."

So that's what Foxx had, and it was more than enough. I didn't need a name to know that this guy didn't come to my apartment to call a truce.

"If he wants me dead, I suggest we give him a shot," I said.

Foxx nodded. "I figured you'd say that."

Which was all he needed to say in return. Foxx hadn't come for von Oehson. He'd come for me.

"It's not worth it," said Julian, chiming in for the first time. He always knows how to pick his spots. "Go be with your family. Go see your little girl."

In other words, go into hiding. Let Foxx dispatch an operative or two to track this guy down.

"Fine," I said. Still, there was one last thing I needed to know. I couldn't imagine that this guy got a good-enough look at me at von Oehson's house in Darien. Even if he had, how was he able to ID me?

I was about to ask Foxx when it suddenly hit me. I already knew the answer. It explained why the Hungarians were cooperating. It wasn't from the goodness of their hearts. It was more like guilt.

"What is it?" asked Foxx. He could read it all over my face. Panic.

I turned to Julian. "If he knows who I am," I said, my voice trailing off.

It only took Julian a heartbeat. "Oh, shit. Then he knows who *she* is, too," he said.

Elizabeth.

CHAPTER 102

THE HUNGARIANS DIDN'T LIKE getting played by Elizabeth and me. Not enough to kill us, but more than enough to make sure we didn't interfere with the killing of Brunetti and von Oehson. Security stills from our visit to the consulate had been shared with their hired gun. Now they were being leveraged in the worst possible way.

C'mon, c'mon, c'mon, Lizzie... pick up! Answer the phone!

After five rings I got her voicemail. Instead of leaving a message I hung up and immediately called again. Five more rings that felt like a lifetime. "Call me as soon as possible," I said after the beep.

"Maybe she's still asleep," said Foxx, looking at his watch. "It's only six-thirty."

"Only if it was Sunday," I said. "She's up. She's definitely up."

Julian looked at me. He could see my panic growing by the second. "What do you want to do?"

No sooner did he ask than my phone rang. It was Elizabeth.

"Hey, sorry," she said. "I was just pulling out some laundry from the dryer. It's early. What's up?"

"Are you on speaker?" I asked. She hates when people put her on speakerphone. Even more than I do.

"Yeah, I know. Do you mind? I just want to fold these sheets before they start to wrinkle."

"No, that's fine," I said. "I need to talk to you, though."

"I can fold and talk at the same time, Dylan."

"Not over the phone."

"What's wrong?"

"I need to tell you in person."

"Okay. How about lunch?"

The last thing I wanted to do was scare the hell out of her. I just needed to get over to her place as fast as possible. I could explain everything when I got there.

"It can't wait until then," I said. "I'm going to come over now, okay?"

"No, it's not okay. What's going on?"

I wasn't so much scaring her. Pissing her off was more like it. "Frank Brunetti's dead," I said. Silence. She didn't respond. She didn't say anything. "Are you there?"

"I'm here," she said.

"It happened yesterday. It's not public yet."

"How is it not public?"

"That's a longer story. But last night someone also tried to kill von Oehson. I was with him at the time."

Again, she didn't say anything. "Are you okay?" I asked.

"What?"

"I said, are you okay?"

"Yeah. I'm just taking it all in."

It was a lot for any time of day, let alone first thing in the morning. Still, that was only the half of it.

"Listen, there's more," I said. "But not over the phone, okay? Don't go anywhere, I'll be there in about a half hour."

"All right, sounds good. I'll see you then."

"Are you sure you're okay?" I asked. "Besides everything I just told you?"

"Of course I'm sure. I mean, yeah, besides what you just told me," she said. "Everything's peachy keen."

CHAPTER 103

FOR THE LIFE OF me—literally—I didn't know how she did it. Keeping her cool. The composure. Waiting for exactly the right moment to tip me off without giving herself away. Or, at least, that's what I was hoping.

Did he catch on? Did he figure it out?

Either way, I was walking into an ambush. There was no other choice. No path around it. He had Elizabeth. He got to her so he could get to me, and I was about to deliver myself on a silver platter. There would be no negotiation. Any chance for that had come and gone. When pushed to the brink, all that remains is your most primal instinct.

Kill or be killed.

Can I help you? no one asked.

The security provided by a doorman is only as good as the size of the building. When there are hundreds of apartments, there's no checking the IDs of everyone coming through the revolving doors. There's no waiting to be buzzed up. Just walk through the lobby like you live there, and no one says a word. I always told Elizabeth how I thought that arrangement was a little risky, given her line of work. Of course, it was nowhere near as risky as her line of work itself. "Besides, I like my place," she'd often say. "It gets great light."

She lives on the twenty-third floor. It's the corner apartment. The living room faces east.

I stepped off the elevator and headed left, all the way to the end of the hallway. With my back against the wall next to her door, I reached out and knocked with my left hand. I shoot with my right.

There was no response, no sounds of approaching footsteps. I knocked again, waiting.

"It's open," came her voice, calling out.

One, she was nowhere near the door. Two, she would've never just left it open for me. Three, that's the number I was counting to in my head. One, two, three . . .

I flung the door open as hard as I could from the side, hoping to draw his fire. He might have been a pro, but reflexes are often just that. Sure enough, he squeezed off two shots through a suppressor on movement alone, the bullets piercing the hallway wall opposite the door at roughly chest and head high. Immediately, I swung around, coming in low, crouched behind the barrel of my gun. All I was looking for was a barrel pointed back at me.

What I got instead, what I saw, was his gun pressed tight against Elizabeth's head.

He had her in a choke hold, her body blocking his. I had no shot, and he knew it. He was twenty feet away, standing in the middle of her living room with the blinds closed, and even though I could barely see his face, I could tell that he was smiling. He was in charge.

"Drop it," he said.

"You first," I said back.

Just because he was in charge didn't mean I was going to make it easy for him.

338 · JAMES PATTERSON

He jammed the end of the silencer hard, grinding it into Elizabeth's temple. She winced from the pain. "I'm not going to tell you again," he said. *"Drop it."*

"Don't you do it," Elizabeth pleaded with me. "Don't you dare."

But it was my only move. This was the play. "As soon as you let her go is when I lay it down," I said. "You can kill me as many times as you want, but only after you let her go."

Sometimes you have to say the quiet part out loud, but this wasn't one of those times. He already knew. He couldn't shoot us both. If he killed her, I was killing him. But he didn't have to tell me the flip side, either. Someone had to go first in this stalemate, and that someone was me.

Slowly, I lowered my arm as I kneeled to the ground. I could see the tears falling from Elizabeth's eyes. "No," she said. *"Nooooo."*

I wanted to tell her that everything was going to be okay, but that was a promise I wasn't sure I could keep.

I didn't want my last words to her to be a lie.

CHAPTER 104

I RESTED MY GUN on the floor. My arm was outstretched, but my fingers weren't letting go of the gun just yet.

He could shoot me first, but he had no guarantee I wouldn't fire back. I knew Elizabeth would do her part to give me a target. I think he knew it, too.

"Was it worth it?" he asked.

I understood exactly what he meant, but this was about buying any time that I could. He was still holding Elizabeth, using her as a shield. The barrel of that suppressor was still pressed against her head. "Was what worth it?"

"Dying for some asshole billionaire."

"I could ask the same of you," I said. "Sorry about the flat tire."

I watched as his smile, what I could see of it, widened. Still, as he shifted his feet I could tell he was suffering from more than mere cuts and bruises. He was pretty banged up. He nodded. "The things we do for money, huh?"

"I promise you I was getting paid more," I said.

That tested his smile. He tightened his choke hold on Elizabeth, her head snapping back. "Yeah, that was a pretty good shot," he said. "Hitting my tire at that speed?"

"Just lucky, I guess."

"Do you think you can do it again? Get that lucky?"

"What did you have in mind?" I asked.

"I'll bet you all the money you got paid that you can't get off a shot before I put one between your eyes."

I remembered what Foxx had told me. *He likes to play games.*

Most men are mountains of confidence built to conceal insecurity at their core. But sometimes the core is just as cocky. There was no tricking this guy. I couldn't distract him with a gym coupon in my wallet. Nor could I distract him with insults, get him angry enough so as to lose his cool and then his focus. But what I did have was what he'd already revealed. Him and me? This was extremely personal. Because I'd already outplayed him once, he wanted the chance to return the favor.

Pride goeth before a fall.

I didn't wait to hear the rules of his game. I gave him my own. One, in particular, I was sure he'd like. I would do what he never thought I would do.

I let go of my gun.

Elizabeth watched helplessly as I pulled back my arm, my hand at least two feet from the trigger.

"Your turn," I said.

He never hesitated. He threw Elizabeth to the ground, whipping his arm at me with his elbow locked. He had me dead to rights.

"Right back atcha," he said.

It was my move. That's what made it a game. He wouldn't shoot until I reached for my gun.

I looked at Elizabeth. She looked back at me. I could see it on her face. For the first time she was realizing there was something a little different about me. All things considered, who could blame her for not noticing until now?

Finally I could promise her that everything was going to be okay. Only I didn't have to say a word. All I had to do was wink from behind my new glasses.

She lives on the twenty-third floor. It's the corner apartment. The living room faces east.

Fire away, boys.

CHAPTER 105

IT TOOK LESS THAN a second. The blinds barely even moved. More important, his trigger finger never moved at all.

He dropped to the floor in a shower of blood. Foxx took out his heart, the .224 Valkyrie cartridge entering through the back a few inches below the clavicle. As for exactly where on the head Julian's jacketed hollow point fired from his Bergara B-14 hit, the answer was *somewhere*. Suffice it to say, there wasn't much left of the guy's head for the coroner to make any determination.

Not that an actual coroner would ever get anywhere near the body. Or the police, for that matter. After Foxx and Julian took off their thermal headsets, which had a sync feed to my glasses, they packed up their rifles and vacated the otherwise unoccupied apartment on the twenty-third floor of the building across the street. The super had let them in after Foxx made a couple of calls. As for the cleanup crew, they were on standby.

Ninety-nine out of a hundred times, when you see a van for a carpet-cleaning company driving around town, it's actually a carpet-cleaning company. But that time? The one that pulled up in front of Elizabeth's building less than thirty minutes after the shooting? That was no carpet-cleaning company.

Although they did roll up Elizabeth's living room rug to carry out the body.

His alias was Dr. Hans Kestler. He had an American passport, a Social Security number, even an Uber account. As for his real name, or anything else about him that was true—those details would take some additional digging. People in his profession spend their lifetime concealing their identity with layers of forged documents, misdirection, and a tenacious dedication to picking up every bread crumb behind them that they might ever drop. Eventually we'd find out more, and for Foxx's sake, I was hoping the information might in some way help with an unsolved file or two down in Langley. Until then, it was a classic case of the contract killer's credo. You die just like you live—as if you never existed.

Meanwhile.

The four of us were sitting at Elizabeth's kitchen table once the cleaners had left. She'd made a pot of coffee, and we were all partaking. "Cream or sugar?" she asked.

"How about some whiskey?"

That, of course, was Julian. It was also one of the best ideas he'd ever had. As fast as you can say Jack Daniel's, the four of us were drinking coffee and whiskey. Never mind that it wasn't even nine a.m. yet. We'd earned it.

"What do you want to do about von Oehson?" I asked Foxx.

He reached for a little more Jack to add to his mug. "Well, let's see," he said. "The guy stole fifty billion dollars from— technically—an ally of the United States, and jeopardized our relationship with their intelligence agency while we scrambled to get them their money back without creating the top story of every newscast in the civilized world. He nearly got you killed, more than a couple of times, and forced me to risk getting my ass hauled before a congressional oversight committee in order to save his ass and yours. And don't get me started about the headache that Frank Brunetti's death creates, no matter how Machiavellian we might all be feeling about that. Personally, I have about a dozen different ideas about Mathias von Oehson suffering an unfortunate accident while deep-sea diving or helicopter skiing or whatever it is that filthy rich guys are doing these days for leisure. But I know that look on your face, Reinhart. You've got an idea or two of your own."

"As a matter of fact, I do," I said.

CHAPTER 106

MY FIRST STOP WAS city hall for a sit-down with the Honorable Edward "Edso" Deacon to thank him for giving me the cover I needed to borrow Elizabeth from her boss, Evan Pritchard, and the Field Unit within the Joint Terrorism Task Force.

"I really pissed Pritch off, keeping him in the dark like that," said the mayor, before breaking into a laugh. He and Pritchard had had their run-ins in the past. "Trust me, I'm the one who should be thanking you."

"All the same, I want to express my gratitude," I said.

"You mean, by explaining why you needed the favor from me in the first place?"

"Not exactly, but I promise you're going to like this."

"Okay," he said, making a show of putting his feet up on his desk. "What are you giving me?"

"It's what you're giving Mathias von Oehson," I said. "A key to the city."

Deacon squinted. "That sounds an awful lot like you're asking me for another favor, Dylan."

"Not after I tell you why," I said.

My next stop, after city hall, was the last place I'd ever expect to find Allen Grimes during a workday. That is, actually at work. But there he was, just as his assistant, Vanessa, had told me, sitting in his office on the editorial floor of the *New York Gazette* building in Midtown. "I know," said Vanessa, when I called looking for him. "I'm just as surprised he's here as you are."

But maybe not as surprised as Grimes himself when I shut the door to his office behind me and told him why I was paying him a visit. I had not one, but two scoops for him.

"Frank Brunetti is dead," I said.

"*What?*"

"He was killed outside his restaurant yesterday afternoon as he was getting into his limo. One shot to his head from a long-range rifle. The triggerman was a contract killer. He's now dead, too."

Grimes was staring at me, stunned, until finally it occurred to him that he was a reporter. He frantically began searching the drawers of his desk. "Wait, wait, wait..."

"Forget about the recorder," I said. "We're off the record."

"No way. We can't be."

"Fine. We're not, then. But you're not going to write that story."

"The hell I'm not." So said his mouth. The rest of him, however, was quickly catching on to how confident I sounded. "Okay. Why not?" he asked.

"Because your paper needs two confirmed sources to run it, and you'll never get the second source."

Grimes could always read between the lines with me. When I said stuff like that, I wasn't the professor with a PhD in psychology, I was the former CIA operative. All the more reason why he didn't need to ask the obvious question. *How could this news not have gone public yet?*

"Why are you telling me, then?" he asked instead. "And what's the second scoop while we're at it?"

I explained why I'd told him about Brunetti. Then I reached into my pocket and handed him an envelope.

"What's this?"

"That's a statement that the mayor's office will be releasing to the press tomorrow afternoon. Somehow you've managed to get a copy of it in advance," I said, getting up to leave. "Merry Christmas."

After making a quick call to Julian to confirm that all the arrangements had been done, I made my third and final stop of the day. Home sweet home.

"Daddy D! Daddy D!"

Annabelle came running to meet me at the door, jumping into my arms. If she were any older she would've asked why there were tears in my eyes. As for Tracy, who turned the corner into our foyer a few seconds behind her, he didn't need to ask at all.

"I'm so sorry," I said.

"What for? Spending the night in a CIA safe house has always been on my bucket list," he said. Then he smiled and hugged me. We all hugged. It was another Annabelle sandwich, this one maybe the best one ever. "So how much are you legally able to tell me?"

"I don't know, and I don't care," I said. "You deserve to hear all of it."

Which is exactly what I told him over a bottle of red as we cooked dinner. All of it. Everything.

And I saved the best part for last.

CHAPTER 107

I REALLY WISH I could've been there to see von Oehson's face at the exact moment he found out.

Instead I had to make do with trying to picture it, although admittedly that was still pretty damn good. I even mentally opened the window in our living room at one point, sticking my ear out into the cold, to see if maybe, just maybe, I could hear von Oehson cursing my name at the top of his lungs from his palace apartment in the sky on billionaires' row.

Of course, the real question wasn't whether he would throw a tantrum and curse my name. It was what, if anything, he would do next. My money was on his doing nothing—except smile for the cameras. That was what I envisioned, what he'd ultimately decide. In his otherwise lightning-fast mind, there would be a slow reckoning, that as far as a price to pay for all his crimes and misdemeanors he was getting off on the cheap side.

Of course, for a man worth twenty-four billion dollars, *cheap* is a relative term.

That next morning, Mathias von Oehson woke up to learn, courtesy of the *New York Gazette*, that he had donated two billion dollars to the city of New York to fund a new prekindergarten education program for low-income families in all five boroughs.

Furthermore, this wasn't one of those spread-out-over-ten-years donations. This was two billion—the whole enchilada—already paid in full to the city to fast-track major construction and massive hiring at the start of the new year.

That was another moment I would've liked to have seen in person. Von Oehson, in full panic mode, checking the balance of his numerous bank accounts, most of them offshore, that were indeed a total of two billion dollars less than they were the day before. Funny thing about those wiring instructions he used to steal the money from the Hungarians. Turned out they also worked in reverse. All it took was some tinkering from Julian, along with the proper routing numbers for the city of New York coffers, courtesy of Mayor Deacon.

How did we settle on two billion as the amount? I figured one billion for each week's notice von Oehson initially gave Harlem Legal House to vacate their offices when he leveraged me into working for him. Yeah, that felt about right.

"It is my distinct honor to be awarding Mathias von Oehson a key to the city this Friday, a city that he has so greatly enhanced for generations to come, thanks to his phenomenally generous donation," said Deacon, as quoted in the article. This was according to the press release, "a copy of which the *New York Gazette* has obtained in advance."

Within an hour after the news broke, the mayor took to Twitter to further codify the transaction. "A gift to more than a million children has been placed under the city's tree," he wrote, before adding that it was his honor to work personally with von Oehson on the arrangement. Politicians never miss an opportunity to get in a plug for themselves.

All the better, though, to further leverage von Oehson. What was he going to do, ask for the money back? Claim that there'd been some kind of mistake?

No, not a chance. While two billion was a ton of money, his reputation would always be worth more. Lest there be any doubt, his two-word text to me that same afternoon summed it all up.

Well played.

A von Oehson man always knows when to cut his losses.

Who knows? Maybe he'll even hang that key to the city on his wall.

For everything that's ever been written about the idea of justice, its meaning will never be something that you can fully understand through words alone. Its full definition will always be something you feel. In your head. In your heart. In your gut.

My gut was telling me that justice had been served.

Not perfectly. Not permanently. But still just enough to feel it.

I'd been played, manipulated, and, for a good stretch, outmatched. There aren't that many dumb billionaires in the world. Yet, in the words of the ancient Greek philosopher Epictetus— and at the risk of a serious eye roll from Elizabeth for quoting a famous dead guy—*It's not what happens to you, but how you react to it that matters.*

In short, von Oehson had his masterpiece.

In the end, I had mine.

THE FINISHING TOUCHES

CHAPTER 108

'TWAS A FEW NIGHTS before the night before Christmas.

That was our compromise, although I'm fairly certain Tracy would've held his ground were it not for the fact that I'd already bought the tree. The poor thing stood there naked in its stand for days. Actually, I take that back. About Tracy, not the tree. Since we were turning our tree-decorating tradition into a party to celebrate not only the survival of Harlem Legal House but its newly planned expansion, Tracy understood that we needed to accommodate the holiday travel plans of the guests on our list.

And what a list it was. In addition to many Harlem Legal House attorneys, we had CIA operatives (past and present), a couple of federal agents, and one high-priced female escort. Oh, and in lieu of two turtle doves, there was a new couple deciding to go public.

"I *knew* you were sweet on him," I whispered while taking her coat.

"Shut up," Elizabeth whispered back, softly enough so her date wouldn't hear her. She smiled. She couldn't help it. I'd never seen her look so happy. Come to think of it, I can't remember my being so happy for someone after I opened the door and saw her and Danny Sullivan arriving together.

"Here, this is for Annabelle," said Danny, handing me a gift-wrapped box.

"That's so nice, thank you," I said. "You didn't have to do that."

Elizabeth leaned in. "Wait until he tells you what he got her. You'll wish he hadn't."

I shook the box, but that was just for show. All I had to do was think back to the night I first met Danny at the Sky Rink at Chelsea Piers. "What's wrong with ice skates?" I asked.

"Exactly," he said, giving Elizabeth a nudge. "She acts like I got her a Barbie meth lab, or something."

Elizabeth rolled her eyes and laughed, and I immediately knew. These two were meant for each other.

Speaking of couples, "Wait. Who's that with your dad?" asked Elizabeth, looking over my shoulder. "Is that who I think it is?"

It was. Josiah Maxwell Reinhart had driven down from New Hampshire with his houseguest, Ingrid, whose days as "Jade" working for Vladimir Grigoryev were officially over. I'd love to report that my father miraculously talked her into a new line of work, but that's a Disney movie that's probably not going to get made. He did, however, take her hunting and teach her how to make his infamous squirrel stew, which, thankfully, doesn't actually contain squirrel. The name derives from his making huge batches at a time and storing it, like nuts, for the winter.

"That's right, you never met Jade," I said, following Elizabeth's eyeline to the strange juxtaposition of my father standing with a very tall and very beautiful Russian woman in her mid-twenties, as they chatted with Julian. "You only met Betty."

For the record, Paulina—Carter's Betty, his standing Tuesday date—was also no longer working for Grigoryev. Her unconditional "release," along with Ingrid's, was granted without much fuss by Grigoryev once he was made aware of the connection between my entanglement with him and the demise of Frank

Brunetti. The criminal underworld is a zero-sum game, and the loss of an Italian mob boss with a firm grip on the five boroughs meant a significant gain in power for the Russian *pakhan*. Letting two of his girls go their own way was the least he could do for me, as was returning Vincent Franchella safely home to his family in New Jersey. I hoped Franchella's days of hookers and hotel rooms were over.

"Come, try the eggnog," I said. "I made it myself. It's absolutely horrible."

Elizabeth and Danny joined the party, and soon all of us began decorating the tree. Everyone took a turn hanging an ornament on a branch. I watched, enjoying every moment of it, while ever mindful of the irony. Suffice it to say, the man responsible for bringing us all together didn't exactly score an invite. Not that Mathias von Oehson would've ever been angling for one. If he never laid eyes on me again for as long as he lived it would still be too soon for him. I would imagine that Julian, who was very much enjoying his new Italian toy, felt the same about von Oehson. There's nothing quite like a Ferrari to turn a near hermit into a man about town. Once he got the new windshield installed, Julian was taking that baby out for a spin on a daily basis. I should know—I joined him a few times to get another turn behind the wheel.

"Okay, Annabelle. Are you ready, sweetheart?" asked Tracy, handing her the last ornament.

We hoisted up our little girl as she raised the star she'd made from a paper plate (with a scissors assist from Tracy), decorated with silver glitter (with a glue assist from me). As for the Cheerios that somehow managed to get mixed in with the glitter, that was all Annabelle.

"Higher, Daddy D! Higher, Daddy T!"

As Tracy and I lifted her higher, I couldn't help but think in that moment of how lucky we were. How lucky *I* was. The void in my younger years, created when my mother died, had been filled with family, friends, and purpose. I knew what it felt like to love and be loved. Best of all, the future was literally in my hands. Her name was Annabelle, and she was the greatest gift of all.

Smiling and giggling, our little girl placed her star on top of the tree. It was sideways. It was off-center.

It was perfect.

FROM AMERICA'S MOST BELOVED
SUPERSTAR AND ITS GREATEST
STORYTELLER —

A THRILLER ABOUT A YOUNG
SINGER/SONGWRITER ON THE RISE
AND ON THE RUN,

AND DETERMINED TO DO
WHATEVER IT TAKES TO SURVIVE.

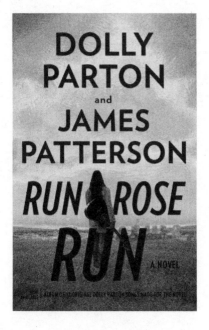

PROLOGUE

The Louis Seize–style mirror in the bedroom of suite 409 at the Aquitaine Hotel reflected for little more than an instant a slim, fine-featured woman: wide blue eyes, clenched fists, dark hair streaming behind her as she ran.

Then AnnieLee Keyes vanished from the glass, as her bare feet took her racing into the suite's living room. She dodged the edge of the giltwood settee, flinging its throw pillow over her shoulder. A lamp fell with a crash behind her. She leaped over the coffee table, with its neat stack of *Las Vegas* magazines and tray of complimentary Debauve & Gallais truffles, her name written in chocolate ganache flecked with edible gold. She hadn't even tasted a single one.

Her foot caught the bouquet of Juliet roses and the vase tipped over, scattering pink blooms all over the carpet.

The balcony was up ahead of her, its doors open to the morning sun. In another instant, she'd reached it, and the hot air hit her in the face like a fist. She jumped onto the chaise longue and threw her right leg over the railing, struggling to push herself the rest of the way up.

Then, balanced on the thin rail between the hotel and the sky, she hesitated. Her heart beat so quickly she could hardly breathe. Every nerve ending sparked with adrenaline.

I can't, she thought. *I can't do it.*

But she had to. Her fingers clutched the rail for another split second before she willed them loose. Her lips moved in an instant of desperate prayer. Then she launched herself into the air. The sun flared, but her vision darkened and became a tunnel. She could see only below her—upturned faces, mouths open in screams she couldn't hear over her own.

Time slowed. She spread out her arms as if she were flying.

And weren't flying and falling the same?

Maybe, she thought, *except for the landing.*

Each millisecond stretched to an hour, these measures of time all she had left in this world. Life had been so damn hard, and she'd clawed her way up only to fling herself back down. She didn't want to die, but she was going to.

AnnieLee twisted in the air, trying to protect herself from what was coming. Trying to aim for the one thing that might save her.

ELEVEN
MONTHS EARLIER

CHAPTER

1

AnnieLee had been standing on the side of the road for an hour, thumbing a ride, when the rain started falling in earnest.

Wouldn't you know it? she thought as she tugged a gas station poncho out of her backpack. *It just figures.*

She pulled the poncho over her jacket and yanked the hood over her damp hair. The wind picked up, and fat raindrops began to beat a rhythm on the cheap plastic. But she kept that hopeful smile plastered on her face, and she tapped her foot on the gravel shoulder as a bit of a new song came into her head.

Is it easy? she sang to herself.

No it ain't
Can I fix it?
No I cain't

She'd been writing songs since she could talk and making melodies even before that. AnnieLee Keyes couldn't hear the call of a wood thrush, the *plink plink plink* of a leaky faucet, or the rumbling rhythm of a freight train without turning it into a tune.

Crazy girl finds music in everything—that's what her mother had said, right up until the day she died. And the song coming to AnnieLee now gave her something to think about besides the cars whizzing by, their warm, dry occupants not even slowing down to give her a second glance.

Not that she could blame them; she wouldn't stop for herself, either. Not in this weather, and her probably looking no better than a drowned possum.

When she saw the white station wagon approaching, going at least twenty miles under the speed limit, she crossed her fingers that it would be some nice old grandpa pulling over to offer her a lift. She'd turned down two rides back when she thought she'd have her choice of them, the first from a chain-smoking lady with two snarling Rottweilers in the back seat, the second from a kid who'd looked higher than Mount Everest.

Now she could kick herself for being so picky. Either driver would have at least gotten her a few miles up the road, smelling like one kind of smoke or another.

The white wagon was fifty yards away, then twenty-five, and as it came at her she gave a friendly, graceful wave, as if she was some kind of celebrity on the shoulder of the Crosby Freeway and not some half-desperate nobody with all her worldly belongings in a backpack.

The old Buick crawled toward her in the slow lane, and AnnieLee's waving grew nearly frantic. But she could have stood on her head and shot rainbows out of her Ropers and it wouldn't have mattered. The car passed by and grew gradually smaller in the distance. She stomped her foot like a kid, splattering herself with mud.

Is it easy? she sang again.

No it ain't
Can I fix it?
No I cain't
But I sure ain't gonna take it lyin' down

It was catchy, all right, and AnnieLee wished for the twentieth time that she had her beloved guitar. But it wouldn't have fit in her pack, for one thing, and for another, it was already hanging on the wall at Jeb's Pawn.

If she had one wish—besides to get the hell out of Texas—it was that whoever bought Maybelle would take good care of her.

The distant lights of downtown Houston seemed to blur as AnnieLee blinked raindrops from her eyes. If she thought about her life back there for more than an instant, she'd probably stop wishing for a ride and just start running.

By now the rain was falling harder than she'd seen it in years. As if God had drawn up all the water in Buffalo Bayou just so He could pour it back down on her head.

She was shivering, her stomach ached with hunger, and suddenly she felt so lost and furious she could cry. She had nothing and nobody; she was broke and alone and night was coming on.

But there was that melody again; it was almost as if she could hear it inside the rain. *All right*, she thought, *I don't have* nothing. *I have music.*

And so she didn't cry. She sang instead.

Will I make it?
Maybe so

Closing her eyes, she could imagine herself on a stage some-where, singing for a rapt audience.

Will I give up?
Oh no

She could feel the invisible crowd holding its breath.

I'll be fightin' til I'm six feet underground

Her eyes were squeezed shut and her face was tilted to the sky as the song swelled inside her. Then a horn blared, and AnnieLee Keyes nearly jumped out of her boots.

She was hoisting both her middle fingers high at the tractor trailer when she saw its brake lights flare.

Was there ever a more beautiful color in the whole wide world? AnnieLee could write a damn ode to the dazzling red of those brake lights.

As she ran toward the truck, the cab's passenger door swung open. She wiped the rain from her eyes and looked at her rescuer. He was a gray-haired, soft-bellied man in his fifties, smiling down at her from six feet up. He tipped his baseball cap at her like a country gentleman.

"Come on in before you drown," he called.

A gust of wind blew the rain sideways, and without another second's hesitation, AnnieLee grabbed onto the door handle and hauled herself into the passenger seat, flinging water everywhere.

"Thank you," she said breathlessly. "I thought I was going to have to spend the night out there."

"That would've been rough," the man said. "It's a good thing I came along. Lot of people don't like to stop. Where you headed?"

"East," she said as she pulled off her streaming poncho and then shrugged out of her heavy backpack. Her shoulders were killing her. Come to think of it, so were her feet.

"My name's Eddie," the man said. He thrust out a hand for her to shake.

"I'm…Ann," she said, taking it.

He held her fingers for a moment before releasing them. "It's real nice to meet you, Ann." Then he put the truck into gear, looked over his shoulder, and pulled onto the highway.

He was quiet for a while, which was more than fine with AnnieLee, but then over the road noise she heard Eddie clear his throat. "You're dripping all over my seat," he said.

"Sorry."

"Here, you can at least dry your face," he said, tossing a red bandanna onto her lap. "Don't worry, it's clean," he said when she hesitated. "My wife irons two dozen for me every time I head out on a run."

Reassured by news of this wife, AnnieLee pressed the soft bandanna to her cheeks. It smelled like Downy. Once she'd wiped her face and neck, she wasn't sure if she should give it back to him, so she just wadded it up in her hand.

"You hitchhike a lot?" Eddie asked.

AnnieLee shrugged because she didn't see how it was any of his business.

"Look, I been driving longer than you been alive, I bet, and I've seen some things. *Bad* things. You don't know who you can trust."

Then she saw his big hand coming toward her, and she flinched.

Eddie laughed. "Relax. I'm just turning up the heat." He twisted a knob, and hot air blasted in her face. "I'm one of the good guys," he said. "Husband, dad, all that white-picket-fence business. Shoot, I even got a dang *poodle*. That was my wife's idea, though. I wanted a blue heeler."

"How old are your kids?" AnnieLee asked.

"Fourteen and twelve," he said. "Boys. One plays football, the other plays chess. Go figure." He held out a battered thermos. "Got coffee if you want it. Just be careful, because it's probably still hot as hellfire."

AnnieLee thanked him, but she was too tired for coffee. Too tired to talk. She hadn't even asked Eddie where he was going, but she hardly cared. She was in a warm, dry cab, putting her past behind her at seventy miles per hour. She wadded her poncho into a pillow and leaned her head against the window. Maybe everything was going to be okay.

She must have fallen asleep then, because when she opened her eyes she saw a sign for Lafayette, Louisiana. The truck's headlights shone through slashing rain. A Kenny Chesney song was on the radio. And Eddie's hand was on her thigh.

She stared down at his big knuckles as her mind came out of its dream fog. Then she looked over at him. "I think you better take your hand off me," she said.

"I was wondering how long you were going to sleep," Eddie said. "I was getting lonely."

She tried to push his hand away, but he squeezed tighter.

"Relax," he said. His fingers dug into her thigh. "Why don't you move closer, Ann? We can have a little fun."

AnnieLee gritted her teeth. "If you don't take your hand off me, you're going to be sorry."

"Oh, girl, you are just precious," he said. "You just relax and let me do what I like." His hand slid farther up her thigh. "We're all alone in here."

AnnieLee's heart pounded in her chest, but she kept her voice low. "You don't want to do this."

"Sure I do."

"I'm warning you," she said.

Eddie practically giggled at her. "What are you going to do, girl, scream?"

"No," she said. She reached into the pocket of her jacket and pulled out the gun. Then she pointed it at his chest. "I'm going to do *this*."

Eddie's hand shot off her leg so fast she would've laughed if she weren't so outraged.

But he got over his surprise quickly, and his eyes grew narrow and mean. "Hundred bucks says you can't even fire that thing," he said. "You better put that big gun away before you get hurt."

"*Me* get hurt?" AnnieLee said. "The barrel's not pointing at me, jackass. Now you apologize for touching me."

But Eddie was angry now. "You skinny little tramp, I wouldn't touch you with a tent pole! You're probably just another truck stop hoo—"

She pulled the trigger, and sound exploded in the cabin—first the shot, and then the scream of that dumb trucker.

The truck swerved, and somewhere behind them a horn blared. "What the hell're you doing, you crazy hobo bitch?"

"Pull over," she said.

"I'm not pull—"

She lifted the pistol again. "Pull over. I'm not kidding," she said.

Cursing, Eddie braked and pulled over onto the shoulder. When the truck came to a stop, AnnieLee said, "Now get out. Leave the keys in and the engine running."

He was sputtering and pleading, trying to reason with

her now, but she couldn't be bothered to listen to a word he said.

"Get out," she said. "Now."

She shook the gun at him and he opened the door. The way the rain was coming down, he was soaked before he hit the ground.

"You crazy, stupid, trashy—"

AnnieLee lifted the gun so it was pointing right at his mouth, so he shut it. "Looks like there's a rest stop a couple miles ahead," she said. "You can have yourself a nice walk and a cold shower at the same time. Pervert."

She slammed the door, but she could feel him beating on the side of the cab as she tried to figure out how to put the truck into gear. She fired another shot, out the window, and that made him quit until she found the clutch and the gas.

Then AnnieLee grabbed hold of the gearshift. Her stepdad might've been the world's biggest asshole, but he'd taught her to drive stick. She knew how to double-clutch and how to listen to the revs. And maybe songs weren't the only thing she had a natural talent for, because it didn't take her long at all to lurch that giant rig off the shoulder and pull out onto the highway, leaving Eddie screaming behind her.

I'm driving, she thought giddily. *I'm driving!*

She yanked on the horn and shot deeper into the darkness. And then she started singing.

Driven to insanity, driven to the edge
Driven to the point of almost no return

She beat out a rhythm on the steering wheel.

Driven, driven to be smarter
Driven to work harder
Driven to be better every day

That last line made her laugh out loud. Sure, she'd be better tomorrow—because tomorrow the sun would come out again, and tomorrow she had absolutely *no plans* to carjack an eighteen-wheeler.

CHAPTER

3

⌒

R uthanna couldn't get the damn lick out of her head. A descending roll in C major, twangy as a rubber band, it was crying out for lyrics, a bass line, a song to live inside. She tapped her long nails on her desk as she scrolled through her emails.

"Later," she said, to herself or to the lick, she wasn't entirely sure. "We'll give you some attention when the boys show up to play."

It was nine o'clock in the morning, and already she'd fielded six pleading requests for Ruthanna Ryder, one of country music's grandest queens, to grace some big industry event or another with her royal presence.

She couldn't understand it, but people just failed to get the message: she'd *retired* that crown. Ruthanna didn't want to put on high heels, false eyelashes, and a sparkling Southern smile anymore. She wasn't going to stand up on some hot, bright stage in a dress so tight it made her ribs ache. She had no desire to pour her heart out into a melody that'd bring tears to a thousand pairs of eyes, hers included. No, sir, she'd put in her time, and now she was done. She was still writing songs—she couldn't stop that if she tried—but if the world thought it was going to ever hear them, it had another think coming. Her music was only for herself now.

She looked up from the screen as Maya, her assistant, walked into the room with a crumpled paper bag in one hand and a stack of mail in the other.

"The sun sure is bright on those gold records today," Maya said.

Ruthanna sighed at her. "Come on, Maya. You're the *one person* I'm supposed to be able to count on not to harass me about my quote, unquote, career. Jack must've called with another 'once-in-a-lifetime opportunity.'"

Maya just laughed, which was her way of saying, *You bet your white ass he did.*

Jack was Ruthanna's manager—ahem, *former* manager. "All right, what does he want from me today?"

"He wouldn't tell me yet. But he said that it's not what *he* wants. He's thinking about what *you* really want."

Ruthanna gave a delicate snort. "*I* really want to be left alone. Why he thinks he knows something different is beyond me." She picked up her ringing phone, silenced it, and then threw it onto the overstuffed couch across the room.

Maya watched this minor tantrum serenely. "He says the world's still hungry for your voice. For your songs."

"Well, a little hunger never hurt anyone." She gave her assistant a sly grin. "Not that you'd know much about hunger."

Maya put a hand on her ample hip. "And *you* got room to talk," she said.

Ruthanna laughed. "Touché. But whose fault is it for hiring Louie from the ribs place to be my personal chef? You could've picked someone who knew his way around a salad."

"Coulda, woulda, shoulda," Maya said. She put a stack of

letters in Ruthanna's inbox and held out the paper bag. "It's from Jack."

"What is that, muffins? I told Jack I was off carbs this month," Ruthanna said.

Not that Jack believed anything she told him lately. The last time they'd talked she'd said that she was going to start gardening, and he'd laughed so hard he dropped the phone into his pool. When he called her back on his landline he was still wheezing with delight. "I can't see you out there pruning roses any more than I can see you stripping off your clothes and riding down Lower Broadway on a silver steed like Lady Godiva of Nashville," he'd said.

Her retort—that it was past the season for pruning roses anyway—had failed to convince him.

"No, ma'am," Maya said, "these are *definitely* not muffins."

"You looked?"

"He told me to. He said if I saw them, I'd be sure you opened them. Otherwise he was afraid you might chuck the bag in a bin somewhere, and that'd be…well, a lot of sparkle to throw away."

"Sparkle, huh?" Ruthanna said, her interest piqued.

Maya shook her head at her, like, *You just don't know how lucky you are.* But since lovely Maya had a husband who bought her flowers every Friday and just about kissed the ground she walked on, she was considerably fortunate herself. Ruthanna, divorced seven years now, only got presents from people who wanted something from her.

She took the bag. Unrolling the top, she looked inside, and there, lying at the bottom of the bag—not even in a velvet box—was a pair of diamond chandelier earrings, each one as long as her index finger, false nail included. "Holy sugar," Ruthanna said.

"I know. I already googled them," Maya said. "Price available upon request."

Ruthanna held them up so that they caught the light brilliantly and flung rainbows onto her desk. She owned plenty of diamonds, but these were spectacular. "They look like earrings you'd buy a trophy wife," she said.

"Correction," said Maya. "They look like earrings you'd buy a woman who made you millions as she clawed her way to the top of her industry and into the hearts of a vast majority of the world's population."

The office line rang, and Ruthanna put the earrings back into the bag without trying them on. She gestured to Maya to answer it.

"Ryder residence," Maya said, and then put on her listening face. After a while she nodded. "Yes, Jack, I'll pass that information along."

"He couldn't keep his little secret after all, could he?" Ruthanna asked when her assistant hung up.

"He says they want to give you some big giant honor at the Country Music Awards—but you'd actually have to go," Maya said. "And he'd like me to tell you that you really shouldn't pass up such a perfect opportunity to wear those earrings."

Ruthanna laughed. Jack really was something else. "That man can buy me diamonds until hell turns into a honky-tonk," she said. "I'm out of the business."

ABOUT THE AUTHORS

JAMES PATTERSON is the world's bestselling author and most trusted storyteller. He has created many enduring fictional characters and series, including Alex Cross, the Women's Murder Club, Michael Bennett, Maximum Ride, Middle School, and I Funny. Among his notable literary collaborations are *The President Is Missing*, with President Bill Clinton, and the Max Einstein series, produced in partnership with the Albert Einstein Estate. Patterson's writing career is characterized by a single mission: to prove that there is no such thing as a person who "doesn't like to read," only people who haven't found the right book. He's given more than three million books to schoolkids and the military, donated more than seventy million dollars to support education, and endowed more than five thousand college scholarships for teachers. For his prodigious imagination and championship of literacy in America, Patterson was awarded the 2019 National Humanities Medal. The National Book Foundation presented him with the Literarian Award for Outstanding Service to the American Literary Community, and he is also the recipient of an

Edgar Award and nine Emmy Awards. He lives in Florida with his family.

HOWARD ROUGHAN has cowritten several books with James Patterson and is the author of *The Promise of a Lie* and *The Up and Comer.* He lives in Florida with his wife and son.

His best stories
are the stories of his life.

The Stories of My Life

James Patterson
by James
Patterson

COMING JUNE 2022

JAMES
PATTERSON
RECOMMENDS

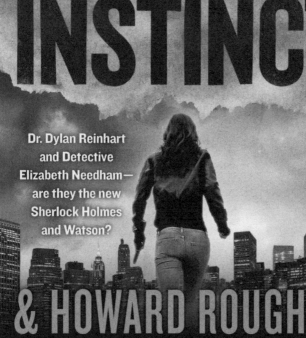

JAMES PATTERSON

KILLER INSTINCT

Dr. Dylan Reinhart
and Detective
Elizabeth Needham—
are they the new
Sherlock Holmes
and Watson?

& HOWARD ROUGHAN

KILLER INSTINCT

The murder of an Ivy League professor sends my smartest crime fighter, Dr. Dylan Reinhart, back to the streets of New York, where he reunites with his old partner, detective Elizabeth Needham. A heinous act of terror and a name on the casualty list rock Dylan's world. Is his secret past about to be brought to light?

Dylan literally wrote the book on the psychology of murder, and he and Elizabeth have solved cases that have baffled conventional detectives. But the sociopath they're facing now is the opposite of a textbook case. I've come up with a test that they have no time to study for—and if they fail, they die.

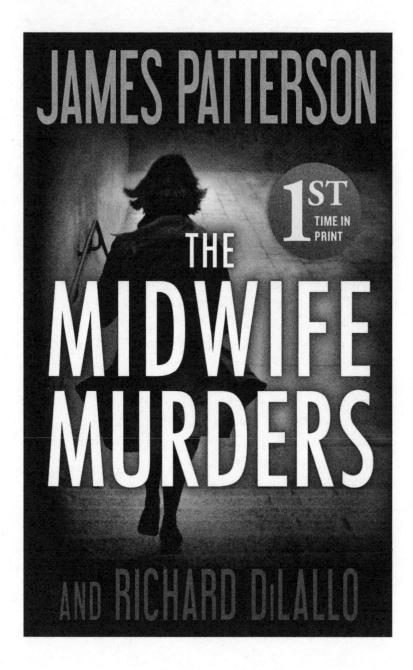

THE MIDWIFE MURDERS

I can't imagine a worse crime than one done against a child. But when two kidnappings and a vicious stabbing happen on senior midwife Lucy's watch in a university hospital in Manhattan, her focus abruptly changes. Something has to be done, and Lucy is fearless enough to try.

Rumors begin to swirl, with blame falling on everyone from the Russian mafia to an underground adoption network. Fierce single mom Lucy teams up with a skeptical NYPD detective, but I've given her a case where the truth is far more twisted than Lucy could ever have imagined.

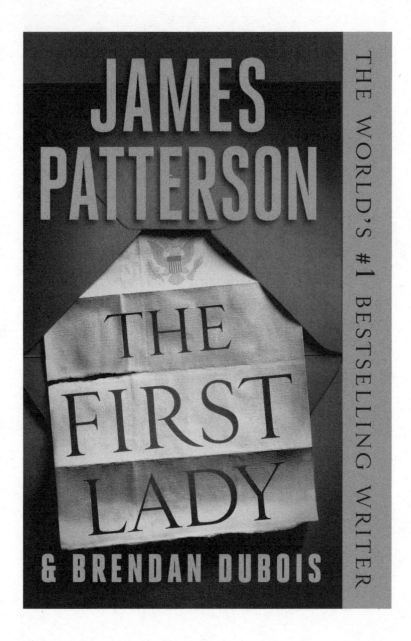

JAMES PATTERSON

THE FIRST LADY

& BRENDAN DUBOIS

THE FIRST LADY

The US government is at the forefront of everyone's mind these days, and I've become incredibly fascinated by the idea that one secret can bring it all down. What if that secret is a US president's affair that results in a nightmarish outcome?

Sally Grissom, leader of the Presidential Protection Division, is summoned to a private meeting with the president and his chief of staff to discuss the disappearance of the first lady. What at first seemed an escape to a safe haven turns into a kidnapping when a ransom note arrives along with what could be the first lady's finger.

It's a race against the clock to collect the evidence that all leads to one troubling question: could the kidnappers be from inside the White House?

JAMES
PATTERSON
& ANDREW BOURELLE
THE
WORLD'S
#1
BEST-
SELLING
WRITER
TEXAS
RANGER
OFFICER
RORY
YATES
COMES
HOME—
TO A
MURDER
CHARGE

TEXAS RANGER

So many of my detectives are dark and gritty and deal with crimes in some of our grimmest cities. That's why I'm thrilled to bring you Rory Yates, my most honorable detective yet.

As a Texas Ranger, he has a code that he lives and works by. But when he comes home for a much-needed break, he walks into a crime scene where the victim is none other than his ex-wife— and he's the prime suspect. Yates has to risk everything to clear his name, and he dives into the inferno of the most twisted mind I've ever created. Can his code bring him back out alive?

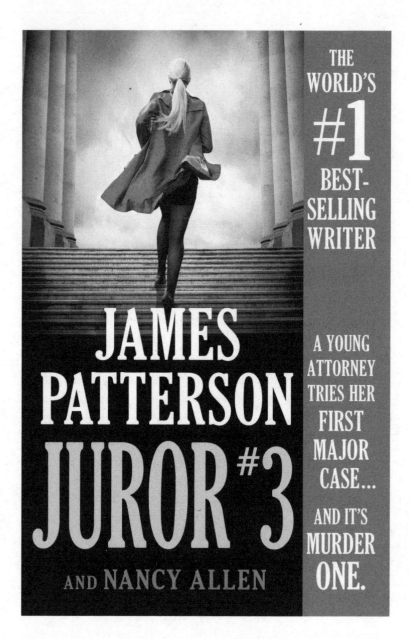

JAMES
PATTERSON
JUROR #3
AND NANCY ALLEN

JUROR #3

In the deep south of Mississippi, Ruby Bozarth is a newcomer, both to Rosedale and to the bar. And now she's tapped as a defense counsel in a racially charged felony. The murder of a woman from an old family has Rosedale's upper crust howling for blood, and the prosecutor is counting on Ruby's inexperience to help him deliver a swift conviction.

Ruby is determined to build a defense that sticks for her client, a college football star. Looking for help in unexpected quarters, her case is rattled as news of a second murder breaks. As intertwining investigations unfold, no one can be trusted, especially the twelve men and women on the jury. They may be hiding the most incendiary secret of all.

For a complete list of books by

JAMES PATTERSON

VISIT
JamesPatterson.com

Follow James Patterson on Facebook
@JamesPatterson

Follow James Patterson on Twitter
@JP_Books

Follow James Patterson on Instagram
@jamespattersonbooks